A Whisper

OF

Fate And Flame

Igniting Change

Tabitha Bull

To my dad for always supporting me and loving me for who I am. To my sisters for speaking an unspoken language of love. To my Love for picking me up when I need it most. And to my best friends who don't have any clue how much they do for my soul.

Ses

Avaris · bellon

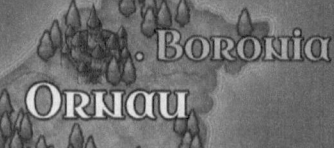

· Deadlands

M

· Te

· Boronia

Ornau

In

Archipelago

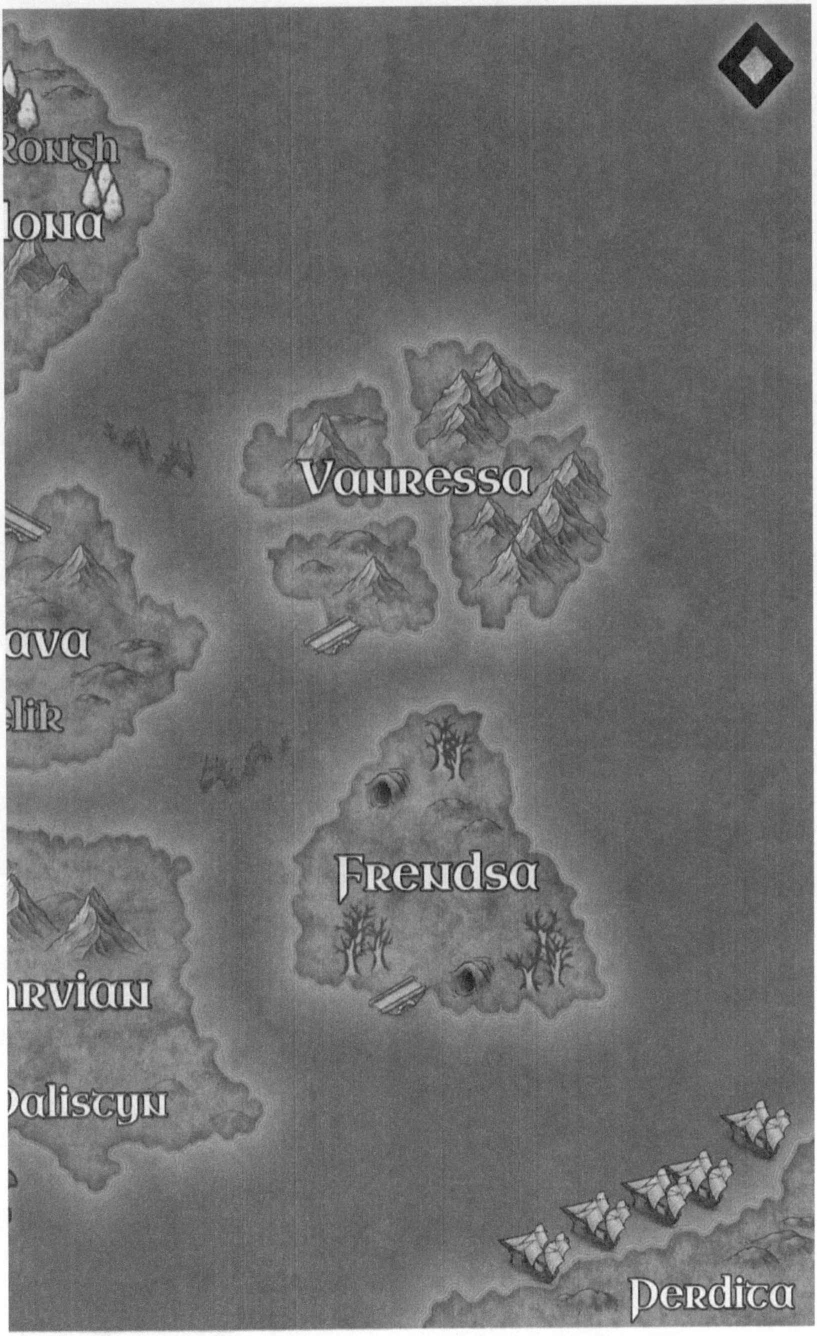
Vanressa
Frendsa
Perdita

PART I

(The Unraveling)

Chapter One

The air has always been thicker after walking outside the shop into the bustling street heading for the tavern every afternoon. People walk around, pushing past others to get the cheapest ingredients for winter meals. Winter is always a struggle for supplies, especially around the part of town I live in. My shop is on the edge of our little town, only a few hundred people. My shop, if you could even call it that, is open to anyone who wants to waste their rations of coins on quilts and bottles, or vases. My Aunt Prim used to own it when she was younger, selling all her beautiful crafts to the lavish and rich townspeople who used to live here.

Now it's just me running the dilapidated parlor, untouched for the past few months. Occasionally I'll have someone come in because the sign I made a couple of years back looks interesting enough to see what's inside. On average I sell five or six items a day when it used to be about forty, at least that's what Aunt Prim tells me.

She likes to give me business advice, as she was once the owner of the previously frequented building. She would make these wonderful blankets, where each square of fabric would tell a story. She would like to convince customers that if they slept with the blanket, wrapped up tightly enough, their story would be embroidered on the blanket as well. If that ever happened, I'm not sure, but civilians loved to hear her tell of the ancient tales of the past.

She gave me her old books that would tell of these stories, almost god-like stories. Authors who thought it was important to document the rulers of their time. Part of me likes to believe the tales, though the reasonable part of me doesn't think anything other than they're just a bunch of nonsense.

There's a story called *Grown Soul*. It's about a woman who went to find her lost husband after he disappeared from her bed in the night. She found him tied to a tree and beaten, with a sign saying *Liars don't become bargainers*. The tale claims that she was in such despair of losing her husband, that she wept until she merged with the tree, letting her soul become one with the earth and her dead husband. Legend says that if you can find this tree, and ask her for a favor, she will grant you one. With no price. However, you only get one favor. The story doesn't explain how extensive this favor could be, so that makes me wonder if I ever found the tree, how far I could go with my wish.

As my Aunt has gotten older, I've been getting more worried about her. It's just been me and her, and I need to find ways to build the shop up financially. I can't do that unless I conjure up the talent my aunt once had before her hands started to deteriorate. Sometimes, she'll make a blanket or a shawl and ask me to put it on the shelf. I have to explain every time that there's no room anymore because no one is buying our products. She scolds me for not having any hope left.

My hands have always been shaky, and even when they're not I can't seem to make a straight line with thread. I could never be as good as my aunt with her threading and quilts. However, there's not much of a point in trying to be as good as her because there's no room on the shelves for more projects. I will sometimes use clay when we can afford it and create vases, paint them, and fill them with flowers during the spring. I'm much better at pottery than I am with threading.

Aunt Prim has raised me since I was a baby, she's all I've ever known. She was passed down this shop when she was in her twenties by her father, and his father before him. One day, her father got a letter saying that his sister had fallen ill, he had to leave to see her. He said he would be there for a couple of months at most, but he never came home. She got a letter saying that her father was killed by a manic stranger, a stab in the chest. She was heartbroken, but was strong and took the responsibility well as she tells me. She had already been making projects to be sold in the shop for her father and had been sewing since she was a little girl, so she was already prepared to run the business.

Numerous decades later, she found me on her doorstep with a note wrapped inside my covering. It read: *Please take care of this child, I'm unable to. I wish you well, and may you always be accompanied.*

She still to this day, doesn't know who placed me there. She's taken care of me since then, trying to turn me into a strong woman like her. I can't say that it's going well because I can't even keep a shop in business like she could.

I've always wondered who my parents were, but I never let it get to me. If my mother and father couldn't take care of me, at least they made sure they left me with someone who could. Of course I'm upset that now, being nineteen, they haven't come back. Even for a visit and to leave shortly after. I wouldn't even mind if they were to only write to me, at least that way we could have some sort of relationship. Maybe they didn't want me and they lied on the note my Aunt Prim received. Maybe saying that they *couldn't take care* of me was a ploy to ease their consciences of giving away an innocent baby.

However, I'm happy with where I'm at. Since the shop has started to go downhill in sales, I made a backup plan. I started to work at the tavern that of course still has plenty of customers. People get lazy in this tiny town in the winter, they don't want to hunt for their own food or drink their filtered water. They instead come into the tavern to eat and drink ale or wine and waste their nights away smelling like rotting corpses and slimy mud.

Today was fast-paced as there were many drunken soldiers from the island's army coming to Ihrvian to celebrate the anniversary of the War of Stone and Mountains that we won about one hundred years ago. There were a few soldiers who fought in the war who are still here today and celebrate with the new army recruits every year.

It's a tradition to celebrate the victory of the war every full moon in August since the war was won on a night just like that. We don't celebrate on the same day every year. Instead, we base it on the moon. Unlike every other holiday, it's not annual on the same date. Why this one is different, I'm not sure, but it's always been that way. I've always appreciated the day, but working in this tavern for the past two celebrations has been excruciating.

The smell of the tavern is thick and heavy. The groggy people, either already asleep or half-slurring their words, the smoke, and the ale's scents all mix letting me know that the night is over. It has to be easily past two o'clock in the morning, though the clock is so far away and the air is so thick that I can't tell the time.

I kick the chairs of the knocked-out drunks who came for cheap drinks, as they're always cheaper when celebrating Stone and Mountain night. I start to wash cups as angry customers stroll out the swinging doors, cursing at the also drunken man or woman bumping into them on the way out. I sigh as I watch the last woman trip over her ankles to walk back home. I finished drying the cups and let my caramel braided hair droop down my shoulder, itching my tired scalp and closing my eyes to the relief. I throw my apron off and lay it over the counter and lock the swinging doors on my way out.

The breeze that calls the start of winter pushes on my face, sending a shivering splinter of cold down my whole body. I've never minded the cold weather, but it would be nice if I remembered a coat or a shawl of some sort. The thin white and brown rags will have to do for now, which is usually what it has to be.

The shop, which also doubles as mine and Aunt Prim's tiny studio apartment, is only a few blocks from the tavern so I can easily commute from place to place quickly. It makes it especially convenient so I can get to Aunt Prim quickly, and she isn't left alone too long. She's a strong woman and can do things well for herself. She's perfectly capable of feeding and bathing herself as of now, but as age starts to weigh on her I like to stay close just in case. She is almost one hundred thirty years old now. She refuses to let me celebrate her birthday, but this year I got her a sapphire necklace. No matter her refusal, I always give her a little something. She's always been the person to protect me and make sure the evils of the world don't get to me. The least I could do was get her a birthday present.

The walk home is quiet and peaceful as there aren't many people in Halistyn, my home town. Ihrvian still carries the weight of winning the War of Stone and Mountains. Halistyn is right on the shore of Ihrvian, facing south. Ihrvian is the southern island, out of the seven, where the late Perditaian king's troops were sent to fight us in battle. Ihrvian is known for the fact that the soldiers were able to hold off the king's troops and protect the people of all the islands, Ihrvian, Frendsa, Ornau, Avaris, Vanressa, and Seglona.

The king was trying to break down the safe waterways, otherwise called bridges, that connect our islands and then merge all of them to the Middle Island, Mava. Our archipelago was under attack and the Duke of Ihrvian, Cabal, was able to command his troops to trick the king and kill him. However, Cabal's troops were too late and outnumbered. The king was able to destroy the flame in the center of Mava, cutting all bridges and pathways to any of the islands, marking the end of the war.

Since the war killed many of Ihrvian's people there aren't many people left on this island anymore. That's why the shop is so abandoned. Aunt Prim was in her twenties when the war ended. People were still here and buying product, and the business was flourishing. However, after a couple of decades people got scared of another war as no one had heard of the dukes or duchesses since the end of the War of Stone and Mountains. It's still that way even now, and people have learned to govern themselves, to a degree. There's more violence and unfairness in all the islands, but we all know that we need to stay alive, no matter how selfish we feel.

I don't know much about the archipelago because Aunt Prim doesn't like to talk about how things were for the few decades after the war. She says the only thing that kept her alive was the customers at the shop, giving her money for food, and me being left on her doorstep. Whenever I ask her questions like where she was during the war or if she had any family, she explains that I don't need to know, that it's all in the past now. It's hard to accept that she doesn't want to explain, but I understand why.

I'm about halfway through my walk to the shop when I catch a glimpse of two dark figures in the alley between two buildings to my right. I stop where I am and I lean against the wooden planks of the building behind me. I peer to my right and see a taller man giving a shorter, stouter one a bag of what looks like to be coins. They both chuckle about something the taller one said and then the short man pulls out a white bag glimmering with a hint of purple. Dragmist.

The dragmist dealings have gotten more and more frequent in the past couple of years as people continue to leave Ihrvian because they're still scared of war or have been run down and too poor to continue living on the island. Halistyn is one of the most populated towns in Ihrvian and there are still barely any folk here. Even the few pixies that roam the forests have ventured off to other islands. I doubt any of them have ever made it to another island, not many do because of the long and labor-inducing journey.

With all these humans and faeries and creatures leaving the island, it makes it easier for folks who don't have anything to live for to create and deal dragmist.

I stop looking, worrying that if I make myself known they will come after me and cover their dealing tracks. I've only ever witnessed one other dealing before and I ran. This time I don't have a chance to run. They would see me, and I would have to fight. Though they both look human, that doesn't mean anything. I'm not small, but I don't know if I could beat two men with how low we have been on food lately. My muscle is not built to the potential of what it could be right now.

I lower my chest and raise it again in slow quiet motions, trying to ease my breath. I peer past the corner again and see that they are still talking, opening the small pouch of purple dragmist. They take turns quickly inhaling the mist and chuckling. The next thing I know, the stout man with his back toward me is putting the coins in his pocket and turning around, strutting out of the alley and toward my hiding place.

My legs don't move, but I look to see if there's anyone around that could help me. My eyes become blurry with fear when I don't see anyone near. I lift my right foot up and quietly unwrap the dagger from my bootstrap. I always have it with me since working with all the ale-ridden tavern customers and it's finally coming in handy.

I grip the cool metal handle so hard I see my knuckles turn white in the blurriness. The short man's footsteps get louder and louder making his way closer, only meters away from me, though I'm too cowardly to check. I could fight him, one short man who is under the influence of dragmist, and might be unarmed. I'm prepared, I have a weapon, and I'm sober.

I could do this.

The footsteps come to a halt. I only hear breathing and the shuffling of cloth.

"I knew you'd be here, girl." I hear the short man say, his throat sounding hoarse and crooked like he hasn't spoken in years.

I stay still, I don't dare to respond or turn to my right and try to attack.

"Tell me, did you see what my ghoul friend and I did back there in the dark, hmm?" he sneers, slyly and smooth, like a snake. *Ghoul,* the human feasting creature, that's why he was so tall. "I knew you'd be here. I can see seconds into the future, sweetheart."

I grip the dagger harder. Dwarves usually are born with a minor ability, so this doesn't surprise me at all. However, he might know what I try to do next, that's what scares me. "You should have been more careful walking around this part of town."

I don't respond and only try to keep my breath steady, I feel my sweat trickle down the side of my face and almost drip down my chin.

"Tell me, why doesn't a pretty thing like you want to talk? I'm just a smaller-than-you dwarf, girl. Don't be scared." He chuckles. I have to make a decision now, run to my left, back to the tavern, and wait out the night, or face the dwarf and risk my life. If I stay out here longer I'll for sure freeze to death.

"What do you want?" I ask, my voice not short of shaking and anticipation. He can hear how scared I am, I'm sure of it. "I won't tell anyone about the dragmist, I swear."

Before I can say or do anything more, the shorter man wraps around the corner, grips my wrist that's holding the dagger, and kicks the back of my knees down, making me fall to the floor face first losing my dagger. I feel his knee into my back and I try to reach for the dagger while pushing my back up against his body weight. I feel him falter and squirm above me but then a separate person's foot is stepping on my hand that's reaching for the knife. I let out an involuntary yelp and freeze still.

"I heard you talking. I was hoping it was a witness, and a human as well?" I look up to see the ghoul smiling down on me, tears welling in my eyes from the cold and the pain. "I get some nice mist and dinner in one night?"

He kneels, pushing more weight onto my wrist while the dwarf keeps my legs and arms pushed to the hard ground. The ghoul lifts my chin and looks down at me, bearing his sharp ghoul teeth. "Could use some more meat on her, but I don't have the time to feed her for weeks. Meals have become sparse since humans keep running off, just to die out in the ocean. Such a shame."

I can't move. I can't see clearly. I can't hear as I feel my heart pumping so hard it might shatter the gravel road below us.

"P–please, let me go home," I say, trying to sound confident and force the tears back. They both laugh at my begging, gripping my limbs tighter as I continue to shake. I look up into the ghoul's sage blue eyes and sneer while the tears trickle down my cheeks, my body unable to contain the fear any longer.

I hear a faint scuffle in my left ear that isn't covered by the dwarf's arm. Wincing at all the pain in my body, I look to my left past the ghoul's feet a few meters behind him. I see a white streak of light moving closer, and faster. Very fast. I feel the air thicken like it's pushing on me harder than the two men pinning me down.

Panic shoots through me but it all turns into shock when I see the ghoul's head tumble to the floor, his body following not too long after. His torso lands right on his head, crushing the skull and bone under his scalp. All of it in the blink of an eye.

I only close my eyes, trying to squirm away from the blood while the dwarf begs for his life for a short moment, realizing what might become of him as well. I almost take my chance to run until I feel my head, neck, and shoulders get warm and all of the one hundred fifty pounds of the dwarf drops itself onto me. *Blood.*

I struggle to get up, realizing I'm too out of shape for anything aside from working at a tavern. I look away from the ghoul, noticing the spine and bone exposed from the clean cut that ended his life. The white bone pokes out of his neck, a striking contrast against the rouge flesh.

I push the dead weight of the beheaded dwarf off of me and slowly stand up, gripping the dagger I was so close to reaching just one moment ago. I grimace and bite back the urge to let myself be sick right in the pile of blood. Breathing through my panic, I grip my wrist to stop it from shaking. I look around with my back against the wooden wall, the same wooden wall.

Nothing.

I see no one. The white flash is gone and the air is thinner again. The bodies of the dwarf and the ghoul lay there, each in two clean pieces spilling with blood. The adrenaline falters after a few minutes of me trying to keep my dinner in my stomach, the pools of blood only growing larger by the minute.

I have to think about what I should do. I didn't kill them, I shouldn't have to clean them up, right? And they were trying to feast on me like I'm some piece of meat just because I'm human. No sane creature would miss them, right?

I've been here for too long. I have to leave before someone sees me and thinks I did this, blaming it on the dagger or something of that sort. I take my blood-covered overshirt off and tuck it under the ghoul's lifeless body, shivering from the biting cold hitting my arms and back. I grip the dagger hard and stammer back on my feet, needing to get out of here as soon as possible.

I start running back to the shop, afraid of having to explain why I'm covered in blood and late to come home. I'll just have to lie and say it was a fight in the tavern. Aunt Prim has always been overprotective and would throw a fit if I had even a scratch from a tree when I was young. I'm grateful for her protection, but how will she react to this? She sure would never listen when I tell her I'm okay.

I feel the pain rise in my feet and soreness in my wrist where the ghoul was crushing it. Running becomes easier and more swift the closer I get to the shop, longing for safety and warmth. A fire.

The pain slowly becomes numbness as the shortness of breath and stinging bite in my feet take over.

I see the shop, and the fear loses its grip on me as tiredness and bewilderment set in. What just happened? I was attacked, but also I was saved? If that is what that was. That white flash of light moved so fast I barely registered it. Was it even alive?

My pale fingers reach the door handle, but before I can be fully happy I'm home, the feeling that something is watching me, lurking around every corner of town, still sinks deep into my limbs.

What *was* that?

Chapter Two

The dusty shop floor welcomes my feet as I step out of my snow-sprinkled boots and stride into the kitchen, which is in the back on the first floor of the shop. I then start the kettle for tea. I always make tea after work, Aunt Prim would know something was off if I didn't. I don't see her anywhere downstairs, meaning she's probably sleeping. It's good news that she's asleep because then I can rinse off the blood, dirt, sweat, and tears from tonight's debacle. Though I could only do that if the water in the pumps aren't frozen, and the way my night has been going I don't think I'll be in much luck with bathing.

I walk away from the kitchen and step over to the shopping area while I wait for the kettle to warm. Yesterday we had two blankets sold and a couple of old vases I had spun with clay a few weeks ago. I'm pretty sure I still have dust fluttering in my nose from when I went to grab them off the shelf. A nice older lady wanted the vase because she said it looked like the one her daughter had given her when she was young. Her daughter had moved to another island, or died trying, a couple of years ago, and she misses her daughter dearly. I happily sold her the vase and she paid twice the amount, mentioning that she knows times must be hard for shops like this. I didn't want to accept, but she insisted.

I walk past the racks of blankets and coats, softly brushing my hand against each seam as I pass each of the interwoven masterpieces. If Aunt Prim and I were somewhere with more folks and more money like Mava in the middle of the archipelago, we would have more luck selling our product. Everyone longs to go there, to the middle.

From what the people on the islands hear, Mava is beautiful with large trees that have leaves of all colors. Mava supposedly doesn't have all four seasons, but only stays in the peaceful balance between summer and spring. The weather is always the same there allowing fruits and plants to flourish. Some islands, especially Seglona, the northern island, have trouble growing plants that are sustainable enough for their populations. Mava tries to help all the islands distribute enough food for everyone when we need it, sometimes even livestock. Though with all the dangers of crossing the ocean, only the earth's largest and toughest ships, as well as sailors, can cross. Even then it's almost a death wish.

I walk to the kitchen in the back after hearing the soft shrill of the kettle. I grab a small bag of mint tea and place it in a mug, pouring the boiling water after it. I lift the cup to my mouth, savoring the sweet taste along with the burning of the water going down my throat.

The weight of all that happened just half an hour ago hits me like a brick. I feel tears well in my eyes again, unsure of why I'm still affected by it. I grip the now warm mug, hoping to feel something else other than the stress of tonight. It was scary, yes, but I don't know why I'm crying over it.

What was that white light? Should I have been grateful that it beheaded the ghoul and the dwarf, or should I have been equally as scared of it as I was of the drug dealers? Did it mean to save me, or was it just getting rid of the filth in the world, and didn't see me there to get rid of me too? Part of me is starting to think tonight didn't happen at all and I'm going to wake up from this odd fever dream and hear Aunt Prim humming an old tune while sewing something beautiful that will never leave this shop.

The scuffle of Aunt Prim's night slippers coming down the stairs pulls me out of my curiosity pit and I quickly place the mug down, running to hide behind a coat rack in the shopping area. I can't let her see me like this, she'll ask questions and I'm a horrible liar. She'd look all over me for a scratch and it makes me wonder if the crushing pain in my wrist will leave a bruise for her to see or not.

"Sweetheart, are you down here?" I hear her ask me while making it down the last half of the creaking stairs, likely looking for me. "You are late. Did they make you run your shift late again? Was it that alcoholic cad, saying those nasty things to you again? You know you should really whack him upside the head and maybe that will teach him to back away, darling." She keeps going on and I stay behind the coat rack. I see her white hair peak above some of the racks, so I pretend I'm trying to find a specific blanket. There's no use in trying to hide, I'll only create more suspicion.

"Yes, Aunt Prim. The alcoholic was bothering me again and stopped me from closing up when I needed to. I'm sorry I'm late." I try to explain with the best assuring tone I can muster. I lose sight of her scraggly white hair and panic rises again, she'll know I'm lying if she sees my upper half covered in crusted blood. Not to leave out the fact that I must smell like the lavatory pipes by now. It's dark enough in here that she might not see though.

Who am I kidding? She notices everything.

"Why are you digging around in the racks, Artea?" She questions from behind me, I turn around quickly with my hands to the side like a child who got caught stealing a caramel.

"I was just making sure everything was tidied up, in case someone wants to buy anything tomorrow, of course." I chuckle nervously, hoping to hide the nervousness in my voice.

"What's wrong, darling?" Aunt Prim glares at me, putting her hands on her hips and biting her lip waiting for my answer. Who knew an old lady could be so intimidating? I almost have to break my neck to look her in the eyes below me. I forget to answer quickly and she reaches up slightly to grip my chin tight, pushing my head up as she takes a close look at the blood and dirt scattered all over my face, hair, and shoulders. "Artea."

The sternness of her voice shoots all the lies out of me, hearing the way she says my name makes me feel like a child again. *Art-ayuh.* I stand still and close my eyes, preparing for the scolding or the lecture.

"Before you say anything, it's not my blood. I got in between two folks fighting and slipped in the blood," I lie. "I'm sorry for hiding, I just didn't want you to worry." She glares at me, trying to decide if she believes me or not. I look at her with a begging in my eyes. I need to finish my tea and go upstairs to bathe because I'm afraid that if I sit here any longer I will pass out from the stench. And I know my lie is terrible.

"Fine." She finishes examining my face and arms. "Go upstairs and run yourself a bath. Don't come out until you are done smelling like death, do you hear me?"

I nod in compliance and flip my blood-soaked hair off my shoulder, walking away to the dim stairs ahead. The 'death' comment hits me in the chest in a weird way that makes me breathe even harder, feeling my hands shake just a little.

Before I can make it to the first step, Aunt Prim continues. "You should stop letting those buffoons in the tavern. How does someone bleed *that* much? And be so ill-mannered to spill on a young lady. Numen, save us."

I quickly walk up the stairs, leaving any chance for my lie to be caught behind. I love Aunt Prim and I hate lying to her because she's given me everything. But I can't tell her about what happened tonight, I can't even decipher it myself. I'm only left with the aftermath.

I make it to the small, dark bathroom and twist the metal knob for cold water as I don't have a choice. Halistyn is too poor for any fae with magic to live here. Most higher to middle-class towns and cities have workplaces dedicated to fae, just to heat the water sources. In a place like Halistyn, no one like a fae creature would want to live here. Tonight presented some good reasons as to why they wouldn't. Only the gross and selfish creatures reside here, like the ghouls, dwarves, pixies, and many more. Being merely human in Halistyn makes you insignificant compared to the evils that can knock on your door. That's why I work in a small shop, a small tavern, and live in a small studio. Making myself known would put me at more of a risk than I should allow. More of a risk than Aunt Prim would allow as well.

I begin ripping my blood and mud-ridden clothes off and stripping myself of the undergarments soaked with sweat. I'm sure I'll have to burn these clothes when I get the opportunity to. When the metal tub is done filling up with the ice-cold winter water, I step in with both legs letting the cold give me goosebumps and shivers down every hair. I force myself to sit down, even though every bone in my body is screaming at me to get into my room, to the fire.

Ignoring my body's cries to defrost, I dip my shoulders down into the water, then my neck, dropping my hair and forehead into the icy liquid. The memories of earlier start to come in thanks to being alone in the quiet of my own head. I start to replay the ghoul's head hitting the concrete with a horrifying thud and crack. I watch his body topple over his head over and over again. I hear the begs of the dwarf, pleading with that white streak of light to spare him. I shiver in the water, making ripples as it ricochets with the sides of the metal tub.

I can't get rid of that feeling that something is watching me, remembering what happened to me tonight. It almost feels like I'm a child whose friend is going to snitch for stealing candy. If me leaving the bodies of the criminals there on the floor is what will damn me to burn, then I deserve it.

The cold seems to swarm me more now than it has in the past couple of minutes. I feel every inch of my body covered in the water as I scrub and scrub, dying the water red. I leave flakes of dried blood at the bottom of the tub, recognizing I'll need to rinse off again if not two more times.

When I finish scrubbing and rinsing off a second time, I drain the tub and rinse the blood down the drain. The cold still lingers like a ghost on my skin as I wrap a towel around my front and let it droop to my knees. The slight warmth is merely comforting, unable to push away the vestige of my shivers. I don't even bother to put clothes on as I walk out of the bathing room and into my room right across the hall, if it even counts as a hall.

It's more like a tiny corridor with three doors. One for the bathing room, one for Aunt Prim's room, and the last one for me. The bedrooms are just as small as the corridor is, with some extra room for a bed. I'm lucky enough to have a fireplace in my room and with the size of the dorm the fire heats the room very nicely. I'm rarely cold if I'm under the right blankets and sleeping with my nightgown on. Unlike the nights this season, I make sure none of those items are constricting me in the summer.

I start the fire after a few good tries and welcome the flames, soothing my shivers as I close my eyes. I've always brought my hands close to the fire, feeling the peaks of yellow and orange dancing around my fingertips, hot to the touch but not hot enough to burn. Something about the warmth and comfort of the fire has always made me feel calm. I'm sure it's because I was left in the cold when I was dropped on the doorstep of this shop. Maybe that's why I appreciate Aunt Prim's blankets so much because I've always resented the cold. Lately though, I've forced myself to embrace the cold on these long winter nights, letting my body get used to both extremes. Something about being able to control how my body reacts to things I can't control gives me a sense of power over myself. With so little control over my life, whether it be Ihrvian, Halistyn, or the people around me, it seems like I have no control. I can control myself, though. At least there's me

Chapter Three

The bell in the middle of the town rings, marking the seven o'clock morning chime. If I listen closely enough, I can hear the rustle of everyone waking up, getting ready to start school or their jobs. This includes me, but mostly my mornings involve standing behind the counter in the empty shop, waiting for my one customer of the day.

I'm sitting up in my bed, trying to let my eyes adjust to the sun on the horizon threatening to blind anyone who looks its way. That's when I hear murmurs and screams followed by gasps and doors slamming. I slide into my mud-covered boots and throw on a shawl and a cream-colored skirt, rushing to find out what the commotion is about. I run down the stairs, meeting Aunt Prim as I run out the door. I assure her that I'll be right back in time to make breakfast and open the shop up.

I forget all about my bedridden hair and my puffy eyes from my slumber as I run to the crowd. I finally realize as I get closer, where they're all standing. Each bystander whispers to their neighbors or rushes their kids back into the townhomes. I halt on my heels and walk slowly now, hoping that for some miracle reason, the evidence of what had happened last night is gone. The closer I get, the more I can smell that a miracle did not come. I stand in the back of the small crowd, but still allow myself to see through the cracks of people's shoulders and heads, all turning in curiosity and horror.

The men's bodies, and heads, are still where I had left them, piled on top of each other in a cruel mix of blood. This was my fault. If I would have just run home, none of this would have happened.

Blood, so much blood.

The edges of the pool have started to crust and stick to the pebbles and withering concrete. Some blood has seeped into the ground and fed the dirt. There's even frost on the edges as the cold winter night took over the soaking liquid.

I try my best to keep my face straight, with an even mix of surprise. Even if the ones dead are filthy creatures like a ghoul or a mean dwarf, this town is small enough that people talk. People see things and word spreads fast. If someone saw me or suspects that I did this, I might have to leave. It doesn't matter if you're friends or strangers, you and your family always come first here. I'm sure Halistyn was a nicer place before the war, before all the nice people got scared off to try and find homes on other islands or towns in Ihrvian. But as of now in Halistyn, selfishness is just as essential as food and water.

I look around the crowd, the circle surrounding the two dead men. The heads stare into nothing as feet shuffle in front of them like they're nothing. I catch glimpses of multiple people, some I make eye contact with who are trying to survey, as I am. A few good looks at the crowd and I'm sure that no one is saying anything about a witness, murderer, or suspects. I take a deep breath, but before I can let it out I catch a glance from a tall man in the crowd across from me who's looking directly my way, and looks anything but happy.

Shit, shit, shit.

I can run, I can get out of here before anyone else acknowledges that I was here. If he thinks I did it, how would I explain that *light* came and decapitated these low-life dealers? He can't believe that a girl just took on those two flesh-eating assholes by herself, does he? I mean, I think I could take on one with my dagger, but two? I'd have a better chance running.

Which you should have done, Artea.

I look away and glance back to find him still looking at me, studying me almost. I keep eye contact and try to look unblinking. He catches my stare and before I can walk away from this mess he tilts his head, motioning to a door leading into a bar I've never been to before. I furrow my brows in confusion and tilt my head to the same door, confirming what I think he's saying. He ever so slightly drops his chin in answer.

Do I follow him? Is he a friend of the men that attacked me last night? Either way, he looks like he knows something. Maybe following him in the tavern would be less dangerous than if I were to go home and get killed in my sleep, which hopefully wouldn't happen. Though, you never know how far someone might go for their family, especially if they think you hurt them.

I nod in acceptance, too scared to put up a fight with yet another man in only twenty-four hours. He turns around and starts to walk towards his left to the bar he motioned toward a second ago. I wait a moment, not wanting the bustling crowd to think anything of me and this man meeting. I make it to the wooden steps of the bar, the man already inside and probably sitting down by now. I push the swinging door open and hear the bell over my head ding with a rusty tang. I lift my shoulders but stay weary, unsure who or what might be in here waiting for me/ To my left there's the main bar with an old man whom I've seen around here before slumped on the counter, asleep and drunk. He most likely had a nice overnight stay. When I peer to the right I see a line of booths and seats meant for dinners and lunches to be eaten, and on top of one of those seats sits the large man.

I crack my knuckles behind my back and let out a sigh I didn't realize I was holding. The man looks at me and gestures to the table with an unreadable look on his face. I pat my skirt down and adjust my feet inside my boots. I was in a rush this morning and I'm sure I look like just another homeless pixie who hides in trees and terrorizes the squirrels. I'm not attracted to this man or anything, but I don't prefer anyone seeing me look like this.

I walk a few yards over to the table and take the black leather seat across from him. I can smell him from here, getting a whiff of pine and rum. It's a pleasant smell but it stabs my nose like a knife. I squint my eyes and study the man. He has a thick coat of hair on his face and hands, as well as black fingernails. He can't be less than seven feet tall with muscles built for chopping lumber. He has slightly curved horns on his head, similar to a bull's head. He looks more human than a bull but seems to be a minotaur or a descendant of one.

Minotaurs are common around here because they're native to Ihrvian. I only know that because Aunt Prim has sewn a lot of quilts with patches upon patches of stories about how the minotaurs had their own legion of soldiers to fight against the king and his army. I don't know much about the war and what happened or who fought, but what I do know is that the king wanted to break the bridges connecting the islands and he used the elvish people from the country below our archipelago to fight the queen of our islands. The queen was fighting him to protect the islands and won the war after Cabal, Duke of Ihrvian, was able to kill the king just after our bridges connecting all the islands to Mava were severed. I wish I knew more about our past but the seas are so dangerous to cross so it's nearly impossible to receive or give any information from or to anyone since the bridges have been taken down by the King of Perdita.

No one has heard of anyone higher up in rank in Mava or from any of the six island's dukes or duchesses. As far as I know, no one has heard from the queen either. Ihrvian got a message that we will be furnished and the queen is working hard to build agriculture back to its peak like it was before the War or Stone and Mountains. That promise hasn't held any merit. Additionally, Mava never promised money and it shows. People might have the correct soil for crops and enough land for cattle, but everyone is still poorer than their neighbor.

I feel my thoughts drift as I judge the minotaur in front of me. His black eyes stare at me like orbs as he waits for me to say anything. This could be an unsettling interaction but nothing about his demeanor makes me worry for my life. He doesn't seem angry or aggressive, just tough to read, and a lot bigger than the average man.

"Well? I assume you didn't invite me here to stare, right?" I ask, looking into his eyes, darting back and forth, looking for a hint of anything at all.

"You would be correct," he says after clearing his throat, letting a deep booming grunt of a sentence out. His voice could shape mountains, and his older age makes it that much more intimidating. "You came running out of your shop quite quickly, didn't you?"

I squint my brow trying to make him think that I was simply worried about the people murmuring outside and the children screaming, running away.

"There was a lot of yelling and I was concerned, yes. Didn't everyone?" I say, glaring at his suspiciousness. If he saw me last night I could be in danger. He might have known the men who were seeping blood on top of me. He might have made me follow him in here to finish the job. I wiggle my right foot around to feel for my dagger and swear at myself when I don't feel it.

I never forget it.

"Don't be so stiff," he mutters, making me loosen my legs trying to hide the fact that I want to get out of here. Now. "The fact that you ran out so fast is interesting in itself. But what made me want to talk to you is all the blood on your boots."

Of course.

The blood on my boots sells me to my ruin.

"I visited the butcher shop the other day, what is it to you…" I lie and fish for his name. Maybe some familiarity would make this guy a confidant instead of my killer.

"Gunter, and we both know that's a load of shit. You were watching the crowd like a crow does to a dead rat." He chuckles at my inability to lie.

"That is vulgar and unnecessary. How did you know I was there? I mean, I didn't kill the ghoul and the dwarf I swear," I ramble on, talking faster than I thought was possible. Some words probably slipped from my tongue, going so swiftly he can't register most of them. "They were attacking me and I got stuck between them. The ghoul went on about how he wanted to eat me and the dwarf was chuckling the whole time, please believe me. I'm sorry if they were your friends–"

A big booming laugh comes from the minoat—Gunter, so loud I think the bar and the neighboring buildings shook with his chest.

"Friend?" he spits out while still laughing with tears in his eyes. "Those demons are the furthest things from my friends. Their filth is ruining Halitsyn and everyone in it," he says as I show him blank wide eyes. "Listen, I believe you. If anything, you did the town a favor by killing those pricks."

"I didn't *kill,* anyfellow." I spit through my teeth, leading Gunter to spread a large smile.

"I'm teasing," he gestures his hands in a calm motion. I loosen my shoulders a little bit as I observe his gray and brown horns poking through his dark black hair. "Though, I do wonder, who killed them?"

"I don't know. They dropped dead in front of me, and on me. I got drenched in blood and had to rinse for an hour to get most of it off of me." I say, looking down as I remember the head dropping to the floor, the pleading, the blood.

"I'm sorry that happened," he drops his chin and it surprises me. Folks aren't usually nice or gentle like he's being right now. I'm used to loud and inappropriate comments or lousy men urinating on the wooden planks of the tavern. The war and starvation, as well as the general hardships in Halistyn make most everyone aggressive. There's not usually compassion. "What is a girl like you doing late enough for those rascals to get their hands on you? Especially a shop girl."

"One, how do you know I run the shop? And two, is that supposed to be an insult?" I gawk at the comment, unsure of what it's supposed to mean.

"Um," he clears his throat. "You came running out of it, slamming the door like you were trying to trap something inside," *Aunt Prim,* I think, but I don't say that. "And it's supposed to mean that you're so pale you could blend in with snow just outside that window there. It also means your muscles look like they're begging for a good pot roast."

"It's wintertime. In *Halistyn*. Do you think I can just go and buy whatever food I wish? No one here has pocket money to spend on blankets or vases, and the tavern is barely standing. Not to mention the fact that I get a tip maybe once a night and it's usually from some prick who wants to bareback with me," I grimace at the memories of all the drunken men trying to touch what isn't theirs. That's what my dagger is for, after all. "So, maybe that's why I look so frail." I spit sarcastically, crossing my arms and kicking my feet forward, reminding myself of a toddler. I silently cringe at myself, hoping he doesn't think I'm as ridiculous as I feel.

I'm ready to get up and walk away when Gunter pulls out a very small black pouch from his pocket. He places it on the table and slides it to me with his hands that are the size of my face. He crosses his arms, motioning to the pouch with his chin.

"What's this?" I ask, slowly reaching for the pouch and undoing the knot while giving Gunter eye contact. As I pull the small, cold, metal object out Gunter explains.

"It's a ring. My wife wanted me to sell it, and pawn it for some money so we could move to a neighboring island like Frendsa or Ornau. Though from what we hear, which is very little, Frendsa is ridden with desert and most people have gone to live in caves," he describes. I've never heard about what lies within Frendsa, I've only seen maps.

"The ring is worth a lot of money, but nobody here has the type of money to give me what it's truly worth. Maybe half, if I'm lucky. I also went to the tavern last night and didn't pay for my drink. You workers were so engrossed with making sure the soldiers weren't breaking everything to notice me walk out without paying. Consider this my payment," he continues to explain. "Plus, I saw you run out of a shop I barely remembered existed with your hair all disheveled. I think you need this more than I do. Especially since I'm going on an adventure I'll most likely die doing."

Those oceans are a long and painful journey. There are hundreds of stories from here about families or friends who have never heard of their loved ones again.

"Oh, don't think like that. If it's such a death wish, why are you leaving?" I ask, genuinely curious, trying to ignore the ring worth my whole life dancing around my fingertips.

"My wife can't take being here anymore. She's unhappy and will refuse to raise children here with this filth lying around in every corner. You're a perfect example of why I could agree with her on it," he says. "I just don't want a ring worth this much going to waste on a boat or to some pawn shop that's as broke as me."

"But, why me? I mean there are more deserving people around here, I'm sure of it." I say, the urge to put the ring on growing stronger by the second.

"Yes, maybe. However, we're leaving tomorrow and I don't have time to wait for someone more *deserving*." He pokes. He gestures to the ring, and I assume he wants me to look at it. I twirl the ring around my fingers as he waves to the bartender to get us a drink. Why is this bar open at seven thirty in the morning? I'm not sure. Though, I could use a drink to calm my nerves right about now.

Why did I follow a stranger twice my size into a bar, and sit with him? Maybe last night made me crazy and now I might as well throw away all common sense. Maybe I imagined last night and this has all been a made-up dream while I'm still fast asleep in my bed.

I'm reminded that this is reality when Gunter gets up and steps to the bar, telling me I can stay here and enjoy the gift from a stranger.

The ring has a delicate and beautiful gold braided band with four different stones. The first green stone is raised higher than the others, its color carrying many layers of pigment. The one to the left is a pale yellow, and the one to the right is a deep blue like a river flowing in a small circle of rock. The last one is a black and brown stone woven inside the gold band right below the green rock. It's almost as if I can feel a story being told within the ring.

I slide the ring on and admire how the jewels decorate my right middle finger. The jewels' colors look even deeper when I take my hand into the sunlight through the dusty window, the sun brighter than usual because of snow glazing the surfaces of Halistyn. I wonder how much I could sell this for if Aunt Prim lets me travel to a wealthier town. Maybe some rich snob would like to wear it instead.

"Hey," Gunter grumbles from the bar across the room, interrupting my thoughts. "I have your drink, kid." I roll my eyes at the comment and waltz to the bar as Gunter has two mugs in front of him. His drink is foamy and tan, so I'm assuming it's beer. Typical. Mine is dark brown and has swirls of pink, red, and purple. Either he or the bartender guessed that, because I'm a girl, I like the fruity stuff. I can take straight liquor just fine, I like it, but I don't mind some lighter flavors with it. I refuse to admit it though as I pick up the mug while he does as well.

"Are you sure this ring is mine?" I ask, making sure he'll let me walk away with this priceless piece of handiwork. Gunter nods and blinks slowly with a little smirk daring to peek on the right side of his face. I raise my glass, inviting him to drink with me. "To new friends." I say as we rattle our drinks and chug them. Gunter looks surprised to see that I emptied my drink in one swallow. I don't do it because I think I'm better than a sipper, I do it because I like to *feel* my alcohol, even if it's gross.

"Hey, can I show you something? There's a sculpture studio in the building behind this bar. They connect with a door just right through there. It's where my wife works." Gunter volunteers, pointing to a corridor past the booths. I feel the alcohol warm my body and seep through my empty stomach.

I was raised to love crafts, so I respond softly. "Yes, let us go see it."

We walk down the hall past a couple of doors when we reach a large wooden door decorated with a golden handle that creaks as Gunter opens it. The candlelight starts to sway as I look at the walls where the candles hang. I start to trek loosely through the door as I feel Gunter pick me up and mumble words that fly past my ears and reverberate through the walls. I try to speak as my mouth feels numb and my throat closes up.

The room gets dark, very dark. I can only sense the tingling left in my muscles from the booze as I lose all ability to feel or hear anything.

Chapter Four

The cold air hits me before anything else, the draft tickling my arms as I roll to my side. The nausea comes next, overwhelming my stomach and head. My body feels like someone spun me around one hundred times and let me fall for eternity. I open my eyes as best as I can and feel for the ground. The soft material under my palms feels like a bed and the light around me is so bright I struggle to make out anything around me.

I find the edge of the bed and fall to the ground on my knees keeping myself up with my arms, pressing my hands hard into the rug below me. I drop my head as the rush of sickness builds up in my body. I liberate the small amount of contents from my stomach, getting sick all over the red and blue carpet, almost hitting my head on a large piece of wooden furniture in front of me.

I sit for a moment, waiting for more sickness to exorcize itself from me. When I feel it's safe enough for me to stand I anchor myself to the bed and push myself up. I can make out the room well enough to see I'm in a bedroom, a *large* bedroom. The presumed bed I woke up on has white sheets and a cream-colored blanket so massive a giant could still have wiggle room.

Panic sets in.

Where am I?

I've never seen this room before nor known anyone rich enough to own anything like this. I look around some more, keeping my composure. Straight across from the bed, there's a fireplace and to my left is an exit with twin glass doors that lead to a balcony. I tumble to the glass doors and twist the door knob. Maybe if I get an idea of where I am, I can find out how I got here. I walk out of the doors, letting my face meet the cool breeze that I felt earlier only stronger now. The sun is out and I can see the mountains and valleys from here. I'm high up, I realize, after seeing the people below walking around a garden.

The garden.

The plants and rocks and small ponds below me are like art. They are intricately designed in patterns and swirls. The ponds are in the middle of rocks that are in the middle of flowers. There are beautiful fish in the ponds, swimming around in perfect circles. The flowers are blooming with pinks and purples. Some are yellow or orange, however, all the colors blend in perfect harmony. Even the trees are shades of red or blue, bright and unusual.

The people are too blurry to be seen from here, but they all have neat outfits on and walk like they're people meant to be here.

I've never seen anything like this before. I've done a lot of traveling around Ihrvian getting cloth for Aunt Prim or finding a new spice for a recipe she would like to try. Sometimes I would get clay for myself and make small models of animals or objects. Clay and spices can only be found in the more wealthy parts of Ihrvian, which Halistyn clearly isn't in. Even with all the traveling I've done, I've never seen something so designed and beautiful.

I look outside as I decide to trail my way back to where I *did* know I was. I remember the attack from the ghoul and dwarf, I remember lying to Aunt Prim, the bath, the bells ringing, and the crowd. I look down at my hand and see the ring holding the four distinct stones, the gold braided band glows in the sunlight.

Gunter. The bar. The drink.

I blacked out.

I turn around from the scene in front of me and dash for the large door behind me. I have no idea where I am and none of this is familiar, the freight builds in my chest with each step I take. I shake the door handle but it doesn't budge. I pound on the door, hard. I pound and yell, and I continue to pound and yell, commanding the door to open. When nothing happens and no one comes, I walk quickly to the balcony.

I yell for help, loud enough that they should hear me. *I'm locked in a room, and I don't know how I got here! I'm locked in a room and I don't know how I got here!*

No one looks up.

I grip the bar preventing me from jumping out of the building until my knuckles turn a shade of white I didn't think was possible.

The door behind me creaks open and I dash to crouch behind one of the sides of the bed, putting distance between me and whoever stands on the other side. I avoid the contents of my stomach as I grip a metal candle stick on a side table to the left of the bed as a weapon. Pain seizes my arm, sending a surging burning sensation up my arm and my neck.

I drop the candlestick, letting it hit the floor with a clunk as I grip my wrist. A small yip escapes my mouth as I look at the red burn. My white skin is raided with spots of red and purple, bleeding only a little.

"Yeah, you're allergic to iron and silver. So, I'd be careful with that," a man's voice creeps through the door. I look up from my red hand and see him leaning against the doorframe. I shoot my hands to my sides and feel for my boots, finding out I'm barefoot.

Great.

I have nothing to protect myself with. Yet.

"Don't worry, I've been given strict orders to not touch you." He lightly tosses his hands up in surrender.

The man has on a uniform of some sort. It's light, almost white but not quite, similar to the bed's blanket. The outlines of the seams are decorated with a gold-yellow thread. He has a strap attached to his side, holding what I assume is a blade or a sword of some kind. He has chest-length dirty-brown hair braided loosely down his right shoulder. His brown beard is clean and trimmed at a length fit for a man in uniform. He's tall and lean, sort of skinny but his suit fits him well enough that I know he has a lot of muscle. His face is completely indecipherable. His gray eyes are leveled, but also glaring with a sort of amusement.

"Are you gonna quit staring and let me introduce myself, or should I come back after the sick pile is cleaned up?" he asks me, with an annoying smirk across his face. I can't help but notice how conventionally handsome he is. Almost sun kissed.

"Where am I?" I demand. He rolls his eyes and uncrosses his arms, standing straight. *Handsome with an attitude.*

"Well, I was getting there. Though, I'm not allowed to tell you anything until you've changed and maybe bathed. We will meet for dinner in two hours. The stylist will be here in about thirty minutes so I suggest you do that quickly." I'm baffled by this man's audacity and bluntness as he turns around to leave.

"Hey!" I yell, and he pauses his steps, turning back around. "You said you wanted to, um– introduce yourself," I say, trying to be polite. This guy could kill me or something and the last thing I need is *that.*

"Well, I'm General Zehlin. I'm the queen's second in command for Mava's military," he answers. Enunciating the *General* part, he tries to hide the titles he's too proud of.

Mava? I internally panic. Mava, the middle island that's seemingly unfeasible to travel to. Am I in Mava? That's impossible though, the ocean is too dangerous to cross and Halistyn is in the south of Ihrvian. The travel time should have taken days if not weeks, I would have woken up by then.

"M–Mava?" I ask, looking him in the eye trying to contain the shivers and panic taking over my legs.

"We will go over it all at dinner," he says, his posture still straight and his face sits impossible to read. "I have things to attend to, please groom yourself and wait for the stylist."

With that he leaves, shutting the massive wooden door behind him. I run to the door and try to open it as I did earlier, and to no surprise it still won't open.

After General Zehlin, as he so proudly called himself, left, I smelled myself. Not only did I smell my rancid body and hair but the sick had been left on the floor long enough to seep into the carpet and pollute the air. I decided to bathe and ignore the spew I left on the floor. The bathroom was equally as abnormally large as the bedroom was with a tub large enough for four more of me to lay comfortably and a sink that I could splash around in. The walls were white and decorated with gold, marbled all around like a pixie sprinkled in.

The size wasn't what amazed me, though. It was hot water. Hot water was as much of a myth as the Sasquatch to people who grew up in Halistyn. Even before the War of Stone and Mountains, Halistyn was still quiet and small. It's much smaller now, but it still wasn't populated enough for a fae factory to heat the water.

The water felt so good on my skin, and it had never been so polished. There was lather for me to use, scented like flowers mixed with the essence of clouds. It was heavenly. I hated indulging in this bath, in the pleasantries. I still don't know where I am or who brought me here. Plus, I'm almost one hundred percent sure I was drugged and kidnapped.

I hated that I was listening to the general, but I did need this. My burn was almost healed by the time I got out of the bath. I assume that there are healing factors in the water.

The cream of the crop was when I tried to take off the ring Gunter gave me, it wouldn't loosen. I assume it was because of the hot water making my hands swell. Though, I wished I could have got it off so I could clean under my middle finger as well.

I analyze my skin in the perfectly clear mirror and see that I don't have any signs of bruises or scratches. The only thing left on my bare body is the ring on my right hand.

The supposed 'stylist' is going to be here soon so I wrap my hair in one of the thousands of towels folded neatly on a shelf and throw a deep purple robe on. I open the grand white and gold door to lead myself back into the bedroom. I pause inside the doorframe when I see a woman laying out clothes on the bed and humming. She doesn't turn around as she speaks.

"Usually when you are given a time, you should be *on time*," she chides, flattening a blue piece of clothing that looks like a silky dress. The more I look at what she's doing, they all look like dresses. Still, without looking towards me she mutters, "Please, take a seat," pointing to a white and gold ottoman sitting at a vanity.

"I wasn't aware I was supposed to do *anything*. I don't even know why I'm here," I sputter, slowly making my way to the vanity seat. I hear her heels cracking against the floor and scoot across the carpet as she approaches me. I see through the mirror that she's holding multiple dresses or clothes of all different styles and colors.

She has an all-black outfit on with nothing standing out to me. She wears a simple and elegant, yet loose dress that goes down to her knees, fitting her figure nicely. Her black hair, soft face, plump cheeks, and lips all make her look my age if not younger. She's beautiful without a doubt and she has a soft voice that projects like an old lady similar to my aunt.

Aunt Prim.

Was she okay? Did something happen to her? Does she know I'm gone? What if she fell or is worrying that I'm gone? I am all she has.

"Who are you?" I stand. "Where am I and what are you doing? I'm aware I can't get out of here and I'm locked in this room. At least one person should tell me what the hell is happening," I challenge, landing my feet heavy on the floor.

"Aside from the fact I'm not allowed to tell you anything, I don't know anything." She answers while hanging up the clothes on a rack by the vanity and motions to the seat again.

"I'm not sitting down to be dolled up for some dinner by an unknown lady, in an unknown building, not knowing how I got here, and on an unknown island. Am I really in Mava?" I slightly beg again, still not sitting down.

She shakes her head and motions to the seat again, insisting on me sitting down. Does she *really* think I'll just sit and look pretty for some dinner? I feel miserable, my whole body is in pain and I feel like I'm constantly going to be sick. My hand still burns from the candlestick earlier and I still can't explain why my skin reacted like that. General Zehlin mentioned I'm allergic to iron, but I'm not. I've touched iron my whole life and it's never burned me.

"I cannot say anything, girl. Now, please sit," she says, standing still and looking at the ground.

"*Girl?* Excuse me but you look younger than me, and last I checked I don't need to do anything a strangefolk tells me to do. Now get me someone who can give me answers. Or find me some trousers and a blouse so I can find answers myself at this dinner the General talked to me about," I demand sternly, knowing I sound childish. "Those dresses are pretty, but I refuse to be gussied up for strangers."

She looks me in the eyes and glares at me but takes a deep breath. "No lady here wears trousers, but I can get you a pair of young men's if that's what you require to attend dinner," she surrenders. "Also I age slowly because of a spell surrounding me given by the queen. I'm certainly decades older than you, to be clear."

I nod in understanding, still taken aback by her beauty. Her face seems sculpted like porcelain or clay. The red tones of her cheeks complement her green eyes. I've always wondered what the queen can do and casting spells doesn't surprise me one bit.

"Will you at least let me groom your hair?" she asks, sounding tired of me already. "I'm only following directions. Getting the ladies of the castle ready is my job." She explains. Her being only a servant makes listening a little easier. If she's not to blame for me being here, I don't need to make her time miserable because of my stubbornness.

"What do I call you?" I ask, drifty closer to the seat in front of the vanity.

"Gachera," she says. She opens a satchel attached to her waist and pulls out a comb. "Chera will do just fine, but I don't mind either. Most people here say my full name as I'm not familiar with many of the castle's people. I just do my job." She points to the seat again. "Now please, sit."

I've barely any clue where I am or what I'm here for but I do know there are royals and castles involved. The only castle I've ever seen is the only one in Ihrvian. It's in the capital where Duke Cabal lived, or might still be living. Though if he is, he hasn't made himself known. Not since the war, that is.

I fidget with the stuck ring on my swollen finger as I feel Gachera lace and weave my hair into all different types of knots and twists.

Someone wants me here.

And I'm trapped.

Chapter Five

Gachera finished with my hair after Numen knew how long, and by the time she asked me to stand up so she could measure my height, my lower back was aching. She told me to wait in here, like I had a choice, while she went to grab some trousers and a blouse.

I walk to the balcony while I wait for the stylist. I give myself time to look outside longer, watching the people walk past the street below me. No one is walking along with another, and they all brisk past as if they're running a few minutes late and have somewhere they need to be. No one nods to any folk as they pass, they just look at the floor and let their coats blow in the wind past their knees.

I peer behind my shoulder at the brown sealed door, grip the railing to the balcony and scream. I scream and scream. I feel my jaw open against the breeze as the warm air leaves my lungs. I yell and wave my hands as I attempt to make my sound reach the pedestrians walking below me.

No one looks up, flinches, or even misses a stride in their step as I belt my chest out into the open air. Left to be ignored, yet still feeling relief as I hear wood creek behind me.

"No one can hear you, sweetheart." I hear the faint familiar voice raise in a hushed mumble.

I flip around to see General Zehlin sitting on the bed picking at one of his nails. I lean against the railing, the cool metal soaking through the thick cloth of the robe. I cross my arms to my middle in an attempt to cover myself up, my midthighs and below, as well as the slight V-shape of the robe on my chest, are open.

He looks away, noticing my lack of attire.

"How did you get in here?" I glare at him, the sun shining to my side slightly blinding my gaze to him.

"I tessered in," he says, still looking at the wall. "I kind of wish I didn't say anything, the light was hitting you in an alluring way."

Gross. At least he still doesn't look at me.

"Tessered?" I ask, moving one hand to my face to block the intruding blaze of the sun.

"I stopped time for a moment to transport here." He says, almost like my question was ridiculous.

"Are you allowed to answer me if I ask, *how?*" I shift on my feet, the urge to sucker punch this man grows stronger every time he opens his mouth.

"I am not, I'm afraid." He says. He opens his mouth to continue something that I couldn't care less about before I interrupt.

"What if I was changing?" I argue walking into the room slowly to get a better look at him.

"Well I thought you'd be done by now, but I take it you were too busy arguing with Chera to take the time to get ready," he remarks with a load of attitude. "And screaming."

"Actually she's getting my clothes now," he stares as I correct him. "Can you leave?" I ask, crossing my arms and stopping a few yards away from the general.

He doesn't respond, he only shrugs and lowers his head to the floor. I see the wooden door in front of us open as Gachera steps in. With her hands full of the clothes she brought me, she bows.

"General Zehlin." She greets as he steps up and walks toward her. He takes her hand and leaves a light kiss on the top of her pale skin.

"Chera, it's a pleasure to see you again. How long has it been since I've gotten to speak with you?" He says, straightening his shoulders as she steps to the side and sets my clothes on the vanity seat.

I wonder how well they know each other. Or how long have they known each other? Garchera said she was much older than I was and General Zehlin looks much too young to be a general. I put the thought aside. Wondering the past of the folks who keep me stuck in a building aren't folks who deserve my pondering.

"Too long I'm afraid." She shakes her head and smiles. "Is there anything I can get you, General?" she asks as General Zehlin makes his way to the door.

"No, don't fret, dear. Just take your time and make our new guest look admissible." He waves his hand as he shuts the door.

Bastard.

I spoke with Gachera about a few things as she tailored the bottoms of my trousers. She claimed they were too long and made me look like a dwarf in a human pair of pants. I asked her a few things, most questions were answered with, *I can't say, wait until dinner, dear.* Yet, when I had asked what in the hell dinner consisted of, she corrected my language and said all I have to do is sit there and listen. She was persistent on the listening part.

Like I *wouldn't* listen.

I'm stuck in a castle in Mava, of course I'm going to listen. *And* share my opinions.

She also mentioned that there's no use in trying to run, that it's not only this door that prevents me from opening it; it's all of them. Windows and balconies included. That's why no one from below heard me when I screamed. She said she truly doesn't know why the castle rejects me and has never seen it before.

I finished getting ready and slipped into a pair of flat dress shoes. I'm the most put together I've been in Numen knows how long. Gachera led me outside the door, the huge corridor outside was covered in purple and red carpet, the ceiling holding a chandelier for almost every door we pass. All the doors look the same, large and brown with golden handles. The walls are all white, with the same gold streaks throughout, similar to the bathroom.

I look behind me as we walk and my eyes meet the back of the hallway where there's a window. I glance at the dusky-pink sky, decorated with puffy clouds before I turn back around and continue to follow the stylist.

The castle is a maze to me as we make our way to dinner, whatever dinner was going to be. The amount of doors and hallways and staircases we pass makes me wonder how anyone makes their way through the castle without having to call for help. Gachera walks down these hallways like she owns them, like she's been through this building her whole life.

After a minute or two of confusing twists and turns, we reach a set of closed double doors, the largest doors I've ever seen. Who or what needs doors five times their height?

Gachera grabs the door handles and it's at this moment that I feel the urge to grab the vase on the small table to my right and smash it against her head, giving myself a chance to run. Considering she's been nothing but nice to me and she says I can't get out, I stay still letting my nerves and bewilderment settle back into my hands and feet.

She swings the doors open and stands to my left, leaving me placed in the middle of the opening, staring. The dining room looks as extraneous as the rest of the building with large chandeliers and undecorated white and gold walls. In front of me, numerous meters away there's a table. Each side of the surface has twenty seats each with large throne-like seats at the ends. I see a woman on the far end from me sitting at the chair as well as a silhouette of somebody else at the closest one. The woman is too far away for me to make out much about her, but she does look older.

I realize I'm just staring, not moving or doing anything. I see the woman smiling faintly and I step forward. I step forward again. Again.

And again.

I can't feel my feet moving, but I can see myself moving closer to the table. I hear the door behind me shut with a light click and turn around to see if there's anything or anyone behind me. With nothing there, I turn and persist to the table. I stop just before I get to the first chair at the close end of the table and look at the woman across.

"Please, Artea, take a seat. We don't bite," the woman speaks, her voice light but infested with age. I only look at her, my throat stuck and dry. The whole situation of not knowing anything is setting in and I feel nausea build up. I take a hand to rest on my abdomen and look at a chair in the middle of the table. "A place in between the general and I is just fine, dear."

General Zehlin. Of course. The brooding prick with no regard for others privacy. If I don't have the choice whether or not I'm here, I deserve some lack of disturbance at minimum.

I finally walk further into the room and don't bother to look behind me at the general. I find a seat in the center of the table and sit down, scooting the chair in behind me. There's some food in front of me on a plate already there. My stomach hasn't stopped rumbling since I woke up, but I think if I ate even a bite of food, it wouldn't stay down long.

"I'm not surprised you don't want to eat, it would seem only natural that your body is trying to regulate itself before anything else." The woman speaks to me, the sound of the general's fork scraping against the plate makes my ears bleed.

"What?" I ask, finally looking up at the woman getting a good look at her face. She has blonde hair with white streaks, her face has light wrinkles but it doesn't sag. There are yellow and brown horns perching slightly behind her head, and curving at the ends. She looks groomed and her dress looks tailored especially for her.

She is a beautiful woman. However, something in her eyes puts me off in the slightest. I'm not sure what it is, but it looks dark. Like she's had a life full of devastation. I drop my shoulders a little and keep making eye contact as I speak. "What are you talking about? Why am I here and who the hell are you?" I say, questions starting to flow out of me. "Why can't I open the doors and why can't anyone outside hear me?"

"Now, now. We will answer all those questions Artea," I feel my stomach begin to twist and go in circles. "We need to explain something about our archipelago, and we need you to listen. Can you listen?" The woman asks me. I'm tempted to say no and throw my plate of food at her face, but I don't. I look over to General Zehlin and he nods toward the woman. I simply nod and look down into my lap, controlling my breathing and counting my fingers as the woman begins to speak again.

"I'm Queen Etiza, and this is my palace. I'm sure you've already met my second in command, General Zehlin. He takes care of a lot of things. Important things. That is why he has been put to task with, well, you," she continues. *Queen* of Mava. "We understand you must be confused, but we had to do this swiftly and safely for your protection. I can answer all of your questions after I explain why we have brought you here."

"Well?" I shoot out, turning my head to her. She has a look on her face that shows me she didn't expect me to say anything at all. I didn't expect it either.

"Yes," she clears her throat awkwardly. "We have found a way to bring the islands together again. Connecting the archipelago once more. However, it is a task, or multiple tasks I should say, that would take a lot of courage and power."

"And what in Numen's name does this have anything to do with me?" I ask, staring the queen down, my frustration starting to boil up and warm my veins. The urge to walk out of here and go back to my room to jump off the balcony and escape grows stronger every sentence that's spoken.

"You have been feeling sick since you woke, yes?" She asks me, surely already knowing the answer. I keep my words to myself, still looking at her. The legendary queen who has held the throne of the archipelago for a few hundred years is sitting close to my right, and yet I still feel no urge to bow to or hold back from her.

She nods, understanding that I won't answer and swallows another bite of meat.

"You're sick because we are cleansing you. You've been rid of your frequent poison of fesch root. It would dull your abilities, and change your appearance to anyone around you, including yourself. Do you know what I'm talking about, Artea?" She continues to talk, the words muffling around the muggy feeling in the room.

"Fesch root? W—what is that? You're not making any sense." I ask, the nausea becoming harder and harder to hold back from the frontlines.

"Your aunt, Prim, she would feed you this fesch root. She would slip it in your tea or supper every day. Without your knowledge, your powers would become inconspicuous to everyone. Your body was changed and morphed into human form." She pauses, letting me process the information.

"Elvish," I mumble under my breath. *Fesch,* I remember reading that word in an elvish poetry book. Reading is my pastime when we don't have any ceramics to paint or clay to shape. The boy in the story was hiding in plain sight from his wretched father and was able to escape him. The elvish boy's name was Fesch.

"Hmm?" Queen Etiza mumbles through her stuffed mouth.

"It's an elvish root. The fesch root. What does that mean?" I ask, eyes starting to tear with the rolling pain pinching all my nerves around my body. I feel the saliva build in my throat, threatening to welcome sickness.

"It means your aunt was hiding your powers from you, dear. Your body is trying to get used to its natural state, that's why you feel so ill," she claims, her words warping around my head like a cloud of smoke. I breathe, trying to calm my body.

Why would Aunt Prim do such a thing? I mean, she couldn't have done that. It would mean that throughout my whole life she's been lying to me. But she's the one who took care of me, she raised me. She's all I've ever known. I raise my shoulders and punch back the moisture in my eyes and the sickness protruding my throat as best as I can. I look over to

General Zehlin for the second time since dinner. He's a beautiful man, his hair still braided and set loosely to his side, and his uniform is the same as well. Though, he doesn't have his overcoat on anymore, letting me see the large arms and stature of him. It makes me wonder what I would possibly do with all that muscle in my arms, how I could put it to use. Maybe that's why he's a soldier, *the queen's* soldier.

I look back at my full plate and take a bite of a biscuit, slightly soaked with gravy. It's moist and salty, the bread more full than any bread I've had from Halistyn. I hide how impressed I am from the absolute explosion of flavor flowing on my tongue as I chew the biscuit.

"Where is she?" I ask, swallowing the dryness and putting my hand to my chest as I push it down my throat, attempting to quiet the nausea.

"Your aunt?" Queen Etiza asks, wiping her chin with a napkin as the general watches the conversation closely. A slight hint of surprise washes over the Queen's face, but is going just as fast. I clench my teeth and close my fists until my flesh flushes lighter. *Who else would it be?*

"Yes, where is she? Explain why I'm here and where my aunt is, or I swear to Numen I will bring this fork through your eye." I threaten, the words rise up and out of my mouth faster than I could even register the feeling coming up.

I just threatened *the* queen of Mava. Not only Mava but the entire archipelago.

"Please, Artea, we aren't the enemy here. I will explain everything to you—"

"You've said that multiple times already." I glare toward her.

"It has taken a lot for me to meet with you personally and if I'm being honest, we need your help. All of Mava, the islands, we need your help," I open my mouth to speak but she puts her hand up, I pause. "You are something very special. I have been looking for you for a long time, Artea."

I scrunch my eyebrows, looking for some way to read her face, the lights become brighter and harder to ignore.

"You see, when you were born, your parents knew you'd be too powerful for this world. They wanted to conceal you, hide you from your true power," she makes eye contact with me. "They hired a halfling to take care of you. Part elf, part dwarf. Your aunt. It was her job to take care of you and make sure you don't discover your true potential. Your mother, she was scared of you, Artea."

"P–potential? Scared of *me*?" I ask, my voice cracking uncontrollably. How could they be scared of me? I don't have any magic or power.

"You aren't human, Artea. You are special. Your father was an elf wizard and spell maker, and your mother is an elvish necromancer. She could raise the dead just as quickly as she would flatten the living." She starts to lean into the table, getting passionate in her speech. My vision gets cloudy.

"Who were they? How do you know this?" A tear makes its way out of my eye and down my cheek.

"Both of your parents were walking evils of this world. The very reason that the islands are disconnected from each other. The reason that families and friends, loved ones, can't see each other anymore. The reason that filth and creatures are crawling around every impoverished town, taking over regions for their own. It's not only Halistyn that's ridden with vile things. We have been watching you, we saw you being attacked," she sighs and looks at me with a soft look in her gaze, dipping her head to the slightest. "When I heard about your birth two decades ago, I was determined to find you and protect you, knowing who your parents were."

"*Who* were they!?" I yell, slamming my fist on the table making some of the tall trays of food shake and the silverware clank as I look at my lap, tears dropping on my trousers. The queen keeps her composure despite my fit, embarrassment rises in my cheeks.

"Your father was the elvish King of Perdita. The one who tore our bridges down, broke our archipelago," she looks down in disappointment. "Your mother was a necromancer but was also an elf. She was one of the southern mainland's fiercest warriors. However, she let the power of being able to play with life and death itself take her over."

"Please, wait." I cough out, the dryness in my throat taking over. The information starts becoming too much.

The room goes silent. The words of the queen looming in the air, constricting me, tighter and tighter.

Is it true that my parents were evil? That the people I've been longing to know or meet, or even speak with once, were the exact reasons that our archipelago is in ruins? *The* king and a sorcerer of the dead?

Where did this come from, and why am I so angry? I've never cared much about my parents before. Maybe making it real isn't what I expected, I never thought I'd hear about them again. Let alone who they were.

However, this doesn't add up.

"If the king died in the war, how was I born only nineteen years ago?" I ask, noticing the pieces don't go together at all. The queen takes a breath, observing my confusion, and my equal sense that I'm being lied to.

"Your mother saved your father with her abilities, and they lived another eighty years in hiding. However, another elvish soldier got hungry. He couldn't stand seeing any other person in power, so he assassinated the king. With magic. How? That's beyond me. It took a whole army to disable the king in the War of Stone and Mountains, so I have no idea how a simple elf did it."

I can only stare at the window in front of me, trying to decide what to believe.

Chapter Six

I gain my breath again, and sit in the tense quiet, fidgeting with the ring still stuck on my finger.

"I heard about your birth from my second, Zehlin. I knew I needed to find you because with parents like that, there's no way you would have been protected as you should have," the queen looks down in sorrow. "I've been looking for you, sensing your energy for almost two decades. And I've found you."

"How?" I question, looking at her now.

"Some magic, but mostly because you're elvish," she faintly smiles. "Our islands rarely inhabit elves, it was easy to sense your unusual essence, even if you were coated by the fesch root."

"Did you have anything to do with the attack that night?" I ask, frustration boiling inside my stomach, remembering the event of the last night I can recall since being here.

"Yes, General Zehlin protected you from the creatures who attacked you. He's been assigned to watch over you the past couple weeks since we found you."

I snap my head to the right to look at the general.

"You've been watching me? For what?" I almost yell toward him. I continue to stare at him as the Queen interjects. "And what about the minotaur who poisoned my drink?"

"Artea, you're special. You're needed. We have a plan to bring the islands back together and mend what was shattered a century ago, by your father," her voice welds my eyes shut, making me think about my whole life. "We need your help to restore our archipelago. Please, Artea, let us guide you. This could be something spoken about in history books thousands of years from now. You could be the hero of the islands, mend the relationships between them, and redeem yourself as the first elvish islander."

I sit with my eyes still shut, the whites dancing around my vision as I clench them tighter and tighter. Did Aunt Prim really lie? Has she been an elf this whole time? Has she been hiding me to keep me from being who I truly am? And my parents, if they were really who the queen claims they were, my whole life has been a distortion, words played through my ears and relayed to everyone else.

I think about my small town, my small life, my insignificance. If my existence, my body, my mind has all been a lie, maybe I can lie to myself too.

"I will help you." I open my eyes, slowly turning my head to the queen, leveling out my nausea. "Under one condition."

"Anything, Artea." The queen beseeches.

"I need to see my aunt. She must be worried sick, I need to be sure that she's okay. Maybe she needs to know where I am." I say bringing my hand to my mouth and chewing on my nail.

"Your aunt lied to you, Atrea," I turn my head to look at General Zehlin who speaks for the first time since I've come into the dining hall. "She kept the truth from you, your whole life. She was hiding you from the world."

"Where. Is. She?" I demand, trying to tug the ring off my finger.

"We can show you, if that's what you truly wish for," Queen Etiza assures me. "But you have to know, she committed treason by hiding an elf in the islands. Let alone she drugged you daily and was an elf herself. There were many crimes committed on her behalf and as the queen, I cannot let it go unanswered."

I wait, looking at the Queen while I continue to shuffle the ring around. I stare her down, waiting to hear her tell me my aunt is being held in the castle, or dead. How could they punish an old woman? She's on her last leg anyway, as much as it hurts me to say it. If Aunt Prim was brought here into the islands only when I was a baby, to take care of me, was all of her history about her dad a lie? Was it a fabricated story that she took over the quilt shop? I've seen her sew before, ever since I was little she's been making quilts and patches, telling stories. Sometimes she would ramble on for an hour about the meaning behind every patch of a blanket.

Most of her blankets would entail the same young boy on many patches. He could fly and he had light brown hair with slight features that were darkened or lightened depending on his circumstances. He was accompanied by a young girl sometimes, other times he would be with an older man who had a violin.

"We cannot disclose where she is, for the safety of you and her." General Zehlin responds to the silence, cutting off my thoughts.

"That's a load of horseshit, and you know it," I point my finger while standing up, glaring at the general who reciprocates my condescending eye contact. "I will not sit here, in the middle of an island I've only ever heard stories of while my aunt has been *taken care of,* then be expected to listen to life changing claims about me that you could very well be making up."

My eyes start to water again, only a little, just enough that I can feel the pressure of emotion hit the back of my eyes. I look down and shut my eyes tight, as simply yelling makes me nauseous now. I open my eyes to see my hands are paler than usual. My fingers are slightly longer and my veins are showing. I can see the changes in myself, the ones happening because the fesch root is wearing off.

A ball in my throat threatens up, and this time I don't push it down or ignore it. The sickness in my head and everywhere else pushes into me like a thousand spikes of metal, getting closer.

I slump in the chair once more, the tears flooding out of me. Pathetic whimpers start to force themselves out of my mouth.

"W–what is happening to me? Where is she?" I cry, more to myself than to the queen or the general.

"We will get to all of that–" I stand up swiftly, the chair falling behind me and making a thud on the ground.

"Bullshit," I tell the queen. "Until I get an answer, a *proper* answer, I'm not doing a single thing for your people."

I start to walk away toward the door Gachera had led me into. I hear the general mumble.

They're your people too.

As if anything in Ihrvian is capable of being saved.

Gachera met me at the dining room door and opened it for me, as I still can't interact with anything in the castle because I'm literally a different person now. I'm morphing into a whole new body every breath I take. The more I blink or talk or even breathe, the more pain I feel creeping up my body.

I look in the mirror of my room, the large one in the too-big white bathroom. My eyes have black circles under them, accompanied by some bruising on my cheek from the night my head was pressed down into the muddy concrete. My skin looks very pale, like I haven't seen the sun in years. Yes, it's winter, but something is different. And Mava is forever stuck in spring, so I'm not cold.

I guess I now know why something is different.

I examine all over my body. My veins are more purple now, faint, but noticeable. My ears are pointed in a slight curve upward toward the ceiling.

This is really happening, you're not human.

All my life I've heard about how evil the elves are and how they destroyed our archipelago. All the stories of the murder that the War of Stone and Mountains brought upon the people of the islands. Especially Ihrvian because it's the closest to the elvish continent, Perdita. Ihrvian was the place where the king was killed too. Or was supposed to be killed.

You're the result of a criminal, a murderer.

What if the queen and the general are lying? They could just be trying to convince me to work for them because I'm an elf. Maybe it's some kind of twisted revenge on the elvish kind. *My kind.*

But that's not me. I'm not an elf, I never have been. How can I be human my whole life and just suddenly change bodies? Change identities? I've seen magic and I've even been healed by our town healer with magic, but I didn't think it would ever impact me like this. Magic, fae and elf magic alike, has always been foreign to me.

Yes, if the queen is telling the truth, I know who my parents were. I know the king is dead.

I hear my bedroom door outside of the bathroom click open, someone's footsteps walk inside slowly. I focus on the sounds, but I hear nothing else. I grab a brush laying neatly on the side of the sink along with some other beauty items. Slowly, I open the bathroom door and see the chest-length brown hair in front of me, and the silhouette of the general.

I step back and slam the door, locking it.

"Why the hell do you keep showing up in *my* room? Don't you have one of your own?" I ask, the neglect of privacy is going to make me do something irrational.

"Yes, I do. But I wanted to check in on you." He responds, still close to the door. He's probably leaning against it right now and I could open it, letting him fall face first into the white and gold crystal floor.

"Want to, or asked to?" I challenge him. He probably was told by the queen that I'm unstable or need to adjust and there won't be a need to convince me when I get comfortable. But I meant it. I will not be doing anything they ask of me until I know Aunt Prim is safe.

"Both, you seemed to have a really hard time in there."

"Seems like someone has a pair of eyes, congratulations." I mentally roll my eyes. "If I'm being kept here, you don't need to sit here and act like you care just because it's your job."

"Please, Artea, I wanted to talk to you. Genuinely, I do."

The way his voice sounds like silk through the door, whispering yet assertive. I feel like he's telling the truth, only because why else would he not? What reason does he have to lie?

"I can tell you the truth," he says, my interest peaks at the word *truth*. "Just open the door. I can be all the way to the other side of the room if that would make you feel better."

I only open the door, seeing him in front of me, his hair slightly disheveled from the day so far, his eyes still full of wake, the greens and grays in them seem to swirl around. He's much taller up close than far away. His forearm is leaning against the door frame slightly above me.

After he sees the door open, we make eye contact as he steps back letting me pass. I try to ignore his presence as I walk over to a miniature desk sitting by the balcony door. It's hard to ignore the fact that he's so tall and built like he chops trees for a living. His hair shimmers in the light, just like the gold weaved into the walls compliments the white.

I cross my arms and look him in the eye. He doesn't move, blink, or speak. I sit on the bed, still looking at him.

Who is he? Did he grow up as a little boy who wanted to be in the military and serve his people? Did he feel obligated by his family? Was he chosen because of something special? Was he forced into this position? I try to read his face as he takes in a deep breath and leans against the bedpost furthest from me.

"Will you let me give you the whole picture, or are you gonna go all sweaty and stare into space on me?" he asks me, and I roll my eyes again.

I gesture for him to continue.

"When the king died, your father, your mother was able to bring him back. Nobody knew that she was on the ship that sailed to the south of Ihrvian. Only the queen and I know what I'm about to tell you and you must swear to keep your mouth shut about it," he clears his throat. "Queen Josephine, of Perdita, is planning on sending troops into our archipelago within some months' time."

My mother, sending troops into my home. I blink and look at the ground, my chest rising and falling without my control.

"We have an insider who gives us information on Perdita when he can. Military operations, trading routes, and other things of that kind. He overheard a lieutenant explaining a travel route for the waters," he explains as my tongue feels gritty and dry against my teeth.

"You mean my mother is coming, and alive? Why risk it with the water? Why did they place me here if she's just going to infiltrate it?"

"We assume they wanted to hide you, couldn't handle taking care of you. Maybe they thought it would be easier to leave you in the enemy's hands to deal with. The king and queen of the elvish continent have always been very selfish people. They tore down the bridges simply because they saw Queen Etiza 'unfit' to be a good ruler," he sighs softly, and as I look at him he makes eye contact with me. "This must be very difficult, I'm sorry, Artea."

My vision goes blurry and I keep looking at the general, trying to keep the shape and face of him in my mind. My entire body starts to feel like it's floating.

"W—what time is it?" He runs over to my side of the bed and I close my eyes.

"It's almost six in the evening, just lay down." I don't know why there's panic in his voice until I start to feel my stomach burn, my arms feel like they're on fire. The tearing of my muscles and cracking my bones spoil the softness of the bed. I can sense the blood inside my new body pumping and pumping, scorching every inch under my skin.

I open my eyes and see a cave, completely different from the room I should be in. In front of me is a pile of ashes. Every breath I take makes the ashes dance in a circle of song. The music plays in a sequence of tunes that I've never heard before, and the pain stops. I shut my eyes tight and reopen them to find myself back in the room, still burning alive. My eyes refuse to close as I feel the smoldering persist.

I hear more voices, though they only go through my head in ringing tones. There's screaming and yelling as I focus on the gold lining in the ceiling above me.

It feels as if my throat is being torn into shreds and my body is being burned across a line of fire, then it all goes black again.

Chapter Seven

(Zehlin)

Artea's screams would have shattered all the windows in the castle if it wasn't for the wards protecting the islands from elves. The noise was suppressed, except for the people in the bedroom, including me. I sat there for what felt like an eternity holding Artea down trying to get her to hear me, maybe if I could have gotten her to listen she would be in better shape.

Right now, I look at her tangled hair laying on the pillow below her head. She's breathing now, no longer clutching her chest as if her ribs were going to extrude out of her torso at any moment.

Gachera heard the screaming from down the hall and rushed in. I asked her to help, yelling over the screams of terror coming from next to me. Gachera was able to find the castle's healer and by the time he came to see if he could help, Artea went unconscious. She stopped breathing and went limp as her skin started to fade into a dark gray, changing the faint paleness into a deep shadow. She was warmer than anything I've ever touched, including my sunlight.

We found that the wards on the castle against elvish magic is what was hurting her, burning her alive. I knew that the transition would happen at some point, however I didn't think her blood would already be riddled with magic. I had thought we had more time.

The warden was forced to take the walls and wards down as Artea is too valuable in the restoration of the islands' bridges. The wards harming her also confirmed that her natural elvish power will come back after her cleanse, whatever those powers will be.

The healer was able to bring her back to a stable state, but she still lies unmoving, breathing lightly as if each inhale is a struggle, forcing the air into her lungs.

I decide to leave the room, but before I do I tell the healer to stay with her. He readily agrees and I rush out of the room. I make my way down to the queen's quarters and knock on the door. It opens responding to the queen's command and I rush in, out of breath. I notice the queen looking at some papers, some scrolls, and some ink as she looks up at me.

"The wards, they're finally affecting her. I had the warden take them down. She was burning, it seemed." I say, the sting in my lungs catching up to me. Iza has a calculating look on her face, she sits still looking at me for a moment.

"Very well, keep the wards down unless she becomes a threat. How is she?" The queen looks back down, resuming her writing. Iza assuming that Artea will be a threat sends a shiver down my spine. She doesn't seem like the kind of person to harm anyone, it seems that she's been tortured enough already.

"She's stable, but my guess is she'll be in a lot of pain when she wakes." I say softly.

"When she wakes up I want you to show her the Candor Flask," she clears her throat. "Let her ask anything she wishes, just make sure she doesn't ask about the flame yet."

"Do you want the truth about her aunt to be revealed?" I question, confused as to why she would let out a secret like that.

"Yes, of course I do. If she will be putting the islands back together and putting herself through all of this for us, she needs to know the truth. Besides, at dinner we told her we would prove it."

I bow my upper half and turn toward the door.

"We are far past bowing and royal pleasantries, Zehlin." She succors me. I nod in response and continue walking.

One of the servants outside the door shuts it for me and I stand still before gaining the courage to head down in the basement, to the alchemy laboratory.

The cold and muggy basement was no place for me, and never has been. It's always been too tight or too dark for my liking, always deterring me from the cold floor of the castle.

I find the door that reads *Concoctions* and open it. The tight rows of shelves upon shelves are covered in dust and bottles of different mixtures of substances. I can't even imagine what the different things could be and do. I weave through the skinny lanes in between the shelves, looking for a purple bottle, with a little man inside.

I scuff past all the smelly concoctions and finally, I hear a voice. A tiny, high pitched voice, but one, nonetheless. I look toward the sound, reaching closer and closer, twisting through the lanes and eventually, spotting the Candor Flask.

"Finally! Someone's here again! Come here, over here!" I let out a deep groan, the annoying tiny man is already talking too much. I walk over and cross my arms. "Yes! Yes! It's me! Mr. Zehlin, you're back!"

"It's General to you, Torrid." I grunt.

"A–are you here to let me out? Oh look at your muscles, and why, that hair you have has grown so long, Mr. G–General!" Torrid starts to dance around in little circles in his flask. The flask is glass, and small, but Torrid makes the flask look like a mansion. I'm sure I could fit the tiny man on my fingernail if I so pleased.

"Stop the ass-kissing. We both know why I'm here."

"No, no, no. Please, General Mr. Zehlin. Don't ask me another question, I hate answering questions. That's all we do now, I want some fun. Let me out, please!" He begs, pushing my patience even more.

"You know why you're in there. The next time you want to lie to children, telling them that the monsters lurking in Avaris' lands will maul them at night, there will be much worse consequences. You don't even need to eat or relieve yourself. I don't know why you're complaining." The amount of times we caught Torrid being cruel to the children or killing animals for entertainment was far too many. Whoever put him in this flask and left him down here did the whole world a favor.

"It was one time! I'm so lonely, Mr. Zully," Torrid quips with exasperation.

"Yes, usually twelve times means only one time. I forgot," I remark sarcastically. Growing tired of the small man's chatter, I grab the flask gently and carry it up the stairs. "Let's go, buddy."

I hear the muffled yells of Torrid as I make my way back up the stairs, out of the mugginess, and into the wide, bright hallways. I look down to see Torrid covering his eyes trying to adjust to the light. I finally find the bedroom holding Artea inside, assumingly still sleeping. I open the door to find the healer gone and Artea with her eyes open. Quickly, I place the flask onto a nearby table and rush back into the hallway to the healers room.

I find the room and burst in, leading to a light jump from the older man.

"Why is she awake, and not being tended to?" I huff, clenching my fists furious at the recklessness of leaving her alone. I tell myself she's priceless because of her potential to the islands. I ignore the fact that I know that's not the only reason I'm upset. "Do you understand how important she is?"

The healer nods and bows, quickly running past me with his bag and into Artea's room. Not long after, I follow him into the room, grab the flask, and sit on the seat next to the elvish girl.

I hold Torrid up to Artea and he yelps in fear.

"An elf! What is she doing here?!" he exclaims, sitting in the back of his cage.

"Torrid, enough. What happened to her to cause her such pain?" I say, getting straight to the point. We don't have time for Artea to ask anything she's not ready to know yet.

Torrid struggles and closes his eyes, trying to fight the urge of telling the truth.

"T–the power was too much for the wards, you were right to take them down. It would have killed her if you let them eat at her blood any l– longer. Stop!" Torrid's struggle is apparent as he fights to throw the answer to me, quick to run out of breath. Taking down the wards seems to be the right thing to have done, confirming what I already knew.

"Is there any unhealable damage, Torrid?" I interrogate.

"N–no! Give her a few days and she will be ready for anything."

I hold the flask out for the healer to take, and the healer does so swiftly so as to not make me more upset. The healer takes the flask out of the room and shuts the door behind him. I take Artea's hand, gently brushing my thumb against hers.

Her hair is made up of knots from me and a couple guards having to hold her down on the bed while the warden took care of the wards. Her eyes are open, brown and golden dancing inside them as she looks up at me for answers. I'm sure she's confused about the tiny man in a flask, and I'm sure she's even more confused about the reason why she passed out.

"Artea, I know you're awake, but can you speak?"

Chapter Eight

The air is so thick. I can feel the sheets and blankets rubbing against every hair or bit of skin on myself. General Zehlin is sitting in a chair next to me, holding my hand. My flesh burns with every touch he brings to me, but I can't move. That's why it's so hard for me to breathe.

After I ask him to let go, he does immediately.

"I'm so sorry, I didn't think it would hurt," he clears his throat. "How do you feel?"

I let out a little smile. My current situation starts hitting me in all these different directions, it feels like I need to keep my eyes closed before everything takes over.

"Fan—fantastic." I manage to breathe out.

"You need to eat, you've been out for a few hours. You probably have no energy, and you need water."

"I could eat," the general nods at me and starts to get up. "Wait," he waits. "What was that thing in the jar?"

I was barely awake to see the little man, but awake enough to remember it. It was an odd creature. It looked human, like a man. But he also looked a little mad. Like he was driving himself into a deep place of his own mind. He knew things about me, and he was scared of me. Is that what everyone here thinks of elves? I have heard stories, horror stories of elves torturing humans for amusement. I've heard of things from the War of Stone and Mountains, and the king–

Your father.

"He's a prophet. He was known for hundreds of years as the 'Liar.' Seems pretty self-explanatory. He used to lie to children or make them so scared they would run away and never come back. Someone, a long time ago, banished him to a life of truth. Any question you ask him, he has to answer. We still don't know where he came from, but he showed up in the basement years ago, before the war. So far, asking him where he came from is the only question he doesn't have to answer." the general chuckles at the irony. "Torrid. He's a tiny foolish creature. He's not human, and I'm not entirely sure *what* he is, but he's helpful in situations similar to yours. Now we know that there's no extensive damage because of the wards. I'm sorry we didn't catch it earlier, let alone leave you by yourself."

I keep note of the interesting small man, condemned to a life of veracity inside of a small glass bottle.

"I'm okay. Everywhere just hurts. My nausea has gone away though. I feel a little more comfortable in my skin, apart from the boiling blood part. What happened?"

"The wards we have set up for protection against elves were still up since the war, we didn't mean to wait this long to take them down for you but the fesch root wore off faster than we thought it would. And because you're an elf now, the wards acted accordingly. The doors and windows not opening to you was happening because the castle sensed some hint of foreign magic. The wards were meant to kill you."

"Oh, well thanks for, you know, not letting me die." *You're an elf now.* My head hurts too much for this.

He nods and stands up, turning to the door. For a moment I'm disappointed, but a little relieved because I think he's leaving. However, he only whispers to someone outside the door, and the next second he has a silver platter of steaming food while he walks to me once more.

While I'm hoping it's not real silver, he sets the platter down on the foot of the bed and I sit up, ready to eat. As I get up, I have an idea. If Torrid answers *almost* any question he's asked, does that mean he could tell me where my aunt is?

"Could you bring Torrid back after I eat, General?" I ask.

"It's Zehlin, please. And why do you ask?" he questions, adjusting the laces around his collar.

"He could be a way for you and the queen to prove to me that Aunt Prim is safe. If you would like me to work with you, then prove to me that it's worth my time, Zehlin," I say blatantly.

The hunger boils into my throat until I can no longer take it. I grab the fork on the platter and it immediately burns my skin. I yelp loudly and grip my wrist as my skin makes a sizzling sound in reaction.

"Oh, Numen! Artea, I'm sorry." The general scrambles to take the scorching silver away and starts walking to the door. My wound from the candlestick reopens as my skin stings from the touch. "I will get you wooden cutlery, one moment."

"Wait," he turns back around. "I need to keep talking, I'll eat with my hands. The burn isn't even that bad. Stay." I lie about the burn, it does hurt badly but now that I think about it, I don't want to be alone.

He drops the silverware on the far table and sits back down on the seat next to the bed. I grab a roll that's sitting next to potatoes and beef, lathered in butter and seasonings. As much as this place makes me uncomfortable and itchy, the food is delightful.

I've never been by myself, and I've never liked the quietness of empty rooms. It leaves me alone for my thoughts to wander and leaves me worrying or sad, all without distraction. That's why I'm asking the general, *Zehlin,* to stay here with me.

There are still things that need explaining.

"Torrid might be a good way to prove to you that your aunt is safe, and you are sure that's the only way you will help us?" He cocks an eyebrow, making a gesture toward the door where the small man was taken out to.

I take a breath, and nod.

"Then so be it, I'll bring him back. Are you okay for just a moment?" I nod, and take another bite. I blink back up from my meal and see that he's gone, just like that.

No door shut or opened. He tessered. That thing, the way he got into my room earlier. How does he do that? Is it like Gachera's youth spell? Is he magic himself? What kind of creature is he? Is he fae?

When I blink again, he's back with the flask. The tessering might take a while for me to get used to. He walks toward me, and I hear muffled weeping. I look at the flask closely as Zehlin walks to his seat again and Torrid is banging on the glass, screaming and stomping his feet.

"Zully! Let me out before I send Numen's wrath upon you in your slumber! Open the top!" Torrid yells, looking up at Zehlin as he sits down in the chair. I can't help but giggle at the little prophet. His voice is so high pitched, yet he has stubble on his chin and scraggly hair. He's not old, but definitely not young either. "LET. ME. OUT. Don't make me go back down there!"

Zehlin flicks the glass flask and looks at me in a, *see what I have to deal with,* way. While we wait for Torrid to calm down, I chuckle a little more which grabs his attention as he turns to me. The general nods, telling me I can ask my questions.

"Is my Aunt Prim safe? If so, where is she?" I say, leaving no room for chit chat.

"One question at a time, Devil Spawn." Torrid scoffs and Zehlin starts slightly shaking the flask, making Torrid tumble around.

"No insults. Answer." The general says in a harsh tone. The way he handles even the lightest offense makes my cheeks flush. I quickly ignore the feeling and look at the little man.

Torrid stops fighting the answer and stands still.

"Missy Prim is safe. Safe and sound. Dirty and smelly, but not hurt."

"Where is she, Torrid?" I ask in a gentle tone. Part of me feels bad for the small man. Being the size of a rat stuck in a glass bottle for years must be lonely.

"She's in a dark place. Far, far, far from here. It smells like the ocean. She's leaving now. Right now, gone." Torrid closes his eyes tightly, shaking his head and flicking the side of the bottle as he stands. "Cold! Cold!"

I take the flask carefully from Zehlin and look at the creature.

"Hey, hey. It's okay. No need to yell. Open your eyes for me, Torrid." He opens his eyes to my command and takes a few breaths. "Are you always this anxious, when answering questions?"

"Who knows? Who knows? Who knows?" he asks himself, still shaking his head. I don't want to hurt him anymore or make him more riled up than he is already. I hand the flask back to Zehlin.

"Thank you, for your time, Torrid." I give him a light smile even though he shakes his head over and over again. "Please take him back now."

Torrid was very anxious the whole time we talked, and part of me wonders if he's always been like that or if it's because he's locked in a flask. After I asked Zehlin to put Torrid back so he could have a break, we talked about where Aunt Prim was. He explained to me that it's the archipelago's law that we command folks who commit treason to be sent back to where they came from, or to prison for life. I agreed that it was a better option to send Aunt Prim back, though I still can't wrap my head around certain things about this situation.

If my aunt is an elf, why was she always able to touch iron and silver? Was she also taking the root? I mean, she's only half-elf as I'm told, so maybe that has something to do with it.

I have my finished platter of supper that I scarfed down quite quickly, and Zehlin is standing, about to leave the room.

"Isn't it impolite to get a lady food and then leave the dishes for her to handle?" I ask, smiling, as he turns back to me. He walks over to the bed and smirks.

"I suppose you must be right, however I didn't think you'd want me to stay here any longer than needed."

"And what might make you say such a thing?" He bends over and picks up the platter as I watch it disappear into nothing right before my eyes. I've seen magic all my life but Zehlin being able to do these gestures with zero effort is no routine for me.

"You were quite damning when I appeared in your room earlier this morning."

I scoff and cross my arms.

"Well, yes I was. A man went into a woman's room without knocking while he knew she was changing. Of course I was damning, Zehlin."

He chuckles and bows slightly at the end of the bed in front of me, and for a moment I focus on the way the late evening light sprinkles his face, and his brown hair dangles as he bends downward. For one moment I think the cocky general is quite beautiful. Effortlessly at that.

"You have a point. My apologies, Mrs…" He pauses. "I don't know your last name."

"And you assume I'm married?"

"Well, you haven't taken that ring off since you arrived."

"You mean since I was dragged here?" I retort sharply. A sudden pinch of anger rises into my throat. "And yes, I cannot take it off. I haven't been able to take it off my wide fingers. I got it from a minotaur named Gunter. Well, half minotaur. The morning after my attack." While I speak of him, I'm reminded that Gunter is the one who poisoned my drink, and that's what led me here.

"Well, I'm sure it'll make its way loose here shortly. In the meantime, I will let you rest. You, me, and Queen Etiza will have a meeting in the late morning. I'll have Chera wake you and get you ready when it's time." He adjusts his cuffs up to his elbows, and the sight of him gives me more silly aches in my blood, like earlier. I blink the feeling away, and the dread of being alone, and nod.

"Yes, of course. I will make sure to get some rest then." I sigh, looking into my folded hands and crossed legs inside the white cotton blankets. He finally twists the door knob, and I ask him, "How am I so important? Why am I truly here?"

He pauses looking down, all of a sudden cold.

"We will go over everything else tomorrow, Angel."

Why would he ask if I was married if he must have been watching me for weeks? Did he not see Gunter give me the ring? Was Gunter going to try and hurt me so Zehlin took his opportunity to get me to the castle?

He walks away, leaving me and my thoughts to flutter in the dusk, alone.

Chapter Nine

I'm sweating by the time I wake. It takes me a moment to register where I am and why the bed is so soft, but it finally rests in. I'm still in the castle of Mava, with the queen of the archipelago. I sit up, adjusting to the light streaming in through the balcony door and the windows facing the town below. My body feels more sore than it did yesterday, but I don't feel nearly as sick and frail.

Still, the joints and bones in my body feel like hundred pound weights as I get off the bed and walk to the vanity to my right. It seems that I'm awake before Gachera plans to get me ready for breakfast, or lunch. I'm not sure what time it is because I don't have a clock in my room.

On the vanity are some green pills the healer told me I should take once a day, preferably in the morning, until I'm fully healed and they're sure everything is okay. Next to it appears a tall, delicate glass of water that glistens in the early sunlight. It appeared in the same way the silver platter of food appeared in Zehlin's hands. There's a light blue hint of smoke that quickly whisps away after it appears.

Is the castle magic itself? Did someone send the water to me? Am I being watched?

I take the glass of water and observe it for a moment. It looks like regular water, so I pick up a green pill and chase it with the whole glass of water. I was unaware how thirsty I was until the first drop hit my tongue. I get ready to set the glass down until I see it's refilled again, right to the top. I drink half the glass once again and set it down satisfied.

I make my way to the wardrobe door and see my whole closet is filled with trousers and blouses of all kinds. Some have jewels on them, some are lined with gold thread. I walk inside the closet that's far too large for its own good and take a closer look at the items. There are shoes of all kinds. Heels, flats, boots, and sandals.

There are hats and hair accessories and bags, and still some dresses, each in a different color or shade than the last. The closet by itself is larger than the room in my apartment, times four.

I decide not to shower this morning since I did yesterday, and to be frank, my body is so sore I don't want to stay upright longer than I have to. I grab a deep blue blouse that has a gold collar and gold cuffs. I match my top with white, skin-tight trousers. They look perfect for horse riding.

Riding the town horses was something else I used to do to spend my down time during the afternoons. Aunt Prim's shop, or what I thought was her shop, rarely had any customers. For years I had to find other activities to fill my day.

I slip on some brown leather flats and a few gold bracelets to match the shirt. If I'm going to be stuck here I might as well have a sense of style while I do it.

I'm almost out of breath by the time I step outside the closet and back into the bedroom. Gachera is in front of the vanity, placing some hair and touch up utilities on the counter space. She looks to me and nods, gesturing to the seat.

I take my place, as she grabs a brush.

"How are you feeling, Miss?" Gachera speaks as she grabs a lock of my hair and begins to brush lightly. "I see you're up a little early."

"Yes, I seem to have woken up on my own. I'm feeling tired, and sore. Not much different than the past day." I wince at the sudden pinch of the brush as Gachera works through my tangles.

"The queen is very excited to meet with you this morning. There are very important matters to discuss." She smiles faintly as I look at myself in the mirror for the first time since yesterday.

My eyes have sharpened, I look serious. My eyebrows are lighter and arched further, and my skin is much paler, like I was born from ice and cold. My fingers are daintier, and my hair seems longer.

And poking out of my hair as Gachera weaves it into two braids, are my ears, sharp and pointy.

I truly look like the elves in the illustrations I'd seen as a kid. I always thought they looked majestic and otherworldly. The country of Perdita is made up of beautiful creatures and biomes and all things majestic as I described. Perdita is where all the elves reside, the southern continent. I don't recognize myself. I don't look like me anymore, and I definitely don't look as magical as the elves in the illustrations. It feels as if I'm looking at myself through two mirrors, the first one changes my face and the second one mimics my movements.

I face the truth and smile lightly, wondering if my teeth shine, or if they stay dull like the feeling I have in my fingertips. They look the same, no fangs. However, that wouldn't have surprised me one bit.

Snapping out of my thoughts, I notice Gachera pinning pearls into my hair, along with other shiny accessories. She then bats my face with powders and cosmetics of different kinds and we begin our walk into the dining hall.

"The queen has been stressed lately about having to take the wards down. She knows that you are of no harm towards us, but she's worried an enemy might catch word of the wards being weaker. She is very fearful of the island's vulnerability." Gachera speaks as we walk down halls, left, right, and downward. The same dizziness of direction hits me as it did last time.

"I understand, I'm sorry you guys had to do that. Are elves really that dangerous?" I ask, looking at the paintings decorating the white marble walls we pass by.

"Unfortunately so, yes." She sighs and slides her hand into her dress pocket, a very innovative feature. She pulls out a key as we stop at a door, the dining hall.

"She's locking the doors now? It's that much of a worry?" I lower my voice as Gachera opens the door and whispers.

"I'm afraid so, dear."

The door swings open at Gachera's hand and welcomes us both into the dining hall. There is the same large table many paces in front of us with Zehlin and the queen sitting at opposite ends, like yesterday's lunch. I nod to the queen as I walk over to the same seat I sat in previously, right in the middle.

As a servant pulls out the chair, I sit and look at the table. There's a large variety of fruits and cakes, along with eggs and meats and beverage choices. This table alone could feed the masses of my street back in Halistyn. I feel selfish knowing that all this food will be in vain.

My plate is full and colorful and I look around the room, eyeing the paintings and the ceiling, open with pink and purple stained glass above us. The colors leave a beautiful shine on the carpets and on the attendees of this breakfast.

The windows are grand, and the panes are lined with gold and marble like all the other walls. The carpets are black and white with gold lining the ends. And the chairs are white and solid, they look to be made out of some kind of stone. They are tucked with cushions that are also gold. Gold, white, pink, and purple. The flag of Mava has those same colors. It's not difficult to spot the theme in this castle.

It makes me wonder if the rest of the town is the same way.

"I see you look well rested, Artea." Queen Etiza speaks to me in a light tone.

"Thank you, I do feel much better. I cannot recall falling asleep last night. I was so tired." I admit. The shine of the forks stare at me, telling me I cannot eat unless it's with my hands.

"We told the staff to give the lady wooden cutlery, did we not?" Zehlin subtly looks to one of the four servants in each corner of the room, noticing the silver issue as quickly as I did. One of the men nod and practically run to grab woodenware. "My apologies, Miss. You must be starving."

"No worries, General." I cough, and look into my fidgeting hands. "Now, I–"

"We wanted–" The queen and I speak at the same time, I look to her and she nods.

"I was hoping everything, and I mean everything, could be explained. Today preferably." I give the queen a serious, yet understanding look.

"Yes, well of course. Give us any questions. I have no intention of hiding anything, especially since you are so important, and we are so grateful." Queen Etiza looks into my eyes, her blonde hair and horns are splashed with purple from the glass above us, her eyes are deep and sincere along with her words. I'm a little drawn back by the fact that she's treating me like I already agreed to everything. We still have topics to discuss and priorities to go over.

"Well, Torrid was able to let me know my aunt is safe. As long as she is only being sent back, and I will be able to see her again, I do not have an issue."

"Torrid, you saw Torrid?" The queen looks to the general.

"Why yes, Your Majesty. We agreed that it would be a good idea for Artea to get some security on Prim's whereabouts. Remember?" The general looks to the queen from across the table, pausing his eating and exchanging looks to me, then back to the queen.

"Yes, yes my apologies. It seems that my new perfume is still making me hazy. It's very potent, this lavender." The queen chuckles lightly.

I try to ignore the tenseness in the queen. Something tells me that meeting Torrid wasn't talked about, or the queen has changed her mind. I put the thought to the back of my head as I remember there are more important situations at hand.

"Well, as you invited, my first question is, was Gunter involved?" I ask respectfully before she can get another trembling word in. "In my kidnapping, I mean."

The words come out sharper than I expected as one of the servants comes back with the woodenware for me to eat.

The queen takes a deep sigh in and lets it out as she speaks.

"Yes, the drink was tipped. With a root," she says, looking at her food. "We thought it was the only way we could get you here safely."

I take in the information and breathe out. So, I was drugged and taken hostage by my queen. Almost every resident of the archipelago would be overjoyed to be in such a wonderful place. I, however, cannot help but feel some kind of dragging. Like my feet are soaked in a few inches of water each time I take a mere step. I'm grateful for all the things the queen and the general have provided for me. *Or shoved down my throat.* But I can't help but feel used.

They do seem to care about me, and what happens to me. They took the bloody wards down that held the king away for a hundred years. All for me.

"How did I get here? If the bridges that made the waters safe to sail are down, how did you get me here?"

The general clears his throat.

"I'm the only person who has been blessed with being able to tesser. Only a few highly ranked generals in the past thousand years have ever been remarked to have the ability."

"You can t–tesser, as you call it, islands at a time?" I ask, looking at Zehlin, observing the glorified statue.

"It takes much energy out of me. In fact I won't be able to tesser anywhere aside from a couple miles for a few days because of the distance I crossed getting you here." He clears his throat again and makes eye contact with me. "Please, my lady, neither of us intended for you to feel trapped. We simply took precautions."

I glare at the comment and fold my hands in my lap.

"For me? Or for yourself?" I bite. "The precautions?"

There's a stillness in the room, even some of the servants stiffen their already stiff posture. The silence is all I need to hear. Because of what I'm turning into, they needed to take *precautions*. I find myself clearing my own throat, trying not to be offended that they thought of me as harmful. Or worse.

I know my aunt is safe. I know how I got here. I know where I am, what I am, and who I truly am. As much as I can accept for now. There's only one thing left.

"What happens from today? Starting tomorrow, next week, next month, next year?" I look to Queen Etiza. "If I help you, what does that entail for me? Why me of all people?"

The queen stiffens and straightens her back as her eyes look into mine with determination.

"There are seven items of jewelry. One, conveniently on every island. That ring on your hand, that Gunter gifted you, is one of them. Each one contains a certain amount of power. Power that originates from the eternal flame."

"*The* flame? The one that the king put out?" The queen nods and gestures to Zehlin, I shift my gaze to him as he speaks.

"He had a way of taking the power and distributing it among the seven pieces. He had people working with him and hid them in each island while he distracted the lot with his death. Victory had been ours, until the flame went out." He breathes out.

"So, he sacrificed himself, risked death, just to take down the bridges? Can I take the ring off, or is the magic what makes it stuck?" I ask the questions to myself more than the general or the queen.

"It's stuck, I'm afraid." Queen Etiza shakes her head. "But we need your help. And you are the only one that might be powerful enough to bring back what your father stole from so many people. The famine, the poor, the anger. All the things that make living on the islands so difficult."

"You can help us break out of this cage, Artea. You can restore what your parents destroyed, you can restore the islands. Once you equip all seven pieces, we can execute a spell to bring the fire back. Bring the bridges back and prepare for war," Zehlin speaks.

"Why did you ask if I was married, if you knew that the ring was one of the seven?" I ask, remembering the time he was at my door, about to leave. As confusing as General Zehlin is, I still loathed him leaving.

"You weren't ready, and I wasn't going to start a fight about the very future of our islands in front of your bedroom door." The general responds quickly.

My life might have been a lie. I might have taken on a whole new form, a new face and body when I was taken to Halistyn. However, I saw what life on the island was like. For humans, dwarves, tieflings, pixies, goblins even.

All folk deserve better.

I have no one back in Halistyn for me. My aunt is gone. I can do something with the now. The past is simply the past. I can make a difference, even if that means decorating myself and pretending to be something I'm not. I may look like an elf, but I was raised human. A human with a heart. Even if the ghouls and dwarves continue on their dragmist dealings, or the halflings and minotaurs continue to break trees on one another's head, maybe I can still give them a key.

I can renew the archipelago, and allow everyone who's trapped to escape.

If Queen Josephine is planning on sending troops in, we are at our weakest point. The safe water ways are blocked, making the oceans nearly impossible to travel on. If her soldiers push through, and can withstand our waters, there is nothing we could do about it. She could wipe out our islands in a matter of months.

And we couldn't do anything.

I look back and forth from the queen to the general multiple times before I look out one of the windows facing in front of me.

I fidget with my ring while my ears fill with buzz and my eyes well with saltwater. I'm not sure why I'm feeling this way, this will be a good thing.

I hear the breaths of anxiety shoot out of the lungs of the two to my sides as I stand and walk to the ceiling length door.

This is the last time I let fear bend me into something I'm not.

"I will do it. Under one more condition." I insist sternly.

"Anything, Artea." Zehlin speaks from his seat behind me.

"I lead this operation. *It will follow my pace, and mine only.*"

After turning back and seeing agreeing nods from the queen and the general, I open the dining room door that apparently doesn't lock from the inside. They don't stop me as I exit and weave through the never ending hallways as the new keeper of one of seven pieces that will change me forever.

It seems like the only secure place I have is my own mind, and even then I'm starting to feel like I'm losing that too.

Chapter Ten

The next morning, I wake up in the same bedroom as before. The sun streams in as smoothly as it did the previous dawn and the curtains blow as the breeze finds its way into the room. I must have left the balcony door cracked last night when I sat out there due to being unable to sleep.

I toss the blanket off of me and walk over to the balcony where the curtains are shifting. The nausea is becoming more and more bearable every time I stand, I can almost barely feel it now. The city is awake already as folks down below are walking to their destinations, wherever they may be. I bet over half of them work for the city, whether it be media or electricity. The fae here are most likely working overtime because of how many people need warm water and firelight. They are the only ones with the ability to make the water warm without it evaporating or the fire shine bright without smoldering anything.

Magic sure is convenient.

I'm not sure what kind of folks live in Mava. Commonly, different islands are made up of primarily a certain population of people. Like fae, humans, or other creatures. At least that's what all the stories have told. The war could have changed that though. Who knows how outdated the stories from before the war are?

Ihrvian is made up of humans, minotaurs, and dwarves. However, dwarves are kind of everywhere because their ancient relatives would travel all over the islands.

Looking down at the people makes me realize that the wards are down, and they could hear me now. I decide to put it to the test, but before any voice can project out of my throat I hear a knock at the door.

I turn around and close the balcony door behind me, walking to the bedroom door. I open it, which is unlocked now that the wards are down. General Zehlin is standing on the other side, wearing a faint smile. His hair and face are glowing, like he just walked through a pixie's house. His eyes are glowing a shade that looks different from before, almost gray and green.

I catch myself staring, smiling up at him.

"Zehlin, good morning." I greet him, folding my hands behind my back.

"Angel, good morning. Rough night?" I roll my eyes at the nickname and roll them even harder when he comments on my appearance feeling vulnerable in my nightgown. I don't know why he asks, I slept fairly well all things considered.

"How can I help you?" I sigh out.

He reaches into his chest pocket of his perfect suit, pulls out a key, and holds it out. It shines in the light and has an interesting feather symbol on the top.

"Queen Etiza thought it was a good idea to show you the library. We have a lot of documented history of the islands. She wanted to get you familiar with how the islands came to be, how they work, and how we might be able to put them back together."

"The library is locked?" I ask, wondering why such a great place would be locked away from anyone.

"Yes, it has to be. Some of the knowledge in there is too valuable, too fragile, for just any folk to consume. Some of the books were written by past kings and queens, and they contain information they only wanted their descendants to know. Or close trusted friends of their descendants." He explains in a decadent tone, fidgeting with the key in his hand.

"I'm a friend to *the* queen?" I ask, chuckling a little as I speak.

"I'm not sure if you're on friend status yet, but since you're willing to help us, she trusts you." He smiles, and I take the key out of his hand. I'd understand why I'm not on friend status seeing as I threatened her with a fork, but having access to hereditary knowledge is a start.

I take a closer look at the key and I see it's made of a metal that looks like silver, but it's clearly not because I'm *allergic* now, and nothing is happening. The pattern of the key is a feather, each vane delicately engraved into the metal. It also has a few red jewels at the very end. Whoever crafted this key paid a lot of attention to detail, and it looks newly polished, like it hasn't been used in years.

"Are we going now?" I can't help but smile at my new freedom. I was never a true prisoner in the first place, but being able to indulge in the queen's hidden history is exciting as it sounds.

He nods and turns around, almost leaving without me. I walk after him, a new bounce in my feet.

We make our way through the labyrinth of hallways that the castle contains. We eventually reach a door that is a floor lower than the dining room. Zehlin turns the knob and pushes it open, the first and only thing I see is a case of stairs that steeply descends into a dark abyss.

"Is this safe, General?" I ask, still looking down to see if I can make out any shapes in the blackness.

"As long as I'm here, nothing will touch you." He chuckles, smiling at me when I snap my gaze to him.

"Touch me?" I gasp, clutching the key in my hand tighter, as if that would do anything.

"I'm kidding, it's just a staircase." I breathe out a sigh, letting the temptation of knocking him down the flight of stairs fade away. I wonder if he's one for jokes with everyone.

"Well in my defense, I have no idea what Mava looks like outside of these walls. There could be flesh eating ghouls down there. Which, to remind you, I have encountered before," I visualize back to the moment I thought I would never reach the dagger, the moment I thought that I was destined to be killed and dragged back to a lair where I'm someone's meal. "Thanks for that, by the way."

He nods and clears his throat. "I thought you didn't like me watching you," he smiles and I roll my eyes, still stealing glances down the dark stairs. "It was my job, don't thank me."

"Well, still. I owe you one." I shrug.

"If we can get these waterways back up, that's definitely return enough, Angel."

"Would you stop calling me that?" I cross my arms at him, key still in hand feeling cold in my fingers.

"Whenever you stop calling me General," he agrees slyly. Part of me thinks he still won't stop. Part of me doesn't want him to.

Zehlin gestures to the door, volunteering me as the first to go down. I take the first step, and before I continue, I hear a spark of light behind me. I turn and see Zehlin holding a ball of light in his hands. The glow radiating off of him lights up the entire entrance and steps below.

I take a guess and assume it's the same light that he used when he killed the ghoul and the dwarf back in Halistyn. I take a closer look and observe that there are streaks of yellow and white floating around, similar to an orb. The light dances on the wall and reflects on his skin as it moves in a coordination of luminescence.

I look him in the eyes while reaching for the light and I receive a nod from him. I'm in complete awe when I move my arm through the ball of light, hovering just above his hand. There's no heat, no feeling, nothing. It feels like air as I twist my wrist, trying to decipher what this energy could come from. The shadows created by my hand morph dancing shadows on the stone walls.

"I can manipulate light. It's one of my abilities," he says as he makes the ball smaller, but still lets us see easily while we shift to make our way down further.

"One? How many do you have?" I ask. I already know he is able to tesser, as well as tesser other objects. I already thought that was powerful enough, but he has more?

"Only a few. Usually fae are only gifted with one or two abilities. I have been gifted with at least four. Some are smaller than others though." I hear his voice from a couple steps behind me, talking about his gifts like it's a regular day.

"What are all of your gifts?" I ask, hoping he'll answer. As a human I've never had anything remotely ability–like. I get hangovers and sore legs as my gifts.

"Well, I can tesser, as you know, and tesser things that are small enough. I can control light in different ways. Sometimes I can turn it into physical matter, and other times it's just light." So, that's how he chopped off the ghoul and dwarves heads, he turned his light into a sword. We continue to go down, the feeling that this staircase is never ending gets more prominent the more we lower and my legs start to ache. "I can also hear from many miles away, if I wish to. It's not always. And the last one is pretty dull, but I can breathe underwater."

"Whatever do you mean, *dull*? I would love that!" I declare, shocked.

The general is so gifted that he thinks breathing underwater is dull.

"Well, I suppose it works when I want to go fishing."

"You, fish? The queen's second?" I can't help but snicker at the idea of him fishing and yanking on a line trying to get a salmon, it makes my chest quake.

"Yes, I have many hobbies. Is there something wrong with that, Angel?"

I mentally roll my eyes once again, that's just the reaction he pulls out of me. One moment he is handsome and bearable, the next he's handsome and annoying.

"Oh, hey. We are almost at the end, and there will be a door—"

I hear the general warn me about the door a little too late as I slam right into a hard wooden frame, knocking backward onto the floor.

I take my hand and rub my forehead with it, hoping it's not bleeding or bruised from the steps. I also remember I'm still in my nightdress and quickly go to cover myself as I stand up, using what I'm assuming is a stone wall, as my support.

I hear the general clear his throat behind me as I fondle to find the key on the floor. I find it reflecting from Zehlin's glow and look to find the keyhole to open the threshold. Hoping he didn't see anything he wasn't supposed to, I feel my nightgown draping at my knees, telling me I'm fully covered. *That's embarrassing.*

"I think my balance is off because of the, *shift*," I say, trying not to recall the fact that I'm now a completely different person than I was four days ago.

A completely different creature, *Artea. Is that even your name?*

I block out the thoughts and insert the key into the hole, twisting it with one swift flick of my wrist. The wooden door creaks open, sliding to my right instead of pushing open like most doors do.

We start our walk through the stone hallway. There are torches lit, burning a faint purple lighting our way through the dim corridor. All the doors are thick wood and it smells like rotting flesh down here, drowning out my ability to think properly.

As we walk I take note of all the different labels on the doors we pass. *Concoctions, Lockers, Nursery, Cells.*

Library.

Zehlin stops at the door we came here for and twists the door knob, pushing the thick frame forward. He gestures for me to go in first, and the first thing I do is drop my jaw to the ground, unable to take a first step.

The library is rusty and there is a haze of dust floating around, but the sheer size of the room is enough to plaster me to the floor. The ceiling is so far up, I almost can't tell where it stops, and the rows of ancient books go so far in each direction I have to turn my head each way, stretching my neck.

I take a couple strides in and look through the room more. The very tall bookshelves have plants circling the stacks, leaves trailing in all directions. Some shelves have moss and it seems like the dust isn't actually dust, *it's mist*. There is a smell of life, like I'm walking into the opening of a garden. The smell of paper mixes with the mist in a perfumed harmony, and the growth of the plants seems to prosper here.

"Does the moisture not affect the books?" I ask, still gaping at the vastness of the library. We take a few steps in, getting closer to the nearest bookshelf. Light shines in from windows high up poking holes in the wooden planks, illuminating the mist and specks floating in the air. It gives the whole room a yellow and purple hue, and it's the most magical thing I've ever seen. Not that I've seen much magic.

"No. Like most things in Telik, magic keeps the pages from getting ruined," he explains. Telik is the capital of Mava. It's where the castle lies, and it's where I am right now.

"Is there magic everywhere here then?" I ask, knowing the answer already. There's probably magic in the food, water, clothes, and air. Everything.

"Almost everywhere. Mava is very blessed to be a home to many powerful fae. After the war there have only been a few hundred who have been lucky enough to find refuge here, making it across the ocean," Zehlin takes a breath as we reach the nearest shelf and he grazes a hand on the nearest book, his fingers coming off clean. No dust. I'm sure it's the magic keeping them clean too. "Most of the more powerful ones live here to serve Etiza for the greater good. Their powers, including mine, are very beneficial for the archipelago. And with the threat of another war always lurking on the horizon, it's always favorable to be prepared."

I nod to his explanation, not knowing what to respond with other than agreeing. I have no idea what the other islands look like, on top of the fact that I know next to nothing about the archipelago's military operations.

I continue to walk around the rows and rows of books that are clearly centuries old. With the amount of information and pages written in this very room, it makes me wonder how many authors and scribes have contributed to the knowledge this library holds. Still looking up, I aim my voice to Zehlin.

"So, I can read anything I want in here?" I almost break my neck trying to see the top of the swinging ladder that allows a reader to get to the top shelf. Before Zehlin can answer me, I'm already seven steps up the ladder in front of me, chasing after a book that catches my eye.

"Yes, you may. The books that you aren't allowed to read are in the queen's possession. Not even *I* am allowed to touch them." He chuckles as I look down at him, seeing his crossed arms and amused face. "I take it you're a big reader? You seem excited."

I grab a deep green, almost moss-colored, book. It's at least three inches thick and it is lined on the spine with gold and silver. The colors and the decorations are not what catches my eye, however. It's the title.

The Forgery of the Grown Soul.

"I have picked up a book or two." I hold the book in my hands now, as gently as I can I flip to the first page, balancing on the ladder as a vine brushes on my eyebrow. "So, this tale. Is it true?"

"Ah," Zehlin walks a little closer to the bottom of the ladder. He's never looked this short before, and it makes me smile while holding back a chuckle. "Yes, that tale is true. The story written in that particular book is a little dramatic, but true, nonetheless. The daughter of the man and woman in that story had written it."

I remember the story Aunt Prim would tell me about the *Grown Soul*. How a woman's husband disappears in the middle of the night and she finds him beaten and dead. She is in so much agony that she sits with the ground and begs the earth to take her. She eventually is granted her wish and becomes a tree that is rumored to grant wishes. She returns the gratitude she was blessed to others in need. It's one of the most touching stories Aunt Prim would tell and I've never grown tired of it.

I slowly make my way back down the ladder, holding the story carefully in my arms like it's a child. When I make it to the bottom, Zehlin takes my hand helping me take the last step to the hardwood flooring, cushioned with red and green carpet.

"If you already know the story, why are you going to read a book about it?" he asks, naively. "Out of everything else you could pick from?"

"It appears you clearly are *not* a reader." I chuckle, knowing that hearing a summarization of the story will never be as good as reading the whole tale, word for word.

"I am not, it seems like most of it is a waste of time," I scoff slightly, letting him continue. "Why would someone want to read hours and hours of the history of a rock? Or how a certain country came to be? Explanations and summaries are what I do best."

"And… you're the general?" I ask, appalled at his ignorance. "Of the archipelago?"

"By Numen, you are blunt. I never fail to be surprised by your comments," his declaration makes me smile. I guess getting inserted into a castle where formality, fae, and magic are common occurrences makes a townsperson seem blunt. "Especially towards Queen Etiza. When you raised your voice, at both of us, I was shocked. She doesn't let many people get away with that, let alone allow them to walk out on dinner without a talking-to."

"To be fair, you guys did kidnap me, isolate me, detoxify me, and then ask me to save the entirety of our people," I laugh, reminding myself of the sheer obscurity from the last few days. Recalling how my life has taken multiple turns just in a short while is something I continue to try and suppress. "The islands are practically in my hands because you and the queen *suspect* that because my parents are some of the most powerful beings in history, that I might be powerful as well."

We both make our ways toward a middle seating area. There are brown couches and chairs that match the dark oak tables. There are more flourishing plants surrounding yellow firelight and stacks of books. We sit across from each other, a low-set table is placed between us.

"Well," Zehlin sighs, sitting with perfect posture partnered with his perfectly auburn hair glowing in the sunlight. "All we need is for you to help us by growing your strength and gaining knowledge. With that, you might be able to prove us right."

"What if I don't want to prove you right?" I ask him, looking at him in his green, almost gray, eyes. I could get lost in his eyes forever. The way the colors swirl in a mix of shades I've never seen before, on anyone. A tinge of sadness breezes past Zehlin's face after my comment, leaving as quick as it came.

"I would understand." He nods, swallowing hard and folding his hands.

"I still wake up in pain every morning. It's almost like I can feel the fire burning through my veins every time I close my eyes. I'm in pain, and it's only bearable because it's not excruciating all the time, only sometimes. My body is still shifting as well. I have no idea who I am anymore," my voice uncontrollably chokes, and I cover my mouth. Vulnerability is the last thing I need to deal with at this point. "My aunt, who raised me, who made me the person I used to be, is now a stranger. An elf, a liar."

We share an extended glance as tears force their way out. I was just laughing a minute ago about books and now I'm thinking about my entire future. Are elves usually this emotional, or will it shift away too?

"How am I supposed to restore everyone, if I don't even know who the one saving it even is?" I quickly wipe my eyes and take a shallow breath. Zehlin is only looking at me, and I don't blame him. If I were him I wouldn't know what to tell me either. A girl is switching species right in front of his eyes and even as powerful as he is, he has no idea how to help me or ease the pain. "Who am I, Zehlin?"

He only looks at me and raises his hand. He conjures his light again, a faint flicker of bright light starts to form, getting bigger and bigger every time I blink until he's holding a small ball of sunshine.

"This," he points to the orb with his other hand. "This is what allowed me to find out who I was. Maybe I can do that for you too."

"You can't help me, I need to learn how to do it for myself."

I stand up and watch the shadows fade out and the light from Zehlin's hand dissolve back into the air.

I continue to hold *Grown Soul* in my hand and turn away for one moment, looking out the windows above me. I blink and sigh away the sudden breakdown I almost had. I should do anything *but* look like I can't handle this.

I take a breath and force my eyes to dry, saving the questions and uncertainties for another day. "Aside from reading, what is the first step to gaining all seven pieces of jewelry?"

Chapter Eleven

Zehlin went over the fact that I already have one of the pieces of jewelry and that we should sit tight and figure out if I have any ability other than poor balance. The chance of me being a full bred elf and not having any abilities is very unlikely.

So, we talked.

Zehlin said he talked to the queen and they agreed I should be 'worked on' before I travel anywhere. Traveling can be so much more smooth than I ever thought was possible if Zehlin truly can tesser as far as he says he did, traveling could be scary fast for us. This would also give us a head start when it comes to Josephine and her soldiers.

Your mother.

The thought of preparing for a war to protect my people from my own mother is something Artea from one week ago would laugh at, hysterically.

He says that he can take me with him as well. It feels like an unreal luxury knowing I could travel an island's distance in only a moment's time, avoiding the terrifying ocean and death traps I've learned to be scared of my entire life.

Zehlin also explained to me that the queen, scholars, and others have read a good amount of the content in the library and were able to come up with the theory that each island has one piece of jewelry.

And all *I* have to do is collect them all.

We are walking up the stone steps and Zehlin has his trusty light in hand, and I have *Growl Soul* in mine, but then I stop for a moment.

"I have a question." I declare.

Zehlin stops his incline and turns around slightly, dropping his shoulders. "You seem to have a lot of questions," he says, smirking two steps above me.

"Yes, well, all of this is very abnormal to me. So cut me some slack, General." His eyes sharpen, waiting for my response. Part of me wonders why he seems to hate me calling him General. Isn't it respectful? "When I get all the pieces, which I won't be able to take off, what's next? What will getting the pieces accomplish?"

He turns back around and continues the path upward, I follow eagerly waiting for his response.

"Well, we haven't found a certain spell yet, but we are hoping that if we end up back in Mava after collecting the pieces, we can go to the cave," he told me about the cave earlier while we were looking at some of the books. The cave is where the flame burned. The flame was what kept the bridges up and made the oceans safe to travel. "Then we can perform the spell and bring the flame back. When the king put out the flame, he needed something to contain the magic it withheld. You're wearing one of them right now. One of seven."

"So, we need a spell that will return the magic back to its rightful place," he nods as we approach the door. "And the super important spell that we need doesn't exist."

Zehlin opens the door and fresh, dust-free air hits my face as we are above ground again, feeling the cool air of the castle's hallways.

"It's not that it doesn't exist, we are pretty sure it does. We just haven't found it yet." He shrugs as he closes the door and gestures for us to walk to our right.

"Okay, that makes total sense. Do you guys have any proof that it exists? Like at all?" I ask harsher than I intended to. If I'm going to permanently attach seven pieces of jewelry to myself, I need to know that it will be worth something.

"Wizards and spell makers, like the king, don't make a spell to contain magic without pairing it with a spell that can reverse it. They'd give up power that way, and the king didn't like giving up an opportunity of power. It's not how he did things."

"But the war was over a hundred years ago? How do you know how the King of Perdita did things?" I ask because he talks about the king like he knows him personally. The thought of that sends shivers down my body.

Zehlin clears his throat and straightens his posture as we walk, showing clear signs of being uncomfortable. Did I ask the wrong thing?

"I worked with him." He says looking to his right, away from me on his left, as stiff as a board.

"How old are you? How did you work with him?" My mouth almost hangs open.

"You and your Numen damned question." He shakes his head while shoving light chuckles out to hide his discomfort and shifts his gaze to the floor.

"I'm all alone over here. The least you could do is avoid hiding things from me. And the way things are sounding, we are going to be with each other for a while." My mind wanders, making me wonder how long this jewelry mission is going to take. I'm not even allowed to leave yet because I need to read and practice whatever it is they want me to before I can go anywhere. Even if I were to leave, I don't have anything to go back to.

"I'm about five hundred years old," I barely get enough time to process his age before he continues. "Queen Etiza and King Ector were military partners for almost three hundred years until The War of Stone and Mountains. Until he betrayed her."

Ector.

No one has mentioned his name until now. My father's name is Ector. The man who left seven islands to be left in ruin has a name. It's a weird feeling to put a name to someone like that, I feel like I only wanted him to stay *King*. That way he's not real, that way I don't have to face him and the fact that I'm trying to repair everything he tore apart.

But my father *is* real.

And so is my mother.

I've always wanted to know who my parents were, but this isn't what I had in mind.

"So, the archipelago and the elves were rivals until the queen and king mended it, only for the king to break it again?" The idea of the king breaking that alliance off doesn't make any sense to me. As far as I know, he tore apart the islands just because he wanted to.

"Correct, and no one knows why he did it."

After multiple staircases and doorways, we made it to my room so I could get changed into some real clothes. I decided to wear a knee length silky lilac dress that compliments my new paleness. My caramel hair was tied up in lilac ribbons thanks to Gachera. She was more than happy that I was wearing a dress. I've never minded wearing dresses, I just didn't feel like looking nice for strangers. But, as of now, the only stranger is the queen. I'm getting more comfortable playing dress up now that I know what I'm in for, however horrible it is. I don't know how long I'll be able to enjoy this kind of wardrobe, so I'll enjoy it while it lasts.

Zehlin then escorted me out of my room after I slipped my flats on and Gachera left, we then walked through the castle and headed back downstairs.

We finally stop at the dining room door. I recognize the door by its carvings of leaves and lilies all the way to the ceiling that seems to go up forever. "Breakfast time." He says it like he's hungry.

The door opens without him touching it, revealing a servant opening it from the inside. The same long dining table sits in the middle of the room, covered in breakfast meals and sweet treats. Queen Etiza sits at the very end as she usually does and I observe her as I walk in, heading to my usual spot in the middle.

"Artea, good morning," the queen addresses me as I take my seat, and I notice that I have woodenware set out for me this time. I'm sure that was enforced by the queen, and I hope no one got in trouble for leaving silver out for me last time. The queen also seems pleased to see me in a dress from the wardrobe, which I'm sure was handpicked by her. I don't really want to know why all the clothes are my size, including the shoes, but it's magical Telik so I don't question it. "General, how did the tour go?"

"The tour went well, Artea already found a book to read." Zehlin takes his seat, pointing to me as he adjusts his perfect suit and perfectly braided hair.

"Oh? What book?" the queen asks me, reminding me I left it in the room when we got back for me to get ready.

"It's called *Forgery of the Grown Soul.* It was a classic when I was a girl. My aunt would tell it over and over because I never got enough of the story." I look back to last week, when my only worry was waking up to the town bell in time to make tea for Aunt Prim and open up shop.

Now my only worry is the fate of all seven islands.

"Ah, yes. That book is very deep, and tragic," the queen points out, taking a bite of her sausage while nodding. "My great grandmother knew the daughter of the woman who wrote that story. I aspire to be as good as a ruler as my great grandmother was. The islands prospered under her throne."

Queen Etiza smiles down at her plate as she thinks, the thought bringing her comfort.

I almost ask her about the past ruling until I feel my body get pushed against the back of the chair behind me, thrusting the air out of my lungs and preventing me from breathing in. My vision goes black immediately giving me no time to prepare and the worried voices of the queen and the general vade away turning into distant cries, like raindrops.

I can feel my body grip the arm chairs and I can hear the crystals from the chandeliers above me rattle like leaves in a storm. I still can't open my eyes as I hear faint voices I don't recognize.

I can't make out what they're saying, but outlines of figures start appearing in the distance and black void slowly surrounds the rest of my view. It almost seems like I'm getting pushed closer and closer, unable to move my legs, until I'm stopped.

Two people are in front of me, neither acknowledging me staring at them. There are seats and a table, as well as a desk with ink and quills matched with half written letters. It's like a chunk of a room is being shown in front of me, like a picture, but it's playing out in front of me. A moment in time.

One of the two people I see is a man, young and strong, and appears to be human. He's in a gold and white suit, with light brown hair treading down his shoulders. His eyes are gray and green, and the closer I look, the more I realize.

Zehlin.

I'm watching Zehlin in front of me, but he looks so much younger. Almost younger than me, and definitely not human.

The second one is an older man with black hair wearing a white uniform that has at least six different medal tags on his right and left shoulders. He is definitely ranked in a place of authority, and he doesn't look pleased.

"Yes, Father, I'm trying! I didn't mean–!" Zehlin yells out in desperation but is cut off by a flooring back hand slap from his father.

"I don't take any Numen damned trying, boy!" He shouts against his son through gritted teeth, pushing back a strand of hair into place. He gets extremely close to young Zehlin who already stumbled back into the desk trying to hold himself up from the hit.

"I–I understand, I'm sorry." Zehlin stands up, wiping blood from his chin as he stands tall but still looks down.

"King Xeon is dead because of you! Do you know what this means?!" The father yells even louder this time, making Zehlin shake as sweat beads on his brow and blood continues to drip down his chin.

"Y–yes, sir." Zehlin pauses and swallows before answering. "Princess Etiza will be placed as the queen of the archipelago, sir."

"Yes, that's right." The father steps back one pace, folding his hands behind him and breathing in. The air feels thinner as Zehlin's father backs away. "The thirty-four year old fae princess is now going to be ruling. Tell me, why is that opposite from ideal?"

I watch Zehlin scramble gently for something on the desk behind him hidden from his father's gaze.

"Because every ruler must be at least one hundred years old before they are allowed to be on the throne, sir." The young lieutenant now holds something behind his back, something I can't see. The idea of one hundred years being the minimum truly puts the separation of humans and fae into perspective. Humans rarely ever touch an age that high.

"That's right, and it's because of you that our islands will have an inexperienced queen. She's not even married yet." The father clears his throat as I start to feel hands on my body outside of this scene playing in my head. I can almost see my knuckles and wrists turning white from my gripping of the arms on the dining chair. "You screwed up. This is all because of your terrible orders. I hope you die before I do, so you never become general. Mava's military would crumble under your command."

The father, general I assume, puts a hand aggressively on Zehlin's shoulder and the young lieutenant starts to scream and bends down to his knees, fighting the gripping pain he's receiving. I see his shoulder start to turn blue and white as icy mist rises away from his father's hand.

He's freezing his arm, to stop him from his future duties.

I fight my chair, forgetting that I can't do anything, I can only watch. I can't turn my head, I can't yell, I can't move at all.

I'm stuck to spectate the abuse.

Before I try to pull myself out of whatever scene this is, Zehlin takes his right hand and stabs something into his father's side, over and over again. The general lets go of his son's shoulder, letting it slowly gain its color back.

The general screams and screams as red slowly stains his white uniform and he drops to the ground in one quick movement. I see Zehlin is pushing him down, still twisting the sharp object into his abdomen.

"I will be a better general than you ever have been," Zehlin takes the object, which I now see is a quill, and puts it against his father's neck as he chokes on blood and tries to fight Zehlin off, grabbing his face and neck. I feel more and more hands on my body, pushing me out of this trance from the past. "And I pray Numen forgives you."

Zehlin's arm raises high into the air.

The window in front of my dining room seat comes back into view, my chair is pulled out and there is the healer, the ward holder, and Zehlin touching my arms.

I only look forward, I can only look forward. I don't move, I don't look at anyone else except for the colorful flowers and trees outside the window.

I can't hear them, but I know they're trying to get my attention. They aren't the only ones confused about what's happening to me.

Their fingers shake me and shake me until I lurch forward and let out my sickness worth two bites of breakfast, bringing on the same nausea that I felt when I woke up the first day cleansed from the fesch root.

The carpet gets stained horrid colors mixed with crimson.

Blood.

Fantastic.

Chapter Twelve

I wake up in my bedroom.

Again.

The first thing I feel is the same old sickening feeling I haven't been freed of for days now. The sheets are covering my pale, cold body and I realize I'm still in my clothes from this morning. A lilac dress and ribbons.

The sun is still up as it illuminates through the balcony door and the windows, so that means it's still the same day. Thank Numen.

I sit up slowly, unable to move any faster than I am. My room looks the same, and no one is in here waiting for me either. I take a few deep breaths and fling the covers off of me before getting out of the tall bed, trying to ignore the nausea.

I look in the vanity after sitting down on the stool in front of it. The bags under my eyes are purple and my eye color has turned into a shade of darker brown, a shade that almost looks black. My eyes have always been dark brown, everyone tells me they look freaky or fascinating because of how deep and mousy the shadow is. So, seeing my eyes even darker is disturbing, even to me. My skin is paler, and I have more freckles than usual. The caramel color of my hair has lightened in the spring weather, even though I haven't even been outside yet.

I've been longing for the fresh air, the flowers, and the trees. I almost don't remember if I've heard a single bird sing the whole time I've been in Mava.

I'm slimmer than I used to be because I haven't eaten anything, and suddenly I'm becoming more aware of everything wrong with my body. My lips are coarse because of the dehydration, my hair is frizzy, I have strains on all of my muscles thanks to the tenseness of everything.

The sickness.

The stress.

The shift.

I think back to the things that the queen was describing about my family. I think about the vision I had before I passed out. I think about my aunt.

And then I remember Torrid.

If Torrid knew where my aunt was going, maybe he can tell me other things as well. Maybe he could tell me where Josephine is, maybe he could tell me what the vision was or if it had any ounce of truth.

And maybe he could tell me where the other pieces of jewelry are. Because that seems to be important information right now.

If Aunt Prim meant to partner with King Ector, my father, then that means that she meant to hide my powers too. That meant that she was shifting me into a human mold on purpose, into the human mold that my father and mother wanted me to be. *Forgotten, lied to, alone, and powerless.*

Not to mention defenseless.

I got attacked, almost killed, kidnapped, drugged, and locked in a castle all in a few days. Clearly they don't care enough if they're going to let me go through all that, and probably much more if this flame mission will play out how the queen and the general describe.

Of course they don't care about you. You knew that since you were old enough to understand that they left you.

Was I even left on Aunt Prim's doorstep at all? Or were we both shipped from Perdita to live in an odious town on a lonely island, just for me to be lied to and for Aunt Prim to be left alone. Is that even her name either?

I step up from the vanity stool and open my bedroom door. The wards are gone, so that means I'm free to roam the castle, no one has told me any different. I step out into the large hallway, closing the door quietly behind me.

Torrid will have the answers.

There is only one issue.

I have no idea where Torrid is placed. When I first saw him and asked him about my aunt, he told Zehlin to not put him back down there again. And there is only one door that I know leads downstairs.

I find my nightgown that I had on while Zehlin and I went downstairs to the library. There were many other doors, so it makes me wonder if Torrid could be in one of those rooms. I look through the pockets of my nightgown and locate the feather key, clasping it in my hand tightly, letting myself release a deep exhale.

I'll just hope I can remember the way.

I ran through the hallways hoping to hide myself from anyone who could be roaming them like I was. To my luck, I didn't see anyone and I finally made it to the door. I went down the stairs very slowly, carefully feeling each stone step. I didn't have Zehlin's sun orb to give me the advantage of seeing this time, so I had to make do.

I found the wooden door eventually, *without knocking into it*, and I entered the key into the keyhole after using my fingers to find it, unlocking the basement door. It slid to the right, leaving me at the entrance alone, looking at the torch lit hallway with many doors.

I look to the right and see the five doors, all labeled with what I'm assuming is what they contain. The labels are *Cells, Concoctions, Nursery, Library,* and *Lockers.*

My first thought would be that Torrid would be in the cells, but then I remember that he was placed in a glass flask, almost like an alchemy flask. So, that leads me to *Concoctions.*

I walk closer to my left where the concoctions sign is placed, right next to the wooden door. I take my hand to the doorknob and push it open.

The first thing I feel is the cold air pushing against my skin, like something telling me I'm not allowed in here. The room is dark and I can see many rows of shelves in front of me. There are glasses and boxes filling the shelves that are riddled with dust and spiderwebs. The air is muggy and dense, like I just walked into a steaming room full of heat and mist. Yet, it's not hot, it's cool.

I gently close the door behind me, shutting out any other light that might have been shining in from the torches in the hallway. There are a few vials and containers holding bright liquids that shine a neon, but yet lambent color. It gives me just enough light that I can still snake my way through the isles of shelves.

In one corner, I see a desk with vials and pages and ink all over it. This is a scientist's hideout. Is there a scientist designated to this castle? So far, it doesn't seem like anyone has been down here in ages, or at least no one has cared to keep the area habitable for some time.

I walk through the isles, deciding that if I want answers, I'm going to need them fast before anyone realizes I'm gone.

I search the shelves all over, digging through boxes, pushing items aside, no matter how grotesque they look. There are some jars full of teeth, blood, and even what looks like pickled intestines. I'm surprised this room doesn't smell as bad as it looks. Most likely more magic hiding the potential stench.

I'm looking in the room for at least five minutes before I hear a tapping to my left. I turn my head, pushing a box back into place, and standing back up from my kneel. I lightly walk closer to the noise, knowing I haven't been alone.

I look up toward the sound and see the same flask Zehlin showed me a couple days ago, with the little man inside of it.

That seemed a little too easy.

I reach up and grab the flask and see Torrid dancing in his fragile cage. I take a seat on the wooden floor, knowing that I'm going to be covered in dust by the time I get back. I look at the purple bottle and smile.

"Atrea! Devil Spawn! You're here! You have come to save me, pale girl, thank you!" Torrid shouts with pure joy. He pushes himself against the glass and fogs the surface as he shouts. The enthusiasm in his voice doesn't match the words coming out of his mouth.

"Do you need to insult me every time we meet?" I ask him.

"Well, no. My apologies, miss elf girl. I cannot help it, I just talk and talk and talk and talk and I cannot stop." *I can tell.*

I place the purple flask on the wooden floor and look down to Torrid. It's clear he has heard about the bad things elves have done to our islands, and he doesn't like me for it.

"You know I was human my whole life right?" I ask, trying to get on the same level with him.

"Well yes, yes yes. I've heard. The wind whispers things to me, she gets bored and whispers. Whispering all the time. I think she likes me."

I pause, watching him smile thinking about the wind, his eyes glancing into the thick air of the room seemingly daydreaming.

"So, you know that I didn't do anything wrong, right? Not like the other elves?" I connect with him. He nods and looks at me, snapping out of his thoughts. "Then I have a few questions for you. The entire archipelago seems to depend on me and my ability to bring the flame back, and I need your help in finding out a few things. Can you do that?"

Torrid looks down to his feet and slumps his back against the far side of the flask, still facing me.

"I'm not given a choice, Artea. Ask away." He sulks as he fidgets with his fingernails.

I feel distraught for him. He might have terrorized kids, and he might deserve a fate like this, but I still feel bad for the tiny man. He's been in here for a long while, it was only a matter of time before he lost his mind and went mad.

"Torrid, I want to give you a choice." I say, and he looks up quickly as I peak his interest. "I *need* your help. If you want the islands to be safe, and for them to be brought back together again, I need to know some things. And I know you have the answers to my questions. I have nobody, Torrid."

He looks away, and I notice his eyes well with tears as he bites his lip.

"My mother and father died when I was a boy. I barely remember them. Dead, dead. And my older sister was evil. C–creature. She didn't care for me. She let others hurt me, it hurt. I had no body. I have nobody." One tear falls from his face and disappears into his stubble. "I know what it feels like to be lonely, and no one has ever given me a choice before. I don't want to hurt people, I don't want to hurt people anymore. I want to help them, Missy Ma'am."

I put a finger to the flask, then he gets up and puts both of his hands against my finger, closing his eyes.

"So, Torrid, will you help me?"

I get one nod from him as he tries to hide the fact that he needs to let a few more tears slip. Either there is a very emotional man in front of me, or he's so broken that he can't keep it together anymore. I'm determined to help him because I see someone who regrets past decisions, or is a changed man, and it takes a lot of courage to admit when you're wrong. I find that impossible myself.

I can be his first step to helping himself be better, and he can be my first step to figuring out what the hell is going on with this place.

"Good." I pick up his flask and set it on a shelf in front of me, sitting at eye level. "My first question is about who my mother is. Can you tell me anything about that?"

Torrid looks to struggle a little bit, similar to how he did when I woke up from the wards killing me because of my very blood. Burning me because of my new elf body. He seems to be in pain, trying to fight the answer until he takes a few breaths and looks at me. He might be forced to answer the questions either way, but I think he's reminding himself that he wants to help me, and he wants to mend whatever wrong doings he did in the past.

Part of me thinks he has done much worse things than lie to children and make them have nightmares. You have to do something pretty horrible to be kept in a bottle for hundreds of years. I have pity for the man but I still keep myself weary, making sure I don't trust too easily. I was taken here and informed that my entire life was a mixture of lies and secrets, for all I know I could be in complete delusion right now. None of this could be real and I could still be dreaming after my cold bath, blood still crusted in my hair. I could be sleeping peacefully, waiting for the town bell to mark seven and wake me up to open shop.

But instead I'm here, at least I think I am, waiting for my next step to save the islands, asking a tiny man about my mother, someone who I thought I'd never have to care about. I thought my parents would be a piece of who I am that I grieve, but never ponder. It has become a whole different thing knowing that my mother might be out there.

"Josephine, Josephine Lara. That's her name," he stammers in his words, fighting a battle in his head that I will never understand. "She raises the dead, and can also bring death. I have met her once, I have met her. She is a beautiful woman, you look just like her."

No one has ever been able to tell me anything about my parents before, let alone relate them to me. I don't have any time to process what Torrid says before he continues.

"She is in Perdita and married to the King. Your father. Father." He repeats and shakes his head, tears still welling in his eyes.

"Wait," I ask him to pause as I look at him on his shelf. "*Is*, married? As in currently?" I ask, waiting for confirmation.

"Well, yes yes. King Ector is married to Josephine the necromancer elf lady." Torrid scrunches his eyebrows, acting like this was obvious information. Well, of course it was obvious information to a guy who has the ability to answer almost any question.

If the king *is* married to Josephine, that means that he's alive. My father is alive.

In the time I've been here in Telik, which I found on a map located on a wall in one of the thousands of hallways, the queen and Zehlin have told everyone that the king died in the war. All the stories have said that the king died in the war. Everyone in Halistyn knows that the king died one hundred years ago and that's how the war ended. Everyone knows that the king is dead.

I know that he actually died from an assassination after I was born. So, how is he married at the moment… if he's dead?

"Do you have the capability to lie, Torrid?" I ask, glaring in suspicion toward his direction. He looks at me with disdain and rolls his eyes.

"Seriously?" Is all he says while he rolls his eyes and crosses his arms. I don't think I've met a bassier man in my life. I understand why he reacted the way he did, I shouldn't question the man's curse. He's had so much taken from him already.

"Does Queen Etiza know that King Ector is still alive?" I ask. The queen and Zehlin told me that King Ector was assassinated, and that Josephine couldn't get to him quick enough. If they know that he's alive, that means they're lying to me. As if I need this situation to get more complicated.

"No, no, no, no. He's dead in their world. No, they don't." I let out a sigh of relief. I've always been someone who's quick to trust. In Halistyn, I would try and help struggling people in simple ways. Even a smile from someone would be an anomaly, so I tried to do things that could make their day a little better. Trusting people, in a place like Halistyn usually didn't get me in good places, but I still did it, no matter how much it hurts to see so much negativity. Though, I don't blame anyone for their actions in Ihrvian.

The king is the one who made the islands how they are today. I'm told we used to thrive, and now it's worrisome to see folks have a good time.

I suppose it's now time to give up my lenience on others. If my own aunt lied to me my whole life, and kept all those secrets, who knows what the queen and the general could be hiding.

So, I will keep this to myself.

Both my parents are alive. In another continent, across the ocean, and cruel. But still alive. This is my knowledge, and I will keep it. I already feel intruded on, knowing that the queen already is aware of so much about my life. This will be held close, especially if it were to start another war if it got out. We already have the threat of Queen Josephine on our heads, but I don't need to be the reason she comes faster.

"Also, what was that vision I had earlier? With Zehlin?" I ask, hoping he's able to explain it, and maybe the sickening feeling that came after.

"T–that was almost five hundred years ago. His father was the general at the time. King Xeon's, Queen Etiza's father, second in command. He was an aggressive man, and Zehlin killed him. Zehlin had made an order to let less fae protect King Xeon because they were getting sick. A demon hunter made its way into the castle and killed Xeon behind his back. The demon hunter thought that Xeon was inherently evil and then Zehlin's father blamed him for the attack and tried to freeze off his arm to stop any future duties, but Zehlin was quicker. Then there was a new crowned queen and a new general on the same day. Zehlin promised to protect Etiza as best as he could as long as he was alive. Which has been a while, and he still does that very thing. Without fail. The late general was also Queen Etiza's uncle, making Zehlin and Etiza cousins."

I take in the story, allowing myself to envision all the pieces of it and adding it to what I already know. I didn't know that they were related either, but it makes sense why they seem to work well together.

"And as far as your vision went, it's because of that ring. It lets you see certain fragments of the past. Ones that might be important. You can learn to control it, with the right training. You can find specific moments in time that you need to see."

The ring from Ihrvian is giving me visions, so will that mean the other six pieces will do the same thing? I don't dare to ask, because I might cut off the mission if that's the case. I'm only just now getting used to being an elf. It's only been one day I've gone without crippling nausea. This is all I need to know now. I can only add so much to my plate at a time.

However, being able to choose what I could look for in the past could be life changing, not only for me but for many others too. Do elves usually get these powers? Or is it unique to the ring? I let the questions stay in the air and slip through the crack of my mind.

I grab Torrid and place him back on his shelf, clearing a few items out of the way so he can see outside in the tiny window close to the ceiling.

"Wait, no please," Torrid begins, like I expected. "Please let me out, I won't hurt you, I won't, I won't." I place a finger on the glass in front of his hands where he leans toward me in anticipation.

"I'm sorry, Torrid. I already risked a great deal coming down here in the first place. I just can't let you out yet." I say apologetically. "I will be down here more often though. I can keep you company, and you can keep me company too. I don't have anyone else here."

He looks down, giving up on arguing but understanding, nonetheless. I could see a small glint of hope after I said *yet*.

All he does is nod and I smile back, standing up and waving as I walk to the door. The mutual understanding that it's not my place to let him go brings a warm ache to my heart. I make sure I have the key in my pocket before I open the door and make my way back upstairs.

I made it to my room in time just before Gachera came to check in on me. Before she came in I changed into a loose white long-sleeve blouse and an ankle-length, felt brown skirt. The outfit is a nicer version of the rags we wear in Halistyn. No one has any money to travel to the wealthier areas of Ihrvian, let alone money to buy nice clothes when they get there. A part of me feels close to home being able to see myself in what I'm used to wearing. Aunt Prim would sew me beautiful pieces of clothing for my birthday every year. Sometimes it was a dress, others it was pants or a suit. She always made the most comfortable and stylish clothes for me.

I get another small pull in my heart, reminding me that I won't see her again. Going to Perdita is out of the question, I was left here as a forgotten treasure, only to be found by the queen. I was told that my whole life was a cover up, all so King Ector and Queen Josephine could avoid having to deal with me in the future. If I was left as a nobody, maybe I can prove them right and show them just how powerful I could be.

When I'm given the instruction, I will read and I will find the other pieces to put back together what we lost. I will do my best to prove them right, that I should be hidden.

But I will not *stay* hidden.

Gachera told me I was to go downstairs to another dinner meeting with the queen and Zehlin. So, I finished redoing my hair, and of course that made Gachera grouchy. She claims I steal her job and that I shouldn't be the one getting dressed and grooming myself. I let her apply powders to my face to make up for the job stealing and we made our way downstairs.

Now I sit in the dining room alone, waiting in my seat for Queen Etiza and Zehlin to make their way in here. I've never been alone in here before, aside from the servants lining the back walls of the room, the table seats are bare.

After a few minutes, the door opens quickly, followed by multiple pairs of shuffling feet. I turn my head to see Queen Etiza, Zehlin, and another man I've never seen before.

They come closer and mumble apologies for being late while finding their seats. Etiza sits to my right, and Zehlin to my left as usual. The other man sits across from me, all of us creating a diamond shape in our chairs.

The man has pointed ears, but shorter than mine. So, he's fae, like Zehlin. I learned that almost everyone near the royal castle is fae, so it's not surprising. He is very muscular and is about as tall as Zehlin. He has short red hair that's neatly trimmed, and he has jewelry decorating his ears, neck, and hands. The different gems clink together as he adjusts in his seat. He has a white suit on, lined with gold in a similar way to Zehlin's suit. His sharp features and dull eyes make me look away almost immediately.

They're all out of breath and scrambling to get comfortable at the table. I fold my hands in my lap, feeling bare. The man has more jewelry attached to him right now than I've ever owned, Etiza is in a gown like most other times, and Zehlin is postured well in his suit, matching the fae in front of me. I have my unadorned blouse and skirt, with my hair slightly wavy and down. The only thing that I have to compare to them is my ring.

And I didn't have the choice to wear it.

"Artea, we are so sorry for the wait." Zehlin apologizes as he ties his shoulder-length hair back with a string.

"No, don't worry," I shrug off. "I wasn't here long." I look forward to the window, and am relieved to remember that the fae is in my way. The vision from earlier made me sick, and I'm sure the sight of the purple valleys outside would have the same effect.

"We were on a run, to remind Aleck here that he has a job to do. Weren't we, Aleck?" Queen Etiza mentions, turning toward the fae in front of me. He nods and takes a bite of his pre-plated food.

"Yes," he coughs through his chewing. "Can a man not forget a job one time?" He laughs and takes another bite.

"Aleck, have I not reminded you that this is *the* mission? I should not have to go to your quarters and wake you because it's the morning after you partied too hard." Zehlin speaks this time, in the same tone he did when Torrid was brought after the wards burned my blood. His general voice gets the reaction he wants out of Aleck as he looks down and nods.

"Yes, sir," he responds, and the three of them exchange awkward glances across the table. To my understanding, it doesn't seem Aleck gets along with the two of them very well.

"What mission, exactly?" I interject curiously.

"The mission to get the other six pieces. It's too dangerous for us to go alone. And Aleck here is the most talented, and useful, combat fighter." Zehlin looks at me, smiling full of pride.

"I'm only the best when I need to be," Aleck says, shrugging the complement off. I'm assuming there is a lot of history behind Zehlin and him based on the way they talk, almost like brothers who can't help but appreciate each other even when they bicker. "And I need to be decoration for tomorrow night's ball."

"Ball? Like a dance?" My hands almost immediately get slick as I think about a ball. There will be people, important people. At least that's what I read about in the books of the royal family back in my apartment. I'm still not over the nausea and the soreness in my body, I can't imagine what it would be like meeting a bunch of people.

Maybe the queen will let me hide in my room and stay there until everyone is too drunk off their wine to care about the missing elf. Not only am I an elf, but I'm also supposed to save them from death ridden oceans and potential war from Josephine and Ector. I'm supposed to save them from my parents. I cannot show myself to Telik right now, *the* capital of the archipelago.

"Yes, it's about time the people can see their savior. You are more than special, even if there's prejudice against your kind." The way she says *your kind* makes my stomach turn and my fingers go numb.

"I doubt they want to see me," I divert, trying to avoid this situation all together.

"They all think I'm lying when I send announcements or hold meetings and gatherings, they don't believe that we are finally on a mission to save the islands. You will be their beacon of hope, Artea." The queen looks at me with compassion and meaning. Like she truly believes what she says, that I can save them all. I want to save them, I want to help everybody. I want everyone to have money, food, and homes so they don't have to worry about having to starve in the winter.

"Will I just be sitting there? Will there be a speech?" I ask, wiping the sweat onto my brown skirt, looking back and forth from the queen to Zehlin and back.

"We want to demonstrate your power. Please, tell us what you saw in that vision this morning, what the future holds." The queen mentions the vision like it was a regular occurrence yet there is urgency in her tone, calculation in her eyes. I almost wonder how she knows that I had a vision but I know she's the queen and probably knows more than I think.

Future.

She thinks I can see the future. If I correct her, then she knows that I can see the past. Maybe this is a trick, to see if I will lie and hide the truth of my power from her. The power of the ring. I don't trust anyone in this castle enough to tell the truth, I remind myself that I only have me.

Only me.

"I only saw you when you were older. Your hair was no longer blonde, and you were laying in a bed. I assumed you were sick. That was pretty much all." I quickly stew up a lie, a diversion from the truth. I can still see Zehlin's father bleeding on the ground, the carpet stained. I hold my breath, waiting for the lecture or wards to go back up for lying. I don't know why I lie. Maybe because I want this to myself too? Do I want more secrets?

Instead, she nods.

"Do you know why that made you so scared? You were panicking and we had to take you to your room to recover." Zehlin asks me out of concern, and I'm happy it doesn't seem to be out of speculation.

"I'm still pretty sensitive to everything, it's still hard to get up and get dressed in the morning, the soreness seems to affect me all the time. Plus it was my first time experiencing anything like that." I say, playing a card I know will flow well with my story. Etiza's eagerness to find out my vision unsettles me, the way she asked me makes me feel better about lying.

"We read a book on the ring that you hold. It claims to let you see the important parts of the future. Is there anything important you wanted to mention, anything that stood out in your vision?" The queen says, taking her first bite of her meal.

"No, I don't think so." I swallow, glancing at Zehlin while I remember how young he was when he was forced to end his father's life. While he watched him bleed out on the floor of that office. A time that must have changed his life forever.

"Okay, just please let us know if anything comes up. We need all the information possible," the queen murmurs pitifully. "And as for the ball we will be holding dances as usual, but we also would like to give the people of Mava a reason to believe that you're going to try and help them. Like I said, I would like you to demonstrate your power. The people need proof that you can do something other than have pointy ears and pale skin. You need to change the reputation that will already label you as a monster."

The subtle insult passes by me as the worry of using a new power in front of people creeps in on me. Especially people who depend on me to help. I'm not even doing this for the people of Mava, they have everything. This is for the starving and dying ones on all the other islands.

"There will be an announcement as well as your demonstration. Then there will be drinks and dancing for celebration. This ball will be your first opportunity to show the world who you can be, Artea. We have decorations and relations all in order. This is for you, our little whisper of hope."

I take a breath and look at Aleck in front of me, he gives me only an assuring nod. If this warrior believes in me, if the queen of my land believes in me, I will do it.

Even if it burns me from the inside out, and leaves nothing but a whisper of ashes.

Chapter Thirteen

I walk along the empty ballroom with Zehlin, waiting for the guests to arrive. Gachera had woken me up this morning and dolled me up more than she ever has. I have a light gray dress on with long sleeves and feathers trailing down below my ankles. There are rubies sprinkled along the hems, as well as rubies pinned into my hair. My head feels heavy with braids forming a crown of hair, exposing my ears for everyone. Elves aren't the only ones with pointy ears, fae have them as well. However, mine are sharp, as opposed to rounded and tilted.

It seems that all my features are sharper. My nose, my chin, my jawline, and my ears.

My black heels make a loud tapping sound, echoing across the empty, much-too-large ballroom. Something I know that will grab even more attention from the people of Telik.

The point of tonight is to show the people of my islands three things. The queen is willing to be an ally to an elf, for the first time in one hundred years, the general is willing to protect an elf, and an elf is going to try her best to save the people of this archipelago. This is going to be a night nobody is going to be able to forget. It will change the course of their thinking, and it will also change the course of my future.

If I instill hope into everyone who attends tonight's ball, I cannot give up on this. I must go through with it, with everything I have. I look at me one week ago as if someone else were to give me the hope I will give others tonight. I would hate them for giving up, I would hate them for not bringing back what so many lost. I would hate them for deserting everyone that has struggled to even eat in the past century.

I would hate myself for yielding.

So, I stand here with the general of the palace, looking above me at the decorations and vines placed delicately around the room. There are tables and chairs set near the back creating a crescent shape, leaving a large open space for dancing and mingling. Snacks and drinks are placed on all the tables, along with multiple types of wines. Servants stand on the wall lining, marking the ballroom borders and carrying trays. In front of us is an elevated perch with four seats designated for Etiza, Zehlin, Aleck, and me. Etiza's chair is nothing less than a throne decorated in purple gemstones and silver lining, arching taller and wider than the three seats near her own. To the sides of this perch are two staircases on either side, curving up to lead to the chairs.

Zehlin gestures to me, leaving his hand out for my taking. I place my palm in his and he leads us up the left staircase toward our designated seating line. I see Aleck stepping up the right stairs along with us as people should be showing any minute now. Zehlin shows me my seat, placed directly to the right of the throne, next to where the queen will be. Zehlin is on the other side of the throne, and Aleck is next to him. Tonight is all about a message, a message to the people. A communication of hope and future tranquility. The first implantation of something new, of something that will help all people and the ones after them. This is why I'm not surprised I'm placed next to the queen. If I'm going to be creating a message as an elf, why not shoot for the stars and give them a message they would never expect.

I hear doors creek open, and footsteps following after.

They're here.

Everyone floods in, at least two hundred make their way to the seats behind the dance floor. They're wearing mixes of colors ranging from pink to deep forest green. It seems that Mava's environment is made of purple, pink, and blue, but this doesn't stop anyone from showing their true sense of style. Some are in blue or black or white, everyone seems to only wear different shades of one color. The room looks like a paint palette. There are gems and silks paired with sharp angles of silvers and golds. Everyone looks like they're made of glass, delicately shaped into formation and beauty. I haven't even seen the queen wear such extravagant outfits in the time I've spent here in Telik.

Once everyone is settled they look up. To me.

It takes but a moment for them to start turning to the one next to them, whispering words of scandal and worry. I turn red, I can feel the temperature change in my body and my cheeks. I can feel my palms and fingers getting slick with sweat. I know what it's like to be them, to be a human or fae, to see an elf in front of you after all the horrible things they've done in the past. I don't blame them for being scared or disgusted. I don't blame them for wondering why a queen would let such a monster in her kingdom.

She doesn't take long to make her way on the perch, making sure her entrance is stapled and paid attention to. She's wearing a dark gray dress, similar to mine but much more provocative. My dress is long-sleeved and covers everything but my neck, while her dress is dark and cuts her curves in the most beautiful and eccentric way. It's lined with silver and rubies like mine, but the rubies are bigger and the silver is shinier. This, I didn't even know was possible. Her hair is braided and draped down one shoulder, creating a base for her purple and silver crown to lay on. It shines in the glistening light from the windows as the sunset welcomes dusk.

Everyone is in awe like me, I'm guessing this isn't a regular ball. Maybe that's why everyone wears something extravagant, even Zehlin's white suit is charmed with more gold pieces than usual. The queen visually pairs with me perfectly, the light and the dark gray calls eyes to us like a hunter does to prey. I feel bare, and oddly alone.

"Everyfellow, thank you for attending tonight's gathering. This will be a night you will not forget," Etiza starts to speak as she doesn't yet take a seat and stands tall in front of her throne, claiming the posture of a queen. "I have a very special announcement, as you all can guess. Artea, sits here to my right. She is here tonight to prove to you all, we can be saved, our islands have hope of being put back together."

The crowd murmurs, more whispers and even gasps flood the room. I try to look at the crowd, try to keep a straight face, try to maintain proud body language. But it's so hard.

"She is an elf, yes. And the only one willing to save us. She is an exiled soldier from our enemy, the elves in Perdita. She was pinned against a wall for being different, for being good. She was kicked to drown in the ocean for trying to make an alliance with us," her story that I wasn't made aware of builds. Of course I can't just be a girl from Halistyn, I have to be special to be a savior. It makes sense the way she builds me into a character who has always supported the islands, even if I was supposed to be an enemy. In a way it's true, I was born human. "General Zehlin found her, and saved her. Even if he thought she would kill us, or harm our islands. We wrongly held her prisoner in this very castle, until we came to an agreement and we found that she wanted to help."

Stand.

I rise from my chair, the echo of Etiza's voice rumbles in my head.

Be proud, do not tremble.

I stand with a confidence I didn't know I could muster. I can't stop myself from looking at the crowd, from feeling superior to them.

"Artea, please address our people." *Address them, be convincing.*

My voice and thoughts lurch out of my throat. I speak to them loudly, clearly, unable to stop and unable to quiver. *What is the queen doing to me?* I start to feel like I'm looking at myself through a second pair of eyes, like my mouth and hands aren't my own. She's using a power on me, one I didn't know she had.

"I was left by my people," I start to speak. "The ones who raised me to be the perfect soldier. But to them, the perfect soldier is a cold murderer. I wanted change, I wanted to know what happened in the war. What *truly* happened. So, they pushed me away, never letting me back into the borders of Perdita. So, I'm here now, knowing what happened and the injustice that was put upon you and your islanders. There are items that General Zehlin, Lieutenant Aleck, and I, must collect to bring the safe waters back. To reconnect your islands once more. This will take time, but we will succeed. And If I have your support, I will give my life to fight for all of you as well as any folk who is not here today," I don't sound like me, this isn't me. I'm not a leader, but I can't stop. "I will stand for you, will you let me?"

The crowd is nodding, some smiling, some still unsure of what to think. I'm unsure of what to think as well. I sounded like a leader, I sounded like someone the queen of our islands would endorse. Did she know I wouldn't have been able to deliver the aspiration for the future that the people needed? Was she helping me, without warning? This is the perfect cover up, the soldier who will construct a new era.

I continue to stand tall, my shoulders broad and form fitting in my dress. As the crowd settles, some of the whispers die down and the queen takes my hand. I grip it tightly, some part of me is trying to find the reason behind her manipulation. How did she do it? No one prepared for tonight, let alone prepared me for Etiza to get in my head and force me to do a whole speech.

The speech.

Someone claps, an older woman with dark skin wearing yellow and gold. Sitting in the front row, she's decorated in jewels and flowers, just like everyone else is. All the people follow suit, clapping along and standing up once Etiza takes my hand, an image of reunion and healing.

Everyone seems pleased enough to sit back down after a brief moment. Some start to pour wine into their glasses, others talk and argue about the situation at hand. I don't doubt that they are conflicted with trusting an elf. However, they don't know who I really am. They don't know I'm the *daughter* of the man and woman who slaughtered their army one hundred years ago. They think of me as a cast out soldier, barred from the land because she had a true heart.

They don't see the true me, the girl from Halistyn raised human. They don't see the girl who's sick every morning, transitioning into something she's never been. I suppose it's better this way, when we give them hope of elves not being monsters all the time. Hope of a better future, and less war.

The islands and Perdita have always been adversaries, fighting or finding ways to incept each other. Until King Ector and Queen Etiza, for three hundred years, were able to maintain a good relationship between the islands and Perdita. Then the king shredded the alliance to pieces, for something as simple as safe water travels.

And just as my father destroyed everything, I'm expected to fix it. And the people of Mava aren't struggling anywhere near as much as the other islands. From the books I've skimmed over, and my own experience in Ihrvian, Mava is blessed to house all the fae and the queen. I can only imagine how this news could affect everyone else who is truly struggling to survive, not just struggling to get the right crops for their evening feast.

The queen directed everybody to dance and eat, and to simply enjoy their time looking profligate and relishing in the possibility of a new dawn for the islands. The queen has spent the last few minutes pointing out a few people who might be important. There are ladies and lords with claims to land and have closeness with the queen. Some of them, like the woman in yellow and gold, are older than the queen herself.

Lady Ideena, the woman in yellow, has been alive since Etiza's grandmother was serving as queen. That's almost over one thousand years. My mere nineteen feels like a beetle compared to how many years Lady Ideena has lived. Lord Caston, he owns most of the farmland in Telik, and is wealthy because of it. I'm told he has a very heavy influence on the people, and they listen to him for the benefits of food. Not that the people in Telik are in any shortage of food. However, it seems that they always want more.

I lost the ability to stay calm when the queen inched into my brain and forced me to recite a speech that I never thought of. Forced me to say her words. I listen intently to her explanations, but stay vigilant and aware. I decide not to bring it up, as it seems like it's not the time to disrupt the image we are portraying. I leave the concern behind me, keeping my attention on her, wondering what she's thinking of the whole situation.

She goes on and explains a few more important ladies and lords of Telik that attended tonight. She then stands and gains the attention of the room, glowing in the dusk light like a star placed in the deep sky above. She calls for dancing, a ballroom dance with couples and siblings and friends, a dance everyone knows.

Except me.

Zehlin stands on his feet and gestures in front of himself, crossing Queen Etiza for my hand. I stand as well, taking his hand into mine as we walk down the steps. I try to focus on the windows in front of me, keeping my eyes straight and my shoulders up as I notice glances from all over the room. Some people whisper as usual, others look outright shocked.

The general of their entire country is going to dance with an elf.

If my speech that wasn't even my own, didn't convince them, then this definitely should.

I watch as some of the younger women flip their fans in front of their faces, seemingly without shame in front of their dancing partners. They bat their lashes and some of the men dance glances around me, holstering their postures when Zehlin delivers them nods of greetings. Some give slight sneers, yet try to hide the negative emotions in front of the queen's second-in-command. They're all jealous. Jealous of me or jealous of Zehlin, I'm unsure. It could be both.

Zehlin is more attractive than most with his shoulder-length brown hair and thick facial hair that's groomed as nicely as a king's. His suit fits his body well, fit for a general with duties to fulfill.

We take the dance floor among many other couples and pairs, some women are paired together as well, giggling as they get ready for the dancing.

I take a moment, waiting for the song to start, to look at Zehlin. He's looking down at me slightly, my heels allow me to almost match his height. A slight smirk is planted on his lips as his green eyes read my face. We hold hands as his other is placed on my waist, and mine on his shoulder. I wonder what he's thinking right now. Would he rather be anywhere but here? Is he more prepared than me to dance? Is he dreading the future months of preventing war?

The band starts to play and I realize I have no idea what to do. Everyone around me starts to shuffle, including Zehlin.

"Just follow my lead." He says, noticing my nervousness and stiffness. He knows I have no idea how to ballroom dance, nor do I know the difference between the songs. I've read books before, ones that would describe ballroom dances and how each dance had a select style of song to go along with it.

"I don't know what I'm doing." I whisper, looking subtly down toward our feet, trying to match his movement.

"This one is slow, luckily. When I pull, you push. It's simple, Angel." He whispers lower than me as we move side to side, our feet barely lifting off of the floor. Instead, we use our shoulders to guide our movements as we sway side to side. Slowly, everyone dancing forms a circle around the floor and intricately flows following the circle line. We become a flowing ring of intimate pairs. Some smiling, some are holding each other close, ears to hearts. I notice some people looking over to Zehlin and me.

I can't help but blush at the name he calls me, along with all the eyes I have glancing toward me. I continue to stand tall and look him in the eyes as we trace the invisible circle on the floor.

"You're one hell of a brute, you know that?" I say chuckling as I tap his chest weakly.

"Then why do you continue to keep me company if I'm such a brute?" He says looking down to me, forcing me to try and focus on not stepping on his toes.

"I don't have much of a choice, do I, General?" I ask, quirking an eyebrow.

I know I'm helping the queen and Zehlin by choice, but when I dig deeper, am I really given a choice? I can get banished back to Perdita where I was born and be forced to look for a lost family. The lost family that ruined my life and deserted me and my islands. So, that option is crossed out. Maybe the queen would let me live in her castle, the elf with the surrendered potential. Maybe she would put me back in Halistyn and continue to drug me, hide me like I've stayed hidden for so many years.

My time here hasn't been that bad. The pain from the cleansing of the fesch root has not been their fault. So far, the only thing that has raised concern is the queen not telling me anything about tonight, and then controlling my body and voice. I knew I wasn't prepared, but do I thank her or criticize her for such an invasion.

"I know you don't think this whole situation is so bad." He leans down near my ear as the dancers shift and spread out into a checkered pattern. We follow them, being placed right in the middle of the floor. The eyes of spectators who don't dance follow us as well, and I know Aleck and Etiza are watching too. Making sure the message sender, the savior, is still holding her head high.

Like a soldier should.

"And we should be starting to execute your training before we go to Ornau," Zehlin casually mentions.

"Ornau?" I question. "Why Ornau?"

"It's the safest island to roam, and the people there are supportive of the queen and me. It will be a great start for us." He explains as he spins me, which I know how to do. Every girl knows how to spin on the dance floor by the time they're five. Our hands twirl around each other before we go back to holding them and swaying back and forth, surrounded by other pairs.

"And the training?" I ask again.

"Yes, your mind and your body will need to be sharp before you can do what you will be doing. You've already been through a lot with the fesch root cleansing."

Great. More pain to put my body through.

"That's why you were put in that undefined dress, so people couldn't tell that you're not built like a soldier. And considering the fact that you ran into a door proves my point." He chuckles as I slap his chest, hard enough to sting but light enough not to call attention to either of us.

"It was dark!" I yell-whisper. I can't help but smile and flush at the memory of my night gown slipping in front of a gentleman. I can still feel the embarrassment, however the fall was a little funny I will admit.

We danced to a few more songs, and I made a fool of myself even more as they got progressively more complicated. I now hear the music slow down, the band eventually hits a stopping point and we all turn toward the perch. Queen Etiza starts her way down the right staircase, walking as elegantly as a swan. Dusk is long gone by now and the moonlight reflects off of her rubies and dark gown like a beacon.

Everyone shifts to get a look at her, her crown glows on her head and she looks like a proper queen. She looks like the queen everyone would want to lead their country. Zehlin and I stand in the front with people behind us and to our sides. Etiza calls attention to herself just by being here.

Doors to the right of the ballroom, large wooden doors, open. Four Mava soldiers walk in, and placed in the middle of them is a man. Everyone gasps and shifts a few steps back. The man is dragged in front of the crowd, separating the queen and us.

The man has chains around his wrists and ankles that are then connected to his neck. The chains are black and tight around his limbs. He has caramel-tanned skin and tangled brown hair. His skin is smudged with dirt and caked in dried blood in some places. He wears only a pair of knee-length trousers, seemingly made of cheap leather. He is pushed down to the ground on his knees, and only looks to the floor. I feel disgusted knowing I'm wearing jewels and he's forced to wear rags. He breathes rapidly, yet looks defeated.

"Everyone, please listen closely," the queen speaks, projecting her voice across the room over the gasps and the whispers. "The man who kneels in front of me is Duke Mateo of Ornau."

The gasps grow even louder, some sound outraged, others sound scared. I don't find it in myself to make a sound. Zehlin stands stone to my right, giving no sign of surprise. He either has the stance of a general or he knew this was going to happen.

"Duke Mateo, as well as all other dukes and duchesses, were forced to be placed in Mava once the bridges were torn down. This was done by an unknown magic. All of them wanted to go back to their islands, and that would take legions of ships and crew. I had denied them, I had told them that the risk was too high, and that they would all most likely die because of the dangerous waters. They thought I was lying, and tried to kill me and my command once I denied. I tried to save their lives, and in return I received assassination attempts. I have tried over the years to let them be free, but they continue to try and override me. So, they are used as experiments, just as they had tried to use me as a means to their own demise. He has blackout carbide chains on his body, which prevents him from harming any of us with his given gifts."

The murmurs and the agreements are traded through whispers and conversation through the room. The people are unsettled and are starting to get out of control. She doesn't have their attention as much as she did a moment ago. Panic rises in everyone, including me. I never knew blackout carbide existed before now, I guess I didn't know a lot of things until this week.

So, this is where the dukes and duchesses went, this is why there has been a lack of government control. This is why so many places have gone awry. If the queen is telling a lie, me nor anyone else can tell.

"Artea, please step forward."

Walk to me, stand in front of Mateo with your back to the people.

Her words take me over as my feet walk confidently to the man, I look the queen in the eye as she continues to speak to the people.

"Artea, our savior, has the ability to see into the future,"

Do I? I remember that this is one of the few things I can keep to myself, something no one else knows. I can't see the future, I see the past.

"She will see what it holds for us as some of you have demanded a show of her ability."

Put your hand on his forehead, and focus. Use your strength and your ability.

Again, I cannot fight her influence. I have no choice but to do exactly what she says. I place my hand on his head, sweat from his skin mixes with my own. I close my eyes, feeling an odd sense of pain and discomfort everywhere in my body. I can feel the focus pushing out of my arms and into Mateo. If I see another vision from this, it will be different.

I've only done this once before, and it wasn't by my control. It wasn't my intent to watch Zehlin kill his father. I didn't want to see it. I didn't know what the ring was doing to me, I didn't know that it would give me any ability at all. I was near Zehlin, so I'm assuming that's why I got a vision about him. And now I'm draining all my strength into seeing this man's past, into watching a moment in his life. A duke of an island is at my mercy in front of the queen, the general, and all the high ladies or lords of the country. For some reason, I can only feel ashamed.

I continue to push myself, to look for him in the past. I search with my eyes closed, looking for a moment. I use his mind like a map, unable to see anything, but I'm able to feel. I fight to find whatever it is I'm looking for, until I suddenly stop fighting.

Etiza agreed that this process was going at my pace, yet that was another lie.

My vision goes blacker than usual. The moonlight from the windows no longer projects through my eyelids. It's truly black.

The nausea builds again, a familiar feeling I've grown used to now. I can feel myself gripping Mateo's head, and I hear the faint yells of pain coming from his throat before I can't hear him nor the murmurs anymore.

I found it, I found him.

PART II

(Whisper of Ignition)

Chapter Fourteen

The familiar pitch black void sends shivers down my body, I can feel my ankles go numb and my fingertips vibrate with anticipation. I'm terrified. I'm terrified of what I'm going to find from Mateo. I can feel the vision already, I can almost smell the conversation and the terror. It feels as though I'm walking through an endless corn maze, waiting for my prey to arrive, and yet I'm being hunted at the same time.

I hear them, I can hear the arguing and I can sense the anger. It boils and radiates heat into my skin, even though I'm not truly there. Not yet.

They start to come into view, there's a number of people. Voices overlap each other as their bodies take full shape and the room accumulates its form.

I found the vision, it's here and it's mine.

I see Mateo, along with six other dressed up royalties standing around a table. One of whom I can tell is Queen Etiza. There is an obvious argumentative split between the six others, and her. Around the others, which I assume are the other dukes and duchesses of the time, stand soldiers. They're all around holstering weapons, pointing them at the dukes and duchesses. To my understanding, this was before the bridges were torn down.

Etiza's hair is slightly more blonde, the age of her body not catching up to her like it is now. The others are sweating, all furious. Some of them wear cloaks, others are in dresses or fighting suits. Each one has a range of colors on, none of them look the same. Mateo is in a green suit, flexible enough for war. He bears no jewels or wasteful banners of honor. He wears only his strength and his suit. He looks like he's been fighting with dirt and bruises decorating his build, he looks defeated.

"You can't do this! Everything will be ripped to shreds, is that what you want, Your Majesty?" An older man standing across the table yells, his voice booming so loud that as a spectator it hurts my own ears. He's in red, a cloak bigger than a bear's hide hangs down below his feet.

"You know that I didn't have a choice." Queen Etiza speaks low, but authoritative enough to come across.

"You're afraid to lose power, you are afraid of what could happen if we decide that we don't like your ruling. You're afraid of a rebellion," Mateo speaks even lower, raising his eyes to meet the queen. There's six fae against one, and yet they don't fight. She was able to control me like a puppet, she's controlling me like a puppet right now. I can only wonder what more she can do. No wonder they're scared. "You're a coward in a pretty dress, just like your father was."

The queen takes a deep breath and gestures toward a guard. The guard steps forward and carries long black chains, similar to what Mateo currently wears.

"Please, you don't need to do this. Just let us go back to our people!" A young woman starts to cry as the guard passes the chains around to other soldiers. One by one, each duke and duchess gets chained, their jewels or colorful outfits overruled by black restraints. I'm reminded of the vision of Zehlin, where he kills his own father after the late general scolded him for his poor orders. The orders that not only killed his uncle, but killed Etiza's father.

The queen sighs, as if she's letting out a breath of pain and tenseness.

"I brought you all here in order to protect *my* people. They don't need you. And in due time, I will fix everything. I will bring the bridges back as quickly as they were torn down yesterday and you will be returned. I brought you here to prevent any further damage, and any further tyranny.

As queen, I must keep my orders and my islands under control." Etiza looks down at the table in front of all of them, which I now realize is a battle map.

The queen brought them here? What about the unknown magic she claimed caused it in the ballroom? She lied, again.

I hear more subtle cries from the younger woman along with grunts of struggle from everyone else. Slowly they all get dragged out of view, my vision blurs them out, not letting me see that far. The only thing left is the table, a few soldiers, and the queen. Her eyes glow a faint light blue as she continues to glare down. In a moment's time, she swipes her arm across the table, flinging all kinds of markings, pawns, and papers into the air creating an aura of war planning mess.

I can hear Mateo's raspy screaming start to replace the silence of the black void. The table and the queen start to shift into the same perch and Mateo from before. The first item I can make out is my ring as each different colored stone, yellow, blue, green, and black all burn with light. Did the ring do the same thing in the dining hall when I had the first vision?

Mateo's screams lower into deep breaths of pain. He winces and groans, dipping his body onto the ground as he lays on his side, no longer victim to my scrounging. I look up to Etiza, no longer feeling the weight of her words commanding my movement, she's not inside my head anymore. I cannot falter now, I must continue to stand and appear strong. The nausea following the vision is not as terrible as the first time, seeing as I'm still standing and there's no dinner on the tile.

I'm sending a message, if the people see that their savior falls to the ground or shows an ounce of struggle, who are they supposed to lay their trust into? I must show them the soldier they are fooled into seeing, I must turn into the elvish warrior with a fae heart.

I compose myself as I look the queen in the eye, and turn toward the crowd. For a moment, I can swear I see a glint of fear in Zehlin's eyes before he straightens again. Mateo continues to silently measure the pain of what I did to him. If the power from the ring leaves me in the amount of pain it does, I don't want to imagine the anguish Mateo is experiencing. I ignore him, I ignore him for myself and my image.

I won't forget you, because I know something isn't right. The queen lied about the unknown magic that summoned the dukes and duchesses to Mava. *She* did it. She forced them to be there and put them in chains, claiming she was stopping them from creating more chaos than the bridges being down would already manifest. Whether she was telling the truth isn't up to me, I don't know any better.

Give them a story, tell them what you saw.

Her voice pierces my brain, splitting it in two. I don't quite understand how I'm still up right. I can feel myself fighting her again, and this time I'm able to lie, but unable to stop talking. It's like she's only using a small amount of her influence, like some of the control is still left up to me.

She trusts me.

"I saw the dukes and duchesses, they still try to fight and get their unearned freedom back. They will continue to attempt to break the chains and undermine the queen who has so greatly served you all for over five hundred years. They are as tyrannical as they were when the war ended. They're as hungry for power as any tick or virus." I say to the people of Telik, lying to please the queen. I make sure to wear the face of slight disgust as well as triumph, selling the depiction of who I'm trying to be.

Looks of demise and hatred get thrown to the shaking man on the floor behind me. They hate him and the others as well, and this is all it took. He has no reaction as I make up the story, one that never happened and won't ever happen. He doesn't try to explain himself or defend the others, he only lies there holding his stomach. The queen is using me to create a story, and it's hard to tell what she gains from lying. She tricked everyone, she was the one who brought them to Mava. So, why lie?

Unless there's something she doesn't want them, me, or Zehlin to know.

I told her I will tolerate no secrets if I'm working for her, but now it's too late. If I back down from the plan I will have all of Mava after me, Perdita doesn't want me, my aunt and everything I've ever known is unreachable. She planned this out perfectly to get me stuck, again. She has left me no choice but to continue because I wouldn't be safe anywhere else. She's smarter than I thought she would be, but what else did I expect from the queen?

I look at Zehlin as I realize that she's using me, I try to speak to him with my facial expressions. I search for anything in his face, any ounce of understanding or confusion. I get nothing. He stands there, straight and broad like a general should.

He knows, he knows exactly what she's doing. He's in on the plan to use me as a pawn. Maybe the queen's end goal is good, to bring the safe waters back, but using me to execute it is something I didn't know she would do. She made everything sound optional, to make me stay. I should know by now to stop making assumptions as I get proven wrong time and time again.

Part of me wonders if she chose me simply for my potential powers. So far, the only ability I possess is from the ring. She overestimated me, I'm not as special as she and Zehlin claimed me to be. Maybe that's another way they got me to stay, making someone think they're dangerous and powerful can mess with their head. This could be a deathtrap as much as it is a noble pursuit.

The same four guards pick up Mateo, moving his dead weight out the same door they arrived in. My ring stops glowing as I smile gently to the people who ease and start to take their seats to drink faerie wine and inch off the steam that lingers so heavy in this room. Zehlin walks to me and takes my hand. I can't help but feel like a statue under his light grip, my nerves undying. We make our way back up the perch and into our seats, as does the queen.

I don't say anything, unsure of what I would even bring up. How do you confront someone who's been manipulating you and driving their hands into your brain like a glove? I stay still, keeping the same bored look on my face as my blood stills, so still I fear my heart may stop.

Hours later, I lay in my bed. The aftermath of the drinking and the vision didn't mix well. So, I lay undressed in my white sheets, left with nothing but my brain. The queen had asked me what I saw in my vision once the ball was over, I told her that I spoke the truth, that I saw more attempts of rebellion in the future. I didn't tell her that I know that she's lying to me and everyone else.

If she wants to bring the bridges back and restore the islands, why is she lying? And why is she trying to control me? I am more than willing to leave home and risk myself for whatever assignment Zehlin, Aleck, and I must do. I thought I made that clear enough, but I suppose I didn't.

We drank for hours and danced some more. I had to continue my excitement of dancing with the general to keep the persona alive. I had to shove down the fear of being dragged into unconsciousness by the alcohol again, and instead use it to my advantage. The drunker I got, the more I forgot about the fact that Zehlin betrayed me too. He had to have known about trapping me here, otherwise he wouldn't have played into it so well. Whatever trust I had in him is broken now, not that it was much anyway.

I get up out of bed and place a white silk robe over my body before walking out to the balcony. The air is cool but not cold, as always. I know Mava's weather never changes because all the books and people say it. So far, the only thing that I've seen that's unpredictable is the rain, and even then it's warm and light, just enough to give the flowers and crops something to drink.

I sit, and I only sit. I'm not even sure what I'm thinking about while I sit here, looking at the bright moon shining down on Telik. It illuminates almost as bright as the sun, giving me glimpses of all the beautiful colors in the capitol. I catch thoughts of my aunt, wondering if she's okay, if she regrets what she did. The queen and Zehlin tell me to forget about her, but I can't find it in myself to do that. She raised me, no matter how long she lied to me, she still created me like she created her quilts or her vases, I was a craft, a project. I don't know how to hate her, even though I know I should. She hid me from the world for my whole life, hid me from my potential. And yet, I still can't forget her.

Who knows, maybe she didn't lie and the queen and Zehlin are covering up something else, just to keep me here and convince me to stay. As much as I want to believe that, I know it can't be true. No one else could have given me fesch root, no other fellow could have hidden me the way she did. All of this explains why she was hovering over me every second of every day, why she would look at any wound at once, no matter how minimal. She was watching me, making sure no one would find me for who I am and try to take my life for it. Was she protecting me? Or was she truly just hiding a weapon?

I don't have any abilities, nothing like Etiza swears I have. My mother is a ruthless reaper and life giver, and my father is a king known for his relentless power and limitless spell making ability. I've yet to be told what he can do specifically. As powerful as my parents are, I thought maybe something would reveal itself. But I sit here on the balcony, staring at the moon with a ring stuck to my finger. This ring is the only ability I hold, and it makes me assume I'll let the entirety of the archipelago's people down. Preaching false promises is something I might have to become accustomed to.

The lords and ladies I met at tonight's ball all had cold, calculating faces, like they were waiting for the queen to do something, before and after the Mateo situation. Some were old, others were young. I couldn't count how many there were, but it seemed like all of them live here in Telik and are close at the queen's disposal. I still don't know what to think of them. However, I'm curious to know what their authority is when it comes to Mava. Do they simply own land? Or do they have a heavier influence on the queen other than just attending parties and showing face.

I let my thoughts wander as I let the moonlight drink up my energy. Finally, after having enough of my mind's rambling, I get back into bed.

I know what Etiza wants from me, and I know what I'm here for. But I can't help but make sure that what I know is kept close to me, and me only. My mother *and* father are alive. Mateo and the others were taken, but they did not just appear in Mava.

I also keep track of what I don't know. Why would my father break a bond that was so strong? Why would he shatter the alliance between us and Perdita? Why would the queen take the dukes and duchesses away from their islands when they needed them the most? And why did she force me to give a speech? She pushed words out of my throat I never would have come up with on the spot.

She made me the elvish warrior she claimed me to be.

If Etiza's intentions of bringing the islands back together are pure, why does none of this connect? What are they hiding?

Chapter Fifteen

(Zehlin)

For slightly over a month now, I have been directed to train and help Artea become stronger mentally and physically. When she's not working hard with me, she reads about the island's deep history, Perdita's history, and any other book she can get her hands on. Sometimes I will push aside my duties to accompany her for some extra time in the library. She can definitely become insufferable with her questions. I believe she has read more books from the shelves in a month than I have in my life. I lived all the history I've needed, and learned enough over time that reading seems to waste useful time.

Aside from her studies, we spend every morning in the training room. I push Artea to her limits until there is sweat dripping down her chin and back. I make her try something new every day, never keeping a regular routine. She needs to get used to the fact that there will never be a day on our journey that she will get what she expects. We will always have to be prepared for anything.

Ornau, southwest of Mava, is one of the safer islands. There are jungles and waterfalls that create a dangerous environment, but the people there are guaranteed to be tranquil. There are mostly fae, humans, and animals of all kinds on Ornau. The ones who live on the island want nothing more than peace and quiet, so there are rarely quarrels. Aleck, Artea, and I will head there first as we will need all the energy we can spare.

The next island we will go to is right above Ornau, Avaris. It's an island with two layers. There's a black and dead base level, crawling with and poisoned by creatures that could kill with one look. Above, there's a sky city, full of whites and crystals that complement the clouds. The folks there are even more beautiful. Pegasai own the sky, centaurs with wings fly around daily without any effort. Weather controlling fae protect the sky city with all they have, swaying the winds and rain, diverting the threat of constant attack from mother nature being so high up.

Then there's Seglona, the northern island of ice and snow. There are storms and winters so heavy that most of the heat conducting fae live there simply to help others survive. There are minotaurs and dwarves, stowed away in the hidden corners of the woods and frozen over lakes. This island will be the hardest to conduct our way through as the necklace we need to retrieve is inside the steepest and most cave ridden mountain known to our archipelago.

Then Vanressa, the northeastern island immersed into a deep world of politics, struggling to survive. Duke Einar of Vanressa, as all the other dukes and duchess have been, is missing. Taken to a hidden place, and the knowledge of this place has been left to very few for possession. Vanressa's island works differently than the other six. The duke or duchess must have at least four children to continue to hold authority over the island. This way, each child when of age, can rule one of the four quadrants of Vanressa. The four sections of Vanressa are too difficult for one duke to manage, so there must be divided ruling with Duke Einar being the high authority and last say. With the duke missing, there is no one with complete order over the island, leaving it in disorder and chaos with each sibling scrambling for power and trying to claim the place their father had.

Ironically, this is the only island we don't know how to get the ring from. There's nothing written about it, unlike the others. Each island has a ring, necklace, or bracelet assigned to it. Mava, as the middle island, has a crown. There's something written about each of these objects and how to attain it, except Vanressa. But we will cross that bridge when we get to it. Or try to.

Frendsa is the south eastern island, to the right of Ihrvian. It's simply desert there, with almost no water or crops to be harvested. Ever since the bridges were taken down, there have been less and less signs of life. People live in caves to avoid the heat and dryness, but are left facing the deadly creatures that overrule the caves' turns and burrows. Frendsa is almost a dead island.

Hopefully in a week or so Artea will be ready for our trip to Ornau to get the second piece of the puzzle, we need to move fast if we want to mend what's broken.

Artea doesn't talk to me very much, she avoids me when she can. And when she can't, I'm usually creating conversation. I don't mind the quiet though, the quiet lets both of us focus and makes it easier for her to listen to orders on how to move and when to block. We don't talk at all when we're in the library, I question why I still follow her down there sometimes.

I'm no fool, I know why she ignores me and enjoys punching me in the ring. When she can occasionally land a hit. The ball last month, when we announced to the people what we were trying to do, she wasn't warned. I knew that Etiza was going to have her make a speech, I knew that Artea would be coated in a soldier's suit. I knew she would be changed into someone she wasn't. It was best for her to not know that we would give the lords and ladies this image so she wouldn't panic and say something she shouldn't. Etiza having the control was best.

However, I didn't know that Iza would force her to use her vision, let alone on Duke Mateo. I understand the message she was trying to convey, but she went too far. She scared the people and unsettled Artea. I'm sure Artea assumes I'm in on the whole thing, and it's draining not being able to tell her. Iza gave me a direct order to keep my mouth shut. She wants me to maintain the look of us being a partnership, together. We are, sometimes. But when it comes to the night of the ball, her and I have had our fair share of arguments. But even as the general, I can't say no to her, I can only influence her.

I try to get Artea to talk to me as best I can. I attempt to get updates on her health and how her body is handling everything. She's told me she feels stronger with the training, and she definitely looks stronger. Her body is getting more full the more she eats and exercises regularly.

She moves swiftly, no longer stumbling on her feet. Her balance and her coordination could use some work though. She also tells me she doesn't wake up in pain anymore, that she hasn't rolled up her dinner in a couple weeks. This tells me that her physical transformation back to her elvish state is done or close to being done. Yet, she still shows no sign of having a natural born power. The worry of being wrong, and that she might not be able to handle bringing the flame back grows stronger by the day.

Right now, she stands in front of me. Her face glistens with sweat as she breathes in and out, trying to hide the fact that I'm pushing her harder than usual today.

The room is dusty and dim as we have slid back and forth in the ring we both know so well, creating a mist of chalk and sweat. The light from the windows gives the room a slight purple hue along with the yellow kisses of the morning sun.

The ring is a little bouncy and has rope surrounding the edges, the rest of the training room has targets and wooden fighting dummies placed along the floor in random places. Some of my army uses this room, others prefer the training room on the campgrounds already set up for them. However, this room is mostly used by just Artea and me.

Her eyes darken as she waits for me to make my move in the middle of the sparring ring. She's landed one or two good hits on me so far, because I let her. I grin and swing to my left as she makes her move instead, apparently I took too long. She tried to hook my side, but I was faster and she lets out a low grunt of frustration.

"Why didn't you go?" She snarls, hopping from foot to foot as she keeps her arms up and close to her face like I taught her. *Good.*

"I was throwing you off. You're so used to me–," I take my right hand and shove her left shoulder, causing her to tumble off balance, but she quickly recovers. "Making my move when you think I'm going to. You just waited for me to finish my sentence, and therefore left yourself vulnerable. Always expect me to make my move. Always."

She nods and charges at me. Just as I'm teaching her how to expect the unexpected, she catches me off guard. I fall on my back, right to the hard floor of the dusty ring as she comes tumbling down on top of my chest. She quickly stands back up, wiping her dangling, shiny, light brown hair behind her ear. She backs up a few steps and starts to take off her wrist and palm wraps we use for hand sparring.

"Just like that, huh?" I ask her, not expecting her to try and end today's session early.

"Yes, just like that." She mumbles, tossing the wraps in the corner before she starts her stride to the door out of the training room.

"Wait," I hop up from the floor quickly, running after her before stopping a few steps behind her. "Why are you leaving? We aren't finished." She scoffs and turns around, crossing her sweaty forearms.

"You always decide when we're done, now I'm deciding." She tips her head and looks oddly frustrated, like I did something wrong. "Plus I'm tired and I still have to finish reading the third volume in War Strategies."

"Look, I know I pushed you hard today. We can go easier, do some balance work. That was really good, when you pushed me down. You're learning." I say, stepping closer and setting my palm on her shoulder. She doesn't ease to my touch, not like she usually does. This past month has been hard on her, and I've been her rock for it while we train and learn.

"I've *been* learning, Zehlin," my back straightens at the sound of my name on her lips. I can't help but feel almost like a child being scolded, but a man all the same. "Yes, you pushed me today, but that's not why I'm tired. I just want to stop early today, that's all."

I look into her eyes and search for something that will tell me what's on her mind. Did I do something wrong? Did Iza rip through her brain again? Did she read something she shouldn't have? I hate keeping some of these secrets from her, but she'll know eventually why I have to.

Something is wrong today, something is different than all the other days. She would wake up and practice with me, then eat breakfast. She spends some of her free hours in the garden or reading, or both. She would sometimes ask for extra training if she was feeling like it. But every day was the same. We are supposed to leave for Ornau in three days' time, and I can't have Artea getting finicky right now, not when we have already worked so hard and been so prepared.

"All right, do you think you'll want to keep training later?" I ask, giving her space as she grabs her rucksack and water canteen by the exit door before placing her hand on the golden door knob. "We're leaving in only a few days, are you sure you're prepared?"

"As you've told me," she opens the door and starts to walk out. "I'll see you at dinner."

I almost ask her what's wrong, almost ask her what it is that she found out. I almost ask her if she will forgive me.

But I don't know if she will.

She leaves, abandoning the dust to drift after, and leaving me to my guilt.

Chapter Sixteen

The spinning dance in my stomach is back again. But it's worse than ever.

When I woke up this morning, I felt it. I thanked Numen for the fact that training was before breakfast, which I usually have in my room ready for me after I bathe the sweat off. If I had breakfast first, it wouldn't have stayed down for long. The headache and the soreness came soon after, right in the middle of training. The frustration of the pain coming back hit me like a brick, and that's when I lunged myself at Zehlin.

I watched his beautiful face knock to the ground as his wonderful gray eyes widened with shock, and fear. I shouldn't be happy that he was scared of me at that moment. However, a teleporting fae general was scared of me for only a snip of time.

Good, I thought.

I know he knew about Etiza lunging herself into my head and forcing me to be someone I wasn't. I could have done it myself, but she had to take control. What queen wouldn't? We still haven't talked about that day. She knows I'm smart enough not to question her, and I know she's powerful enough that if I did, I might not be able to question anything for much longer. When I looked at him that day, I saw fear. But I did not see shock.

He knew, and he didn't say anything.

But I sit at dinner with Etiza every day. I train with Zehlin every day. I tell myself that even though they lie and things don't add up, this is still for the greater good. We are trying to prepare for a war that *my* parents are going to start, we could bring back economic growth, and I can finally be at peace.

I've told myself that I have no one else, so even if the only people I can work with are liars or magical fae, it will have to do. It will have to make do until the safe water ways are back and I can find a true home. One that doesn't lie to me.

I walk away from the training room, leaving Zehlin to himself and me to my studies. When I make it to my room, I change from my black training suit into a casual blouse and a skirt. I slide some brown flats on and grab *War Strategies; Volume Three.*

I walk down the hallways and staircases that I've memorized well after the past few weeks, and I find the garden exit. I swiftly open and shut the door, the air of the plants and mist hits me like a fresh coast, similar to Halistyn.

I take a deep breath in and slowly walk down the cobblestone pathway surrounded by bushes and flowers of all kinds. They're all shades of purple, blue, pink, or green. It's a wonderful harmony that I feel blessed to see each day. In Ihrvian, it's winter, and I haven't seen proper flowers for months. In Mava, it's always a perfect balance of spring and summer.

I walk through the cobblestone pathways and end up at a fountain, glistening in the morning sunlight. It's beautiful and it's the perfect place to read when I have to. I've been filling my empty time with lots of reading. Mostly it's been old information about past wars or the way the islands are set up. Some books are even fictional retellings of the love stories between past kings and queens. Zehlin wants me to learn as much as I can before our trip, which is in three days I might add.

We've been training not just my body, but my ability too. This whole time I've used it on Zehlin for practice, I've also had to lie and say that it's future visions I'm seeing, not past. So far, none of the visions I've had since the ball night have seemed significant. I guess I've only had about four or five, so I'm still unsure. Zehlin's also tried to get me to exercise whatever natural born powers he thinks I have. He says that no elf has ever been born without power, but since we've spent a month trying to figure mine out he thinks that maybe being on the fesch root for so long has gotten rid of my natural ability. It makes sense, but it's kind of a disappointment.

So, without any impressive powers like Zehlin's sun orbs or his tessering, I'm left with sharpening my brain and my body. I'm not going to lie, I'm doing a great job. I feel myself getting stronger and remembering more and more about almost everything.

Zehlin says he wishes I was more physically adept for going to Ornau, but it's a safer island, so I should be okay. He's acting like we can push together his five hundred years of battle experience into my one month. I'm trying as hard as I can, but practice takes time.

I sit on the fountain edge, looking down at the crystal clear water with reflections of the clouds coasting on the ripples. Before I look back up and open my book, I hear footsteps to my left. I turn and see Aleck walking toward me with his usual careless pace. I nod to him and he takes a seat on the fountain a meter or two away from mine.

"You look like you didn't sleep." He said as he takes the book from my side and opens it up, pretending to be interested in what I'm doing. He quickly gets bored and puts it back.

"Well that's one way to compliment a lady," I lightly hit his shoulder with my palm and chuckle. "I'm starting to feel sick again, like I did the first week I was here." I say, not bothering to hide it.

Over the past month, Aleck and I have confided in each other when we're bored or need someone to talk to. He's fun to have a drink with or ask questions to. He doesn't seem to sugar coat things as he's always blunt and to the point. He's a strong soldier, and Zehlin's best friend, which I now know who Zehlin gets his bolstering ego from.

His red hair is always shiny and he's built like a soldier. Zehlin is taller, but I know Aleck would win in a fight. Aleck's fae ability *is* fighting. His power is the ability to retain battle knowledge and pinpoint his enemies' weaknesses. He's asked me many times over the past weeks to fight him in the ring. I've avoided it because when it comes to hand to hand combat, he's the best of the best. I understand why Zehlin and Etiza want him to come with us for the island journey, just in case we bump into unfriendly folks.

"Maybe you're just ill, or allergic to your own poor balance." He smiles and gives me a soft look. I've described to him how painful it can be for that sick feeling to come up.

"Real sweet," I say before I grab the book and hold it in my lap. "You haven't even seen me in the ring."

"You're right, but Zehlin has a big mouth," he admits, but before I can argue about the fact that I'm talked about, he continues. "About that, actually. Do you think that an amplifier will help with the whole power search thing?" I pause and furrow my brow, cocking my head.

"What do you mean?" I ask him.

"Zehlin and I were talking. There are spells, ones that can enhance any natural born powers, and natural only. The spells are always attached to Etiza. She applies them to others, like with Chera and her young appearance." She told me before that only her closest friends call her Chera, so it's nice to know that she and him are familiar.

I sigh at the thought of the queen having more control over me, especially now that we are close to truly starting our plan.

"Does the spell go away whenever she wants it to?" I ask, wondering if my power would be in her hands and hers only. I still can't get comfortable around her after the ball. The way she invaded me like that, forced that man to be dug through, and lied to everyone. It changed her in my eyes forever.

"Not as far as I know, I'm pretty sure they stay active until she dies. She can't take them away," he pauses and lets out a sigh.

"I knew Chera before she had the spell, and there's a reason she has it. She was born with some grotesque features and people oftentimes would cast her out because of it, but clothes and castles were her passion. She started working as a maid and stepped her way up to stylist. The stylist is an extremely important job, so she needed to look the part. And she was tired of everyone looking at her like a monster. So, the queen offered to make her look not just young, but beautiful."

The way Chera's skin glows in any light, and her hair falls so perfectly right above her shoulders. She's perfect, and the queen allowed her to do her job without the weight of the judgment. And she can't take that away.

But would the queen do that for me? I'd assume so if she wants me to withstand all the pieces to the flame and bring the waterways back. I've read some of the old books from when the jewelry pieces were created, and they all conclude with the same thing. That only someone with the will and strength never seen before will be able to come out of the spell alive. And the person needs to come out alive to keep the flame burning.

So, I assume she kind of needs me.

"I mean, my natural ability that's supposed to be there isn't yet. Shouldn't an enhancer only enhance what's there, not just bring something up?" I ask, looking at Aleck's face, his stubble poking from his defined jaw. His icy blue eyes compliment his red hair, reflecting the water's ripples along with the sun.

"Well, sure. But it might already be there, just so little of it. Or maybe the visions from the ring are overpowering your natural ability. We'd need to talk to Etiza to find any of that out first, and to ask her."

I only nod, and open my book to the page I last left off on. Aleck stands and clears his throat, looking out in an opening between the bushes. The opening leads to fields the size of large estates. The fields hold flowers and crops, as well as landscape for more buildings in the distance. He lets out a deep breath.

"Are you going to be okay?" He asks, still looking out in front of us.

"Don't do that."

"Don't do what?" He turns to me now, a slight smile on his face, accompanied by a scoff.

"Don't make me seem like some Ihrvian girl who can't handle this." I say closing my book again, the thought of reading now sounds boring, and frankly repetitive. I doubt my mind will be able to rest knowing that we're leaving soon, somewhere I've never been, under a fake name, following a dangerous plan.

"Didn't you just say that you're getting sick again? Listen, I do care about you and how you feel, but the entire archipelago is depending on you. If you can't do what you agreed on, it's better to back out than to die trying." Like I said earlier, he's blunt and straight to the point.

"I'll be fine, trust me. It's nothing I haven't dealt with before," I say sarcastically. "And even if for some reason there's a moment I can't handle anything, I have Zehlin and you."

"You're right." He shrugs, wearing his fighting talents on his sleeve without a single ounce of contrition.

"I think I'm going to skip the next couple days of training, conserve my energy. And I might need a packing list." I smile, looking to him as he turns slightly away from me and raises his head, allowing the warm sun to kiss his face.

"We're bringing only one large rucksack per person, so only the essentials." Before I can respond, I hear the gravel and stone crunching beneath boots and fading away. He leaves without another word. Maybe a little *too* straight to the point.

The familiar scent of the basement's dusty and oxygen robbed air soothes my goosebumps caused by the cold stone stairs. The doors labeled with their designated contents eases my stomach's pain and the soreness from training. No matter how often I train with Zehlin, I always find a new spot that can hurt for days.

I walk towards the end of the hall and see *Concoctions*. I know Torrid is waiting for me because we made a deal. I told him that I can't take him out of his flask yet, but I can take him with me in my rucksack for the trip. He needs to get out of this basement, yes, but he also could be useful to us. He can answer almost every question, we might need that at some point. Even if Zehlin and Aleck don't, I probably still will.

Plus, I'm seeing Torrid right before dinner so I know it won't be weird if I show up late. *Oh, I just got caught up in the new* Island Map *book I started.*

I open the door and I already hear little footsteps tapping on the glass. Yesterday, I put him up on the windowsill that almost touches the ceiling so the tapping echoes throughout the room. I walk over to the window and grab the flask, lowering him in front of me as I hold his container.

"Artea! You're here!" he exclaims and hugs the edge of the glass towards me. He's great, don't get me wrong. Just a little clingy. "Are we leaving yet?" I have visited Torrid a lot during the month as I don't have anyone else I can truly trust. Every other day or so I will come and talk to him, sometimes for hours. Usually it's when Zehlin is out doing his duties so I know he won't come check on me in the library. Aleck doesn't even touch the basement and Etiza always has her books ordered into her throne room or office. So, without Zehlin, it's just Torrid and me.

"We aren't leaving today, we're leaving in three. But I just wanted to see you and ask you a few things, if that's all right." I reassure him. Ever since I mentioned that I appreciated it when he *wanted* to answer questions, he's been more than happy to answer for me.

"Yes, yes. Of course." He nods, anticipatingly looking up to me.

"Is it possible for the queen to try and make my natural powers stronger? Zehlin and I haven't been able to train my powers out of me, but everyone swears I have them."

"Well, yes of course. Though it's probably not a good idea." He giggles. "Nope."

"What do you mean? So, I *do* have a natural ability? Why wouldn't it be a good idea to put me to use?"

He drops his shoulders and shrugs. "I don't know, the wind just tells me things. You know as well as I do, Miss, that I'm limited."

"Do you know what my ability is?" I ask, growing more and more curious. Why on earth would it be a bad idea to use my powers? Are they more harmful than helpful? Would I hurt people?

"Your mother and your father, they're your parents right?" He looks at me like I was born yesterday, and in a way, I kind of was. I wait for him to continue and he rolls his eyes. "Elvish powers are different from fae. Faeries powers aren't hereditary, they change over time depending on the person. Families can have similar powers, and a lot of times do. But most of the time, a child won't have the same exact ability as either of their parents. However, elvish powers are almost always hereditary, and can become more prominent over time."

So, that means that my father, who seemed to be a spell crafter, and my mother who was a necromancer, made me. So, do I have my father's or my mother's power? And does more prominent mean that I could be stronger than one of them? All of these ideas scare me. I'm only just now getting used to my new body, now I might change again?

"You've always liked crafting, pottery and clay and silly stuff like that, right?" he asks me, I quirk a brow and he smiles.

"Silly?" I ask, tipping the flask only slightly so he tumbles on his rear.

"Anyway!" He stands back up, continuing his statement. "Maybe that's because your dad makes stuff. You know, like father, like daughter?"

I don't like thinking of myself as a copy of him. He destroyed so much, why would I hope to follow in his footsteps?

"I just don't understand why my ability won't show up. All of this feels like a dream that I can't wake up from. Tormenting, yet peaceful in the same way."

Torrid places a palm on the surface of the glass and tilts his head. "I can come with you and maybe make you feel better. I've had a lot of time to make up stories while I've been in here. And the wind whispers me secrets sometimes when she thinks I'm not listening. I could tell you those secrets and stories when you're sad."

I smile at the kind gesture and raise him back up, placing him on the windowsill. There's only so many questions I'm morally comfortable asking Torrid before it feels like I have an unhealthy advantage.

"You're leaving?" He asks softly, and I fight every nerve in my body to not pick him up and hide him in the oversized closet of mine.

"Dinner is going to be ready soon, and I might already be late. But I'll be back for you when we are going to leave. And remember—"

"Don't tell Zehlin I'm going, don't make noise in the rucksack, and especially don't try to get out of my jar until you're ready. You've said it at least one million times, Miss Artea. You know, as much as I'm already a prisoner, I still feel like you make it more difficult for me." He crosses his arms like a child.

I roll my eyes and let out a light laugh. "You love me."

I ignore whatever dramatic whining he has to say and leave *Concoctions*. Torrid is sweet, and I'm almost sure that he means well. However, I don't think he ever closes his mouth.

I make my way back up the dark stone steps, dreading talking to Etiza about something *real,* instead of just preparations for the journey. It's easy to not think about the things that don't add up when I just listen to her advice, but to ask for her help is going to be another story.

Chapter Seventeen

We sit at the dining room table, all eager for what's to come. "That's a very risky thing to ask, Artea," her voice is low as she swallows a bite of bread, chasing it with a sip of red wine. I've never had a taste for fae drinks, so mine sits full in front of me. "I don't think I've ever tried to perform a spell on an elf, let alone one like you."

I pause cutting my meat and look at her. Her golden dress drapes lightly into the chair below her as her silver-gold hair makes the purple light of sunset dance around her. "An elf like me? We don't even know if I have an ability, aside from the future visions the ring gives me." She still thinks that I see into the future and not the past, I make sure that stays the same.

I haven't seen Mateo, or any of the other dukes or duchesses since the ball. I'm assuming that they're still here, or being kept away somewhere. I can't imagine what it would be like to be locked up from your island, your duty, for over one hundred years.

I still don't know what to think about Etiza taking them away. If they were actually trying to overthrow her, maybe she was right to take them away. And if it's something else, I can't find it. And I'll never figure it out unless I get my hands on one of them. If any of them are still alive.

"Yes, but we can never be sure. Something could go wrong or worse. There's a reason I was chosen to be queen over my brothers or sisters. They're all long gone, but my father chose me to be the one to hold the throne after him. I hold power that not many folks could ever fathom. If it gets used improperly or on the wrong thing, I don't know what could happen."

"We have waited long enough, I don't see how I could be much different than a fae. If we're going to each island, dangerous ones too, we need all the help we can get." I say, my fingers no longer on my woodenware as I switch back and forth between Zehlin and the queen.

"Exactly, what if I activate your natural ability and then you can't control it, or you die and all the power of the ring dies with you. We need you as you are."

"What do you mean the power dies with me?" I ask, turning fully toward Etiza.

"After we got you to put the ring on, we found the spellbook that your father wrote. It has all the information we have found about the pieces and the flame. We also found that once we start the ritual, which starts the second you put the first piece on, if it gets ended before the flame is burning again, there's no hope. The magic will die," she pauses and takes another sip of her wine. "That's how elf magic works, and that's why it's taken us so long to finally be able to try and bring the bridges back. There are so many complicated paths to weave through. You happened to be perfect. And you're right, we need you at your full strength."

If I die doing this, the fate of these islands is doomed. They will forever be without food or end up dragmist ridden, people will be poor and starving. More people will die and even more evil will break its way through.

And the spell already started, meaning there is truly no backing out now.

And absolutely *no* dying.

It makes sense now why Zehlin has been training me so hard, and why Aleck has been constantly on my tail about how I'm feeling, emotionally and physically. I have to carry this through or it all dies with me. I know there are good people like Gunter on these islands. He might have helped the queen kidnap me, but he did it only so he could safely move away from

Halistyn. He just wanted to protect his wife and his future kids. I can make that possible for everyone else too.

I have to.

"Why did you wait to tell me?" I ask, confused why they wouldn't tell me such important information as quickly as they found out. Zehlin starts to speak for Etiza.

"I couldn't accept that we practically doomed you and the rest of our people just with one ring. I didn't want to admit it, and telling you would make it real. So, I decided to try and find a way to break it, but we haven't found anything. And you're right, even if it's dangerous, we still need to try. We need you at your best.

"Your Majesty, if you use only a percentage of your power, just try to dig for something natural inside of her. I have a feeling it'll call to you pretty quickly. Your power is strong, and we think Artea's will be too. Please, we need this as badly as everybody else." Zehlin almost begs his cousin, his eyes carrying a pleading gaze.

The queen lets out a breathy sigh, adjusting her sleeve as she looks down to her plate. If I can get an ability more useful than seeing the past, something that would help me with anything else, I would be extremely grateful. I don't think I'm this powerful elf with hereditary capabilities, but it would be a comfort to know that I'll be traveling across the islands with something other than my hands. It would be comforting knowing that there's something I could control. Something that's mine.

"Okay, we will do it tomorrow morning so you can have two days to recover if anything goes wrong." I smile and cut into my meat again.

"Good, thank you." I nod and bite into the juicy beef, thinking about the possibilities. If I do have one of my parents powers, maybe I can turn them into something good.

Use them for saving the islands, instead of tearing them apart.

I woke up this morning without any sickness, thank Numen. I'm hoping that yesterday morning was a one-time thing, I don't miss that feeling at all.

Zehlin and I are in the training room again, like we are every morning. We're in the ring, diagonal from each other. I have chalk on my palms and wraps around my fingers and wrists, as does he. It's only been fifteen minutes and my arms are feeling sore already. I can taste the sweat on my upper lip and feel the heat under my training suit.

"Like I said, I'm not giving you a break," I tell him. We didn't get to do his difficult training he had planned because I pushed him on his ass yesterday, so I've decided I'll make it up to him today.

"You seem in too good of a mood, where did my Artea go?" He smirks and cocks his head, pretending to look around the room.

While he looks around I take that as my chance. I lunge forward and kick one of his feet out from under him and tuck his arm over my shoulder, pushing him backwards on his back with his arm still wrapped behind me.

His loud grunt of pain, or surprise, fills me with pride. I just took down a soldier with actual skill, instead of just pushing myself into him. I hold him still, or try to, until he breaks free and pushes me off of him. We both stand back up and get into position again.

"You're the one who taught me to never let my guard down? Now you're getting light footed on me? I thought I warned you before we started that I'm not giving you a break," I banter through heavy breaths, jumping lightly on the bouncy floor.

"You're throwing jokes around too? What is up with you?" I would run to him and knock him on his back one more time, but he's right. I'm happy today because I feel amazing, and I might be getting my natural ability back, something that should have been mine since birth.

All of our guesses at dinner last night was that the fesch root made me human for so long that my ability just got watered down, or hid away. Either way, Etiza thinks that with her help and getting cleansed even more from the root, I should have my power in no time. As long as we're safe about it.

"I'm excited for today, okay? And then we leave in two days and I get to go to another island. I know it's for a cause, but I'm still excited just to see everything. I wonder what people are like there, and what it looks like."

Before Zehlin responds, he's right in front of me, doing the exact same thing I just did to him. I land on my back on the ring floor with a grunt, the wind knocking out of me with it.

A sharp pain stabs into my lower spine as he looms over me, holding my arm up like I did to him, pinning my wrist to the chalk covered floor. Except he's stronger than me, and I can't wiggle out like he could. The ceiling is above us as some of his loose hair dangles above me. His skin is covered in a layer of sweat, each inch of his skin touching mine burns like a flame.

"The people of Ornau are very peaceful, and the nasty creatures usually keep to themselves," he lightly whispers, staring longingly into my eyes. I can't help but feel how warm the air around us is getting. I can't help but see his shoulder-length hair fray from his bun as he still holds a grip on my wrist. The dim yellow light of his ability mixed with his sweat makes him appear almost shiny. Like his skin is covered in sunlight.

His gray eyes squint as he smiles bigger. "It's beautiful too. It's very green, with jungle in every corner. Waterfalls are everywhere, splashing down into streams and rivers, that all eventually flows down to the ocean."

I swallow. His face gets closer to mine and panic shoots through me. His eyes start to glare closed and his grip on my wrist softens. I can almost feel our breaths mend together as I begin to close my eyes as well, welcoming whatever might come.

Am I about to kiss him right now? In the middle of our training?

I clearly can't remember that he so blatantly lied to me about the ball and that he only makes snarky remarks or reminds me how bad I am at fighting. I clearly forget that I'm an elf and he's a faerie and I shouldn't even be closing my eyes along with him. I should punch him in the gut.

But I don't.

And before I can even make the decision, we are both back on our feet. He pulled me up with him quicker than I thought was possible.

Tessering.

I forget to get back into position for a moment, letting the closeness of the previous moment ride me over. I feel the heat on my cheeks as the scorching feeling of his hands grip feels like a fresh wound. But a good one. A tingle I would allow to linger for longer than I should want. He had pulled us up, breaking whatever that was like a shattered mirror.

"Hey, let's keep practicing your punches, okay?" he asks, which is more of a demand in this case. I nod, and get into my stance as he bends down to pick up two pairs of gloves. He slips his pair on and then hands me mine. We both get into our stances before we start going back and forth.

I punch and he dodges, and vice versa. I ignore the pain of the hard punches I give and receive. They're all much harder than usual. I know he can sense that I'm not fully here, that I'm distracted by what he just did. Is he distracted as well? If he is, I can't tell. Does he know what he was doing? He was smiling, so he had to have, right?

Are we seriously going to act like nothing happened?

Chapter Eighteen

(Zehlin)

What was I thinking?

She wants nothing to do with me and she hasn't since the night of the ball. I keep my straight face and hold my fists up.

My hands are covered with gloves, hiding the fact that they're radiating sunlight from the eye contact between us two, my power threatening to give me away. The way she was looking up at me, the way she seemed to ignore everything I was explaining and only stared into my eyes.

I bounce on my toes, ignoring the voice in my head that's thinking about her in these ways. She's beautiful, she's strong, but she has only one mission. All she wants is to fix what her parents broke. She hates me for not telling her what the queen would do to her, what she would make her do to Mateo.

I've kept my distance as much as I can all this time. Training and dining, taking walks on the pathways. And yet, it's always been impossible to ignore how magnificent she is. However, that's what all elves are. They trick you into thinking they are beautiful on the inside too. I continue to remind myself that she's an elf, and she hates me.

Two huge reasons that should make me content with ignoring her.

So, why did I look down at her, smiling, and whisper about an island while all I could think about was staying there, that close. I wasn't thinking about Ornau at all, and I doubt she was either. They were just clouded words in a heated moment.

We both have stone faces, yet hers is still a light shade of red. I can't help but feel a little delight in the fact that I made her blush. But she already blushes every time I get close to her. The first time I leaned over her on the bathroom door, the first day she got here. When we were in the library, and I was helping her down the ladder. I'd be a fool if I didn't notice that she gets warm.

And I'd be an even bigger fool if I didn't admit that I get warm too. Being able to manipulate light has its advantages like hiding tattling blemishes like that.

We spared harder than we ever have. I'm sure she needed to let off some steam. I'd be mad at me if I were her too. Hell, I'm mad at myself right now. As much as I would love to get closer to Artea, I can't. And I refuse to distract either of us from the task at hand. She left all my muscles sore while I left bruises and we were late for breakfast. I was upset, and she was even more upset.

I've never gotten carried away like that.

We ate breakfast, and it was more awkward than ever. Iza relayed how she's still scared to do the spell on Artea, but that she will do it because it's needed. For Atrea's survival, and everybody else. Artea just kept quiet, but I could sense the tension. I don't know if it was the heat from the moment still looming over our heads, or if it was the heat from her temper.

Today was the first time in a month that I've seen her truly enthusiastic about something. She's studied because she has nothing else better to do, she's trained with me because we all know it's the best thing to prepare her with, and she can't go out into the city because Numen knows who might try to kill her. No one here likes elves. That's my biggest worry about this mission. That someone would rather kill her than give us the jewelry.

Some pieces are hidden in deep caves, and others must have rituals performed to obtain them. Vanressa's bracelet for example, we must find a way to reunite the four siblings of Duke Einar. The dukes and duchesses were brought to Iza a day *before* the bridges were torn down. This means that King Ector must have still been planning and writing out his spells and counterspells. He saw that Duke Einar was absent and it would lead to a brawl over who gets the control of all four quadrants in Vanressa. Each sibling controls their quarter, but someone needs to watch the whole island. Someone needed to inherit the seat, and there wasn't anyone appointed. Not even in his will.

To get the bracelet, we have to find a way to make all four of them agree on who will lead Vanressa. They've been in their own mini war for the past century, and don't stop even when I try to intervene. So, we have the hardest job to make the most stubborn folks we know get on the same page.

Artea seems excited for Iza to help her potentially get her natural ability back. She will finally have something here that's not fed to her. She's had a lot taken from her, so Iza and I both want to give her this. We also aren't sure how Artea stands on the issue with the ball that night. Is she still mad at us? Does she blame me? She's obviously pulled away from trusting the queen but will it affect the process of getting the waterways back?

That's another reason that Iza agreed to try this, to get back on Artea's good side. Iza says she couldn't risk Artea saying the wrong thing to the third most important people in Mava. The Mava lords and ladies have a massive influence on the population of our everyday fae and humans. Any exposition of lies or theories would ruin this whole process. We need each island's support no matter what. So, even though Artea should have been warned, I feel that it was the safest option, even if it ruined the potential closeness between us two.

What am I saying?

It's only been six weeks. I've known her for six weeks. Eight if you count the stalking weeks.

Right now, she kneels in front of Iza. Her head is bowed down toward her feet, Iza's dress almost too wide in diameter for her arm to reach Artea's forehead. She sits on her knees while breathing deeply, as she was instructed to do. The only people in the queen's throne room are her, me, Artea, the warden, and multiple of the castle's healers and guards. We have no idea how Artea's potential elvish magic will react with Iza's fae magic.

The way her hair dangles past her shoulders while she continues to breathe makes my heart race. Not in a flustered way, in a scared way. Now that she has the first ring, she's the last chance to finally bring everything back together.

I know what Iza is capable of. I fought by her side as her general during the War of Stone and Mountains. There's a reason she's a queen, and an even better leader. Her magic could rip Artea apart, but Artea's magic could do the same.

Still, she kneels and Iza shows ultimate focus. I stand to the side facing them both, ready for anything like the healers and warden are. Iza starts, the purple wisps of fae magic start to drip from her arm and hand, making their way down to Artea's head. The magic makes a tinkling sound as Iza forms it, it sounds as if there's a light rain outside mixed with starlight. Her special power is to create spells so that the person carries it, and there's no breaking it. It's how she fights her enemies. All she has to do is touch them, and the spell kills them. We've always called them spells as it seems like the only way to describe it, however there isn't an official name for her gift.

"You're sure you're ready?" She whispers to Artea. Artea doesn't open her eyes as she nods eagerly.

I hear her start to chant, the ancient language she was born with the knowledge of strikes through. Another reason she calls it a spell. Her eyes are still closed and Artea's breathing quickens as the blood under her skin on her face starts to glow the same light purple as it is around the castle. Her head is no longer looking down, but looking up at Etiza, almost out of need for more.

Etiza's chanting gets louder and more and more blood glows under Artea's skin. Artea's eyes open to show pure black, no white, no brown iris, only black. The magic continues to pulse into her as Etiza is almost yelling, assumingly searching for the natural elvish power. The dark purple veins under Artea's skin start to turn black as she takes both of her arms and grips Etiza's wrist. Everyone takes a step forward but Etiza holds an arm out, stopping us.

"Etiza!" I yell over the sound of the magic, now so strong it starts to shake the throne behind her and the curtains sway in the air. She doesn't move anything except her head, a slight shake.

Purple sparks start to fly away from Artea's body and clothes, disappearing into the floor. She starts screaming instead of breathing. She wheezes, like her breath is running out.

"Etiza, stop!" She holds a finger out, telling us she's close. Her chanting increases and the black starts to spread. The veins under Artea's skin look like dead tree roots, and her fingertips start to appear ash ridden. Like she dipped her hand into the bottom of a fire.

I walk forward up to them, except I'm met with a wall and get knocked back onto my back. The soreness from Artea knocking me gets revisited before I get back up again. She's creating a ward so we can't get to them.

What if she kills her?

Panic rises in my throat as I look to the warden who has never had to stop his queen before. I can sense his fear and panic as well. Would it be a good idea to try and stop her? Artea *needs* to live.

After the warden makes up his mind and takes the first step, Artea drops to the ground, a limp body sprinkled with black and purple. Etiza opens her eyes and shakes her head, adjusting to the light again.

I don't waste any time and sprint a few meters over to Artea's still body. I flip her over and lean her back and neck against my knees after I kneel myself. I press my palm to her mouth and can feel a warm breath, too light for comfort.

She's alive.

The healers, after their shock, run right after me and start working on her. I back up to let them work because what will sunlight or tessering do for her? All of a sudden I feel useless, something I've never felt before.

Four of them start on different parts of her body and green dusty magic quickly creates an aura around her fragile body.

I look up at Etiza while I stand up from the floor and she simply nods while catching her breath. She pauses and swallows hard.

"I found it, I found her powers," she says, looking down as she relaxes herself. "It was fighting me out. It tried to cast me out of her mind. I think that's what the black is from. Elvish magic and fae magic are a deadly match. But I found it and I took it out."

I nod and look back down to her, only seeing silhouettes of her limbs as the green mist continues to block my vision of her.

"Do you know what it was?" She sighs deeply and puts a hand on her forehead.

"We really should have killed her mother when we had the chance, Zehlin."

PART III

(The Breakaway)

Chapter Nineteen

Two wagons pull out in front of Zehlin, Aleck, and me. There aren't any horses or servants to pull them, almost like the wheels have a mind of their own. I can see through the small doors that they're packed with suitcases and rations, as well as weapons and other things of the sort.

We're standing outside the castle wearing silver and black armor crafted for flexibility. It's not hard and stiff war armor, it's armor made from a material found in Frendsa, the desert island. Because there's barely any moisture, the cotton that used to grow there is now mutated to a tough, malleable, and conveniently sword-proof, material. It makes for perfect armor that still allows us to move comfortably, along with some black metal shoulder and chest pads. As much as Zehlin is a stubborn prick, at least he educates me. I don't know what I would do going into this with no idea what to expect or background knowledge.

I look up as petals from the trees fall lightly to the ground, following the breeze. The ground is sprinkled in purple and white specks as we take a few steps closer to the wagons, the petals crunching under my boots.

"How are we supposed to get all this to Ornau, General?" I ask, turning my head to Zehlin. His brown hair is tightly tied back behind his head and his armor is perfectly fitted to his body, carved and sewn in a way that's only fit for a general. *The* general.

His face has purpose written all over it as he speaks. He doesn't correct me on the name this time.

"You underestimate me, Angel." He smirks, and I don't correct him either. I can't help but feel the light redness on my face as I remember the kiss we almost shared. I still hate him for lying to me, and he probably is still lying to me, but Numan, he knows how to get me worked up. I couldn't stop thinking about him, not even when I was sleeping. And I continue to hate myself more and more for it.

"You can tesser all of us, and all of this at the same time?" I ask, my hands gesturing to us and the wagons.

He shrugs and clears his throat. "Well, yeah. I just usually need a few days to rest afterward. But I can do it. It's just a struggle to make sure everything is held on to. Once we get to Ornau, we know a few people who will take us in. It's already organized." I know he has to be touching whatever he wants for it to tesser with him, as long as it's not just himself.

"Does it hurt?" I ask again, probably stalling from having to hop on over to another island that's miles and miles away in only an instant.

"No," Aleck starts. "Nothing ever hurts him. Except when Chera plucks his beard." He chuckles and ties his sword tighter around his back. His red hair looks like something from a book when the dawn light hits it. He decided to wear similar armor, but he paired his with a cloak and gloves, that for some reason have the knuckles cut out of them.

"Pricking my face with that evil tool, just to look *presentable*. Yeah, sure." He shoves Aleck on the shoulder and smiles, only a tiny bit. They both laugh and I smile too.

There's a pause, and we all take a breath. I look up to the light pink and blue sky, clouds coat the horizon like a blanket on a child. Gently and softly.

"How are you feeling?" Zehlin finally turns to me, he tilts his head and we make eye contact. I look at the gloves covering my hands until I slip them off. I sigh and close my eyes before looking at my hands. My fingertips, and a little bit further down, are stained black. The black is like a tattoo, permanent and dark.

We all found out what my power was after the healers got me stable again. I can't explain how tired I am of being sick all the time. After I was healed, I was taken to the garden and I wanted to pick fruit from a bush. Once I did, the fruit turned into ash right after collapsing in on itself. The bush had a few leaves and stems turned into ash as well. It wasn't ash made from heat, but it still looked and felt like ash. Like fireplace dust.

My ability is to drain life. Like mother, like daughter.

The ring's colors glisten in the afternoon sun, almost mocking the darkness of my fingertips. The gold of the ring band acts as a stark contrast to the black, and it feels heavier than ever.

Zehlin said that I can't control it yet, so gloves are what we will settle on for protection. We don't know the extent of what I can do, only that I disintegrated that fruit the moment I touched it. He and Aleck agreed that once we get to Ornau, we can spend a few days trying to find out what else Etiza enhanced.

And if I can control it. The idea scares me, but I know with something like this, it needs to be contained.

"Are we ready?" I look up to Aleck who seems reasonably impatient. I slip my gloves back on and secure my bag on my back by pulling the strings hanging from each side on my shoulders. I quietly hope that Torrid is doing okay back there, and that the tessering won't hurt him. I promised him that if he helps me, then eventually I can let him free. I'm praying to Numen that setting him free won't let out another evil into this world. But what I do know is that time can change people.

I hope it changed him too.

"Yes, at least I am." I nod and walk toward the wagons. I reach my hand out toward him, telling him I'm ready. Aleck takes my other hand. "General?"

Zehlin gives and affirming gesture and looks at me for one short moment, and in his eyes I see determination, alongside a little bit of fear. The fear of a war starting is real. The fears of another ambush, that we won't be able to save them this time, and the fear that I will die, they all surface for an inkling of a moment.

He tries to hide it, but I know why he fights so hard. He feels responsible for everyone, and he seems to do anything in his power to make sure he will keep them safe. He will not be like his father.

We all hold hands and then Zehlin holds onto a wagon. They are connected, so if he takes one with him, he's taking both. Once we are all secured with each other, he closes his eyes. Aleck and I do too, all in anticipation for what's next. I don't know what to expect or how we'll feel, but I hope it isn't more throwing up.

"Do not let go." He says in a low, intent-filled tone.

I feel my feet start to lighten, almost like I'm being picked up by my shoulders. The air grows thicker and the light morning breeze picks up speed, turning into wind. I focus on my grip that holds myself to both of them, just like Zehlin said. I hold on so tight I can feel my bones attempting to protrude from my thin, unfamiliar skin.

I feel my newly tipped ears bend in the wind. I almost try to open my eyes, until the world goes silent. I can't hear anything anymore, and it's the most peaceful silence I've ever heard. Or not heard, if that's what silence is.

Slowly, the silence is filled with high pitched tones and rushing water. I open my eyes, or at least I think I do, to see black. My vision focuses and adjusts to the light after a long moment.

The first thing I see in front of me is the sky, riddled with green trees taller than I have ever seen before. Either I'm still getting used to the tessering, or the trees are truly taller than the castle in Mava. I look over to see a stream, and behind it is a waterfall, feeding it with more crystal blue water paired with white foam. The blurriness subsides and I roll to my side, attempting to sit up.

I'm able to sit up straight, groaning through the pain and tenseness. I don't feel sick, but my head pounds in response to the noises around me. I look behind me after only seeing foliage and spot the wagons. By the wagons are Zehlin and Aleck, each adjusting their clothes and setting their footing. Realizing that I need to look like I can handle things, I stand up quickly and the weight of my rucksack pulling down on my shoulders reminds me I have Torrid. I have to fight the urge to check if he's okay since I landed on my back. Zehlin and Aleck can't know that he came with me. Zehlin hates Torrid, and he doesn't know that I've been talking with him every few days since I've been here. I don't need to give him more reasons to lecture me like a child.

"You good over there, Angel?" I hear Zehlin yell from behind me. I catch my breath and close my eyes before reopening them again. I throw a thumbs up, wincing as I let my organs get back into place.

"I bet you look worse," I chuckle as I take a few steps toward the wagons. "Hey, why was I so far from you guys?"

"You've been sleeping longer than we have. We took a few minutes to get everything together before we head north to Boronia. And I guess we had to wait for you too." Zehlin explains, looking in a direction I'm assuming is north. It's great to know I was left sleeping on the ground, and now that I'm thinking about it I can feel the dampness on my back, and all the way down. I shift trying to get the armor fabric away from my skin. Great for combat, enemies with the rain.

I know Boronia is the military base for Ornau. We decided that we'll set up camp there as it's the safest option. It's also closest to the Bleeding Circle, the place where we are supposed to find a bracelet, the second piece. Thinking about it makes the ring feel that much heavier and stuck, reminding me that I'm, literally, in this for life.

It makes me wonder if the bracelet will give me an ability like the ring did. I don't plan on using it until I have to as I've practiced a little bit on Zehlin. It feels like such an invasion. Do I have to touch the person to see their past? Or can it be telepathic like it was in the dining room when I accidentally saw Zehlin and his father from four hundred years ago?

"Well, is everything in order then?" I say to them both as I look around with my chin up, ignoring the fact that it feels like the world is still spinning. "And are you feeling all right?" I ask Zehlin. He probably is exhausted after carrying all of this across an island, so my dizzy dread can wait.

He's probably just fine, Artea.

"I'll be settled, but thanks for your concern." He smiles. I know he's not fine because both Aleck and him said he would need a few days to recover. "Are you all right? You look like you're going to be sick for the hundredth time since I've met you." I guess this new chapter of my life has taught me that the real world can make weak stomachs.

"First of all, it's technically since you kidnapped me. Second, I'm doing better than I thought I would do. Considering I was asleep on the ground and no one thought to get me up," I roll my eyes as the wagons start to move through a path in the foliage. Zehlin, Aleck, and I walk next to them. We don't have time to waste and we don't want dusk to hit too early. "How familiar are you with where we are anyway? I've seen maps, and we have a few, but how reliable is your five-hundred year old brain? You've had a lot of time to learn, have you not?"

We all continue our walk, the wagons are our guides as they were crafted by a spell maker. They're meant to find pathways, and depending on the direction we want to go, we can show them where and they take us on pathways in that direction. They don't show a direct location, but they can lead us to where we need to go.

"I've lived a long time compared to what you're used to, yes. But you aren't human anymore either. You're going to live a long time too." Zehling shrugs like he's talking about the weather.

"Well, how much longer?" I'm not surprised, but I didn't even think about that. I'm not human, I'm not going to have a human lifespan. The thought terrifies me, but also soothes me. I have so much more time than I thought I would, so much more time to explore and create.

"Could be over a thousand years. Most elves live past that," he looks up to the sky in response to a chirping sound made by a chimp. I know what chimps sound like, especially small ones, because I lived in the forest area of Ihrvian and apes and chimps were everywhere. I look up too, and try to spot the little guy.

They're known to be violent, but Zehlin said this island is relatively tame. Quickly, the wagons stop and Aleck starts to slide his sword out of its sheath, looking all around above us. He starts scouring the thick green treetops for the guilty chimp, or chimps. Zehlin also looks up, leaning against the back wagon, trying to hide his exhaustion.

"What's going on? I thought you said we weren't going to be in danger." I whisper, unsure of what to do. Aleck looks at me and whispers back quickly.

"We said the folks here are tame, not the animals. Animals rule here. We risk walking through dangerous territory if we don't watch where we go." Zehlin looks to Aleck and they exchange a look, along with a nod.

"We're going to keep going, this is the only path to Boronia. We just need to be quiet, and keep watch." Zehlin pushes away from the wagon and all of us continue again. Aleck keeps his sword out, prepared to use his combat knowledge, and extreme advantage, against a few monkeys. The thought of one of our faces being torn off by a territorial ape terrifies me.

"Will I need to take my gloves off?" I ask, taking each step with caution.

"We want to avoid that since you aren't familiar with your power yet, but if it comes down to it, yes." Zehlin says wearily.

"Is there any way you could shift the light, hide us?" I say quietly, looking down to avoid stepping on any dry sticks.

"I can't risk using my power yet, I'm already drained. Just stay quiet and keep moving." He whispers with me, keeping a hand on his sword as Aleck has his focus set on the sky while we move.

I hear a rustle in the foliage behind me for a moment, but I ignore it and continue looking forward. The rustling gets louder until I hear a crack of a branch behind me. I stop on my footing, slowly turning behind me, and when I don't see anything, I turn back around again. I almost start walking once more until another branch snaps. And this time when I turn around, there's a baby chimp walking towards us. I hear Aleck and Zehlin stop too, and the creaking of the wooden wagon wheels dies low.

"Don't. Move." Aleck sternly orders me. I don't move, but I'm also unintimidated. It's about two feet tall and looks anything but territorial as it walks close. It holds still and just looks up at me, fiddling with its hands. He makes a light chirp sound, tilting its head up at me.

"Oh he's just a little guy. Maybe he's hungry." I say, taking one step closer. My one step is quickly followed by the tiny monkey screaming and running up the nearest tree. He continues his wail as leaves rustle and fall from their branches. I look up and can no longer find any of the chimps we saw up in the trees earlier.

"Artea, I would kill you if it didn't affect everything I stand for." Zehlin groans and slips his sword out all of the way, standing up right away from the wagon he was using as a crutch. Aleck is tip toeing around the cargo, watching in all directions. The one small animal's cry soon isn't the only belting screech we hear. I look over to Zehlin and we lock eyes as I mouth *I'm sorry.* How can one baby chimp be such a brat? Telling on others to your parents is such a whiny move.

All Zehlin does is shake his head, and I look away once the sound of more branches crunching and leaves shaking slowly take over. I look up again, tilting my head as far as it will go, looking directly at the afternoon sunlight. The blue sky dotted with green jungle tangles is littered with dark brown and black spots, each contributing a low grumble sound that sounds like an outlandish tribal cry. There's almost a rhythm to it as more show up many feet above us. My heart rate has never gone up faster.

"See? Animals rule." Aleck confirms what Zehlin just happened to mention.

"I can see, yes, Aleck." I whisper, snapping back. The apes of all sizes start making their way down the branches, slowly and methodically. There has to be at least twenty of them. My fight or flight instincts are testing me again, the same feeling from the dragmist situation back in Halistyn hits me like a brick again.

I could run, hide behind a bush fifty meters away and stay there until dark. I know the direction, and I'll just make it by myself and hope that Zehlin and Aleck will wait there for me. Assuming they make it out. There's the best combat soldier and the general of my archipelago with me. What am I scared about?

I could take my gloves off, rely on a power I just now have and barely understand. I don't even know if it would work on an animal, let alone any other living thing. It would break my heart to have to turn these apes into dust like I did the fruit. It would be justified, though.

Hopefully.

Almost as if he can read my mind, Zehlin nods and takes a quick glance at my hands. I throw them into my pocket before unsheathing two small swords from my back. They aren't as big as the ones that Aleck and Zehlin carry, but they are more comfortable for me that way. I'm used to my dagger, so when it's conveniently lost, these are perfect.

I know twenty men with swords would be different to fight than twenty apes who feel threatened. Apes are unpredictable, is Aleck trained in ape fighting? Does his ability qualify for all types of combat, or just soldier combat?

My hands feel heavy, almost as if they know what I'm going to have to do. The weight of the air feels greater than the weight that the gloves introduced. The apes continue their way down towards us, the low rumbling coming from their chests is a warning, and a terrifying one at that.

We all stand still and I keep my hands in front of me, locking my elbows, stiff. The first ape lands on the ground with a thud directly in front of us and the wagons, parallel with our group. My next thought is if Torrid is still okay. I push it away as the giant gorilla-like animal flares his nostrils.

He's large, larger than any other I've seen. He's definitely the leader the way he's presenting himself. Slowly, others drop down and stay several meters behind him, but they're all still on guard. The rumbling has quieted and none of us three make any movement or sound. The leader takes multiple steps closer, never changing his broad shouldered stance or composure. I nearly stumble back, but I'm too tense to do so. I breathe deeply knowing that he could rip my head off and leave me to bleed like the ghoul and dwarf endured. I almost start to feel bad for those murderers.

Who did try to eat me, nonetheless.

He keeps moving to us and shifts his direction towards Zehlin, to my left. Zehlin is weak, and he can smell it. I watch Aleck's body stiffen even worse, but he can't do anything yet. Even I know it could only end in more blood. Best case scenario, they realize we aren't a threat and we can go on our way to Boronia, to safety. Worst case scenario, we all die here and all the training and preparation is left in the dust. My new powers might not even work, or they'll work wrong and I do something I don't mean to.

They're face to face now. The air from the gorilla's nose blows the stray hairs from Zehlin's hairline. He only looks to the ground, waiting for the ape to pass. He's taller than Zehlin, taller than Aleck, and much taller than me.

Before I can think of a solution, the monkey grabs Zehlin by his neck and lifts him into the air. He holds him like he's less than a feather while he sniffs Zehlin's body. He starts to struggle to breathe and his legs spasm under him, kicking the gorilla in the chest.

In not even a moment, I hear the crack of Zehlin's spine hit the tree to his left. The thud, mixed with the crack, breaks the terrifying silence. I flinch, watching Zehlin roll over onto his stomach wrapping his arms around his abdomen. The ape stands still, unbothered by the fact that he threw a grown man like it was for sport.

I panic.

My first thought is to run to him, and make sure he's okay, but I know I shouldn't do that. I also don't need to be any closer to the beast that's in front of me. I look at Aleck and see the same amount of calculation in his demeanor. What do we do without turning into rag dolls?

I see far out in the distance, a figure. It's making its way to us from behind the apes. I can hear their footsteps breaking the twigs and leaves from under them as they walk. Slowly, I start to see more of them. It's a woman, she has long braided hair that lands on her waist. She wears flowing cloth that looks primitive, yet royal. The tan cloth is decorated with blue and green accents around the seams and the neckline. She wears multiple bags, as well as a canteen of what I assume is water around her shoulders. Her face is sharp, yet soft. Her dark skin shines like a golden coffee bean, and she walks like she doesn't have a care in the world.

Before she gets too close, I look to Aleck and Zehlin. Zehlin is still faced to the ground, his groans becoming less and less audible. Aleck's sword is back in his sheath and he sighs, a relieved sigh. She stops a good distance in front of us, but she nods to Aleck. He rolls his eyes and starts walking to the wagon. All of the apes step away and eventually end up behind the woman. The large one sits right next to her side and she sets a hand on his shoulder.

I seem to be the only confused one here as Aleck is now totally relaxed and the woman has a smile on her face.

"You didn't think to tell us you were moving base?" Aleck speaks, irritated.

So, they know each other, well that's a good thing. My panic subsides and I let out a breathy sigh.

"I didn't want anyone here that I didn't expect. I had to throw you off so we could ensure the safety of the base. We didn't technically move it, we only extended the barriers a few miles out or so. Moving base would have been far too complicated. You of all people should have known we would," she speaks like smooth chocolate. Her voice is soothing, yet harsh. I can tell she's dangerous, but even more cautious. "I'm surprised Zehlin didn't recognize Zazu, he's been roughed up by him before."

She looks at the ape, which I'm assuming is Zazu and smiles. I slip my gloves back on before she pays any attention to me and runs over to Zehlin. I kneel to the ground and flip him over onto his back, he groans and blocks his eyes from the afternoon sun above him.

"Are you all right? What can I do?" I ask him, my heart racing faster than I'd like to admit.

"I–I'm fine, yeah." He nods while I help him sit up against the tree he was thrown against. "Fuck you, Mila." He coughs out toward the woman. She laughs and almost offers a hand as well.

Mila and Zazu.

What a fantastic first meeting.

"You could have at least told him not to throw the general against a tree." Aleck says as he grabs some water from the front wagon. By this time, most of the other monkeys have left except a few and Zazu. Zazu shrugs at Aleck's comment, showing clear amusement.

"You know we have healers, Alley. And plus this *general* stole my liquor last time he was here. I planned on getting pay back anyway." She shrugs and walks over to us, the nickname for Aleck makes me almost giggle. She stays closer to Zehlin than she does me, which I understand. I can only imagine the assumptions she has about me.

And then I remember my cover story. I'm not an ex-human who's been lied to her whole life and is actually an elf who has to get used to the world being thrown at her. I'm an exiled soldier who wants to do her best for the islands. Who wanted to bring the alliance back but was met with being left to die at sea. I'm born and raised as an elf. Mila has no reason to trust me, and I can't convince her to either. Suddenly the points of my ears feel extra cold.

Mila and I both help Zehlin up and set him inside one of the wagons. He's clearly agitated that he needs to rest and can't walk at the moment, but he knows it's best. We shut the side door and I can see through the windows that he closes his eyes. His swampy, grey eyes.

"The walk isn't too far from here to the base. It should only take an hour or so. How was the tessering?" Mila asks me as the wagons and all of us start to walk. She drifts to my left and gazes at the sights around us as we go. I pause, surprised she created conversation with me.

"It was… nauseating. But it was quick, so at least there's that." I smile and adjust the straps of my rucksack behind me as I feel for me short swords that are back in their straps as well. I pray that Torrid is left in one piece by the time we get to Boronia.

There's a very casual air around us, like Mila is a good friend. And if she is, it makes sense that we're going here first. Allies are an essential part of what we're doing, and she seems oddly comfortable around me. "Mila, right?"

"Yep, the one and only. You're the elvish girl…" She waits for my name, and I give it to her.

"Artea, Miss." We continue our hike. I make sure to keep my posture wide and straight. I'm a soldier, I don't know anything different. It actually has become easier to do since the training. "From Perdita, I served a few terms before I was run out. And I wanted to thank you, for letting us in here. For giving us a place to regroup."

"Yes, of course. And you can call me Mila, I'm married and I'm not near old enough to be called Ma'am," I nod in response before she speaks again. "This base will always be open to Aleck and Zehlin, therefore it'll be open to those they trust."

Aleck stays quiet as he's on the other side of the wagons, to the right. I see him though, he's looking around, always on edge. I guess when your ability is to fight, you never stop looking for one. I also get a closer look at Mila. Her hair is dark and tightly braided in small sections, her skin is a dark chocolate tone, and her eyes are golden, straight golden. I've only ever seen eyes like that once before in a halfling from a town next to Halistyn. I used to go there and buy clay for my pottery or fabric for Aunt Prim.

I haven't had a thought about her in a while. I guess it's easy to forget someone who lies to you, drugs you, confines you to a shitty town on a shitty island. I've learned to hate her, and my parents even more. They were scared of me, so they made me live a scrappy life with even scrappier people.

I've grown to get excited for this war so maybe I could confront my mother, confront my father. Zehlin, and I'm guessing everyone else, don't even know my father is alive. Torrid told me that they're both alive. Plotting to destroy the islands like they tried to do all those years ago. Do I tell Zehlin that my father is alive? Would it help anything, or only create more paranoia? My body isn't even my own, my thoughts need to stay mine. They are the only things that I can keep close.

"So, are you a halfling?" I ask her, trying to ignore my spiraling theories.

"Yes, how did you know? I didn't think elves were familiar with us," she suggests, but not in a casting-out way. She says it like it is. She says it with impartiality, like I'm just another neighbor, and it's much different from what I expected. And then I remember, I can't tell her I saw one in Ihrvian, in my hometown. I'm a soldier.

"I've had plenty of time to study. I wanted to know as much as I could. Golden eyes are typical in fae and human offspring. So, I took a lucky guess." I project my voice in a similar way that I did in the ballroom, when it wasn't me. "Are you in charge around here?"

"My husband was. Mateo. He's been gone since the war took off, I've heard that all of the other dukes and duchesses have been gone as well. We got married after he assigned me to be the Chief of Command. Then since he left, I've just been here guiding Boronia just in case anything else goes down. Everything feels... unfinished. I'm not a duchess by rule, only marriage, so I've turned down everyone who's come to me suggesting that I should take Mateo's place. I belong here with Boronia, and the people in Ornau can take care of themselves."

"Seems very humble of you, most folks I know would have taken that chance as quickly as they could." We start walking uphill, and as I look up, the hill gets steeper as it inclines. And we still have another mile or two to go before the hill is over. Thank Numen for training.

"Us, in Ornau, are definitely not most folks."

I like her.

Chapter Twenty

The air feels like syrup in my lungs by the time we make it to the top. It's so hard to breathe, but we finally stop walking and get to see the view from the top. Boronia is a terrifying beauty. Everything, yet nothing that I would have expected. There are large houses made of thick logs, not many, but about a couple dozen. Around the houses are more tall jungle trees that have small houses, or tents, built inside them. Some of the treehouses are connected with bridges or rope lines and have ladders that lead to the ground. Some have staircases, others have ladders leading up the small tents.

There are two large wooden and stone buildings with hundreds of transports set around them, I'm guessing as a storage lot. There are large sections made of only stone, where the weapons are probably stored. My guess is that repairing and building is held there, and so much more. I was told a little bit about this place by Zehlin while he was telling me what I needed to remember.

You're a soldier. You are not scared. Military bases are home to you. You're a soldier.

He never stopped saying that.

It almost looks like there are mountains and hills surrounding all of Boronia. Like a protective barrier, hiding a military base right in the heart of a vast jungle. It's the perfect disguise. Always reminding me that I'm not safe if people know who I am, if people want me trapped or dead they might succeed. It almost makes me wonder if he's scared of me too.

I hear the creaking of the wagon door and turn behind me, Zehlin steps out of his seat and stretches his back in an odd way.

"Forgot about me?" He knows no one forgot about him because we all know he'll get healed and that he's breathing. He's been through worse. I've heard him and Aleck joke about a time when he was beaten until his entire body was purple. One smack to the back by a tree shouldn't be too bad.

"No, but I wish I did. You look fresh as ever," I mumble and he shrugs while I notice the path in front of us. It's well cleared out and very smooth. The decline down the hill is steady, it'll be easy enough to maneuver and a relief to my feet.

I don't wish that I forgot him, I wish that we never had that moment in the ring. I wish I never tried to imagine what kissing him would feel like. I wish he didn't make me turn red whenever I think about it too hard. I can't believe that I would have let him kiss me. The general of the archipelago and the one person that could have warned me that the queen was going to control me in front of a bunch of nobles and their families. She hasn't done it since, but Zehlin also hasn't apologized.

I'm glad it worked, and we have Mava's support, but it's besides the point that she dug into my brain like that. And there's no way he doesn't know that I'm still upset about the whole situation, and that I absolutely don't want to think of him that way again.

None of us argue with Zehlin when he says he wants to go down and finish the rest of the walk to Boronia. We make our way down too, making sure the wagons' cargo is safe.

We all made our way down the hill eventually. Halfway down, Aleck had to help Zehlin stay up because he refused to get back into one of the wagons. Once we got to the tall wooden and metal gate, Mila opened it with only her mind. The gate creaked in response to her command and Zazu took his first chance at running into the base and climbing a tree. I lost him when he got too high for me to see. *What an interesting bodyguard.*

"I'm hoping you guys can get comfortable. Those buildings serve no use to you right now," she points to the stone and wooden buildings, the ones filled with weapons. "So, we'll skip that part of the tour. But over here is the heart of our base, Artea."

She gestures down a large alleyway that has other wagons and animals, as well as halflings and fae, humans and pixies. I'm honestly surprised they have pixies around as they're known to steal. There are shops on either side of the alley selling clothes and food, as well as all types of other things. We walk down the way and I notice that everyone is wearing the same clothing as Mila. Hers looks much more neat, but it's the same idea. The tan cloth, the colored fabrics around the seams, and the tassels hanging on dresses or the straps slung around shoulders.

These are soldiers and protectors, strong and fearless too. Yet, I don't think I've felt more safe before.

Zehlin and Aleck look bored because they've been here before, they look at the mud under their nails more than they do around us. The small chimps and dogs walk and stroll around like they are people too. A little white and brown striped chimp even steals a banana from a cart and runs up to the roof.

"Feel free to shop around for things, I know you have a few days before you get going. Just a short walk and we make it to the bunks."

She was right, the bunks were just a couple minutes away from the shopping strip. The bunks are small wooden apartments built into the jungle trees above us. The trunks are unbelievably thick, sturdy enough for homes. Once Aleck and I help get Zehlin up the ladder, we tie our two wagons to the bottom of the tree and make our own way up. It's about six o'clock so it's time for dinner, or in Zehlin's case, a nap.

When we get up there's a small balcony that holds the entrance door. There's a small living space, enough for two chairs, and a metal stove with some pots. Mila told us that this was the only vacant apartment available, and it only has two rooms. Aleck and Zehlin's room has two small beds, and mine has a larger bed. The ceilings are low, but the apartment is cozy and smells of my old bedroom in Halistyn.

I kind of miss being drugged into believing I'm a whole other creature. I miss the fire and the pain of the ice baths, I miss the summers where I dreamed of the ice baths to soothe the trembling heat. I almost even miss the tavern covered in sweat and ale, the wooden floorboards forever stained with them.

But I know this is best. I have found what I've been missing for my entire life. I've found a purpose. I've found people who care about my life, even if I'm only needed to save others. Even if I'm just collateral damage.

I hear one of the boys start the fire in the fireplace sitting in front of the two chairs while I walk into my room. I drop my rucksack and contemplate getting Torrid's flask out, but then I settle with taking a nap first. My jacket and the armor, as well as my armored boots come off. They lay on the floor in a messy pile while I don't hesitate to flip the quilted covers over my body. My gloves stay on though.

My door was left cracked open, but I want it that way.

I'm tired of closed doors.

Chapter Twenty-One

The next morning, I turn over towards the small window in my bedroom. The light is bright and the sounds of the jungle seem to settle my bones. The wind, the birds, the distant waterfalls crashing down into the streams, all sounds I've never been able to hear before today, not truly. I sit up and don't feel any aches or strains on my body from the shift or from training.

No pain from even the hike.

I'm getting stronger by the day and I can feel it. All I need to do is find the bracelet, stay alive to find the others, and help stop a potential breakout of war.

Simple.

I toss the quilts off of my body and let my skin drink up the fresh air. The next thing I do is open my rucksack and dig for Torrid's flask. I find the outline of the purple-tinted jar and let out a relieved sigh.

It's not shattered.

I pull it out gently and see Torrid in the flask, safe and sound.

"It was dark in there!" he yells with all of his voice he could project.

"Shh!" I instinctively look around and lower the flask, whispering to the small man. "Torrid, people can't know you're here. Remember?" He cowers and covers his mouth, nodding quickly in response.

"Good. How was the journey? Are you all right?" I ask, looking around for any bruises or broken bones in the little prophet.

He whispers in response. "I'm fine, just a little sick there for a while. And it was very dark." His voice is shaky like usual, but he's in one piece.

"Do you need anything, Torrid? I need to go outside soon and make sure everything is settled before we try and figure out more about my powers." As I say that, I wonder if Torrid could tell me what the extent of my powers is. What really can I do besides tear a bunch of fruit down. Does it work on people?

"Yes, yes. Well, I would like to stay out in the light please." He crosses his arms, making sure to be extra dramatic.

"Oh right, of course." I walk over to the small window and place him on the window sill. I make sure to cover a majority of the flask with one of my shirts from my rucksack to cover him up. Once he's settled and takes a good look outside, I begin my questions.

"You know that I tried to get my natural powers to arise with Etiza, like we talked about?" He nods. "Well, it worked. Now I have the ring telling me about the past, but now I also have a strange new power. And I had some questions."

"Yes. You can make deals with life." He shrugs like I should have known this already. I suspected it, but still.

"Deals?" I ask, looking at the black gloves covering my hands.

"Yeah, drain and give. Your mother had the same thing, remember?" he asks me like I'm incompetent. I'm tired of him assuming that just because he knows almost everything, doesn't mean I do too.

"So, the fruit that I touched died. But does that mean I could bring it back?"

"Well, yes. But you have to learn how to control it first. Obviously. But sure, you could bring life too. Well, certain extensions of you could." He sniffs the air and makes a disgusted face. "The whispers here, they taste funny. Not like my basement." I ignore him.

"Okay. Thank you. I'm not sure what *extensions of me* would look like though. The controlling part is what Zehlin and I are working on today. I will be back later though. Maybe tonight, we can let you out, hmm?" I ask, shifting his ruined mood, caused by the whispers he hears.

"Yes! Almost half a century I have spent here. I promise I will be good and not trick anymore children. Swear it, Missy Artea." He relays how much he wants out, and he better not make me regret it.

I meet Zehlin and Aleck in the cafeteria. There's a large building next to the stone ones that's meant for soldiers and the base workers to have lunch or other meals. It took me forever to find them as I had to chase down Mila to tell me where she thought they might be. Mila showed me where her office was yesterday as well and told me that she's usually there. I went to her office, covered in beautiful stained glass and vines, and Zazu almost ripped my head off. Mila apologized and led me on my way.

"You didn't even bother to tell me where you were going." I cross my arms when I make it to the table. Aleck's red hair is a contrast in this crowded cafeteria, so it wasn't hard to find them. Zehlin turns to me, he doesn't look as drained as he did yesterday.

"We decided to catch up with some old friends. You were sleeping so peacefully, we didn't want to wake you, Angel." He smirks and looks me up and down. I was able to brush my hair and change my clothes before leaving on my scavenger hunt this morning, but I'm suddenly too aware of my appearance.

"We could hear you sleeping nice and peacefully too." Aleck chuckles, and a few of the other guys sitting at their table chuckle too. I glance around the room and notice different looks from everybody. Some people stare at their food or talk with their fellow soldiers, others are looking at me. Some with curiosity, and others with disdain. I'm an enemy. I'm one of the people that they fought, that could have made their dukes and duchesses disappear, that killed thousands of people. Of course they're judging me, I don't blame them.

I'm one of you guys. I'm not evil. I didn't kill anyone. I won't kill anyone. Please, stop looking at me. I'm human.

But instead of yelling the truth, I keep my posture up and my face still as a soldier as I talk, trying to ignore the stares.

"Real funny, Alley." I shake my head, pointing fun at the nickname from Mila.

"Don't call me that, pointy ears." He frowns and takes a bite of a piece of meat from his tray.

"You have pointy ears too, they're just not as sharp as mine. I don't want to hear it," I roll my eyes and Aleck goes back to eating. "But hey, that's not my point. Zehlin, didn't you say you wanted to try and practice with me today?"

A man next to Zehlin looks at him and laughs before he speaks. "Zehlin, you fighting with a girl or something?"

"It's not like that, Fin. She has some skills she wants to test before we use them on the redcaps later. Just insurance, you know how it goes," Zehlin says, also taking a bite from his tray. He's trying to avoid talking about my powers. If it gets out that I have the same powers as my mother, Josephine, I would definitely have a target on my back. Folks here are already weary, we don't need to piss off an entire military base on top of it. *And what are redcaps?*

"Yeah, whatever. I guess it makes sense if she's going to save our circle of islands. Tell me, soldier, what are your powers? I know every elf has 'em," Fin, who looks like a human, asks me with a glare in his eye. This is a test, a test I'm well prepared for.

"I can see into the future, when someone wants me too, or when I touch them." I shrug. "It's not much, but my real power is the fact that I'm a soldier, just like all of you. And I plan on putting that to use for you all."

"Hey, not to be rude or anything," he says, looking down to his tray for a moment and then up to me again. "But you're our only chance now that you have the ring. Stay alive, or I'll kill you. We've been in this for far too long."

He seems very comfortable at this table, well known, and very comfortable talking to me. This is a good sign. Straight to the point and blunt. It seems that all soldiers are like this.

"You got it, boss. That's my plan anyway," I declare as Zehlin stands up and Aleck gestures to the table, stating that he will stay here. Zehlin and I walk out of the cafeteria without another word.

There's a large training area outside full of people, equipment, and terrain, all suited for the best preparation possible. We haven't had a war in a hundred years, yet these soldiers are fighting like there will be a war tomorrow. There are a couple lieutenants ordering soldiers around through exercises or courses, others are fighting dummies, and some are repairing their weapons or sharpening their swords. Every soldier has muscles larger than any that I've seen before. Their bodies have been crafted to withstand anything and it shows. The grunts and yells coming from them is unsettling, yet also soothing. Ornau seems to be in very good hands.

Zehlin and I walk past all of them, onto a path that leads into the jungle. After a moment, there's an opening. A large circle of dirt that's surrounded by trees and other plants. It's quiet over here, and I'm unable to hear any of the sounds from the training area.

I walk into the middle and look up at the afternoon sun. Zehlin walks to me and looks up too, slouching a little bit. "How are you feeling, since yesterday?" I ask him, noticing the faint bags under his eyes.

"Tired, but not in too much pain. I can feel my power coming back already. I'll just need about two more days." He shrugs. "Are you ready to take the gloves off?"

I look down at my hands for a moment and think about it. Draining life from anything is no feat. I need to learn how to control it before I do something I regret. I slip the gloves off and place them in my pocket. I try to ignore the ring and the way my fingertips are coated in an ash-like color, I try to ignore the fact that I'm different, and I try to ignore the fact that I'm happy to be alone with Zehlin, and I don't know why.

"What's the first thing you wanted to try?" I question him. He mentioned yesterday that there were a few things.

"Well, understanding how powerful you could be." I pause at the remark and almost shake my head. Me? A bartender? A clay spinner? Impossible. *Nope, it's possible.* "We should test different ways you can use it."

"Like what?" I ask him.

"Well, you know how I can do this?" He takes his hand and makes an orb with his sunlight ability. I nod my head and put my hands out like he has them and I close my eyes. "I can make my magic float around me and others, or I can hold it. I can manifest it in many ways. Focus on the way that you can feel the energy around you get absorbed into your palm. Will it, control it."

My eyebrows furrow as I maintain focus on the feeling around me. He's right, I can feel the energy calling to me, almost like it wants me to hold it. It feels like it's been waiting for me. The wind feels to drift a little faster around me as I feel my clothes waving in the air, hitting my skin lightly. My palms get heavier and heavier the longer I ask for the power to come to me. I hear footsteps walk from in front of me to behind me, Zehlin then puts his fingers on my shoulders and squeezes them.

"When I put pressure here, imagine it's the power taking you over. You need to make it listen to you. You need to make it stop pinching you. You're the wielder, you do not listen to your power. It follows you." I can feel the heat from his hands and his breath against my neck. I don't let it distract me though, as I focus on what he means. My palms weigh more and more as I call it to me, and it comes.

I open my eyes.

Nothing.

"You broke your concentration too early. I'll tell you if it comes," he tries to reassure me, but I'm everything except reassured.

"What if my power doesn't work like yours? What if I can't make sunlight swords or magic orbs?" I turn my head to the side, meeting his eyes. The colors inside them dance, almost as if he can speak with them. The heat coming from his body almost reflects the dancing sunlight above our heads. I wonder if he's giving us light on purpose for any reason, and part of me thinks he is.

"Just focus. I've seen what your mother can do. And if you're any fraction of her, I know you can." He presses harder on my shoulders and it forces me to focus on what my body feels, and not the anxiety of my ability.

I've always admired the stories of the fae and the magical creatures like pixies or even ghouls, I couldn't stop reading about their powers. I wondered for so long what it would be like to be something special, to be something other than human. But I was not human, and I'm the daughter of two of the most powerful enemies we have right now. I have a power just like them, and I will use it for good. I will bring life and I will help prepare for this war, and maybe even stop it.

"Keep looking for it. It's there, Angel."

I don't feel the heat from Zehlin on me anymore, instead it's quickly replaced with cold ice from deep inside my bones. I feel the shivers worming their way all over my body, scavenging for something. They're looking for something inside of me and they won't stop until they find it. I shut my eyes harder as the shivers almost start to hurt, making my muscles vibrate in response. My wrists seem to carry more weight, until I open my eyes and see something that makes me stumble into the rock that Zehlin is being for me.

"W–what?" I whisper too quietly. The same black color from my hands is manifested as a small misty cloud in my hands. It's like the ash that I turned the fruit into as it dances in the air around my hands. I keep it in place as the shivering cold rinses away from my body and the black mist stays put. I take a step away from Zehlin and turn towards him very slowly.

He takes a cautious step backwards and I try to not be offended as he looks at the cloud of ash. Every once in a while, I can see the ring from Ihrvian shining in through the darkness. I twist my wrists around before I separate them, using my full concentration on the cloud in front of me.

I want to move it around, not just have it sit on my hands. I know I can because I made it. It's telling me to do something with it, like the cold urges me to not let the energy go.

The energy is calling to me like it's waited my whole life to be summoned, and in a way it has.

I raise my hands into the air and imagine the energy floating above me, dancing around the tree branches like a flock of birds. Just as I imagine it, it happens.

The magic follows my lead as I use my hands to guide it through the branches, weaving it through the twists of green. I decide I want to see what would happen if I lead it to the plants.

I push it toward a small bush on the ground, slowly moving it against the plant. The leaves start to turn gray, not a quick death like the fruit, but slow and methodical.

The magic almost has a mind of its own as I walk a few feet toward it, still holding it against the bush. The black mist veins through the plant, slowly taking over each branch and leaf until all that's left is dust. I close my fists and the black cloud immediately disappears, vanishing out of the air. A large smile creeps on my face, exposing my excitement.

Zehlin walks over to the bush before bending down and dipping his fingers into the pile of dead bush. "Fascinating. But it's only the beginning. I wasn't expecting you to be able to summon like that today. Most fae, and even elves, take days to use their power like that. How did you do it?" He asks me, standing up and walking to me as he glances at my hands.

"I don't know. It was calling me, urging me to do something with it. Like I was unlocking it from its cage," I say while getting ready to slip my gloves back on. "It was easy, almost like breathing." I look at him and see a small smile rising on his lips too.

I furrow my brow and place my hands on my hips while giving him a glare. "What?"

"Nothing, the light just makes you look ready. Well rested, you know?" He starts sauntering back the way we came and I follow.

"As opposed to my usually-looking poorly rested?" I question him, slightly offended.

"I mean, for the while I've known you, you've been sick or reading and training all day. It just seems odd that you look brighter while we are on a mission that could get everybody killed if we don't do it right. Especially you." I look to the ground and nod.

Since we got here it's felt like I could breathe. Almost like Etiza taking the natural power out for me has let me feel not so constrained, like the missing piece has been put in its place. Ornau is beautiful and the people here, despite the worry, have made me feel so welcome. The air isn't so hard to breathe.

The death threat from Fin wasn't too bad, it definitely could have been worse.

"Yeah I guess you have a point. Oh, and hey, what were the redcaps you mentioned earlier in the cafeteria?" I ask him. He mentioned that we're preparing for the redcaps when Fin assumed we'd be fighting. Not like we don't fight, but it made me curious. I haven't been told how we're going to obtain the bracelet from here, only that it's a bracelet and that it should be easy to get.

Zehlin starts to explain as we continue walking. "The redcaps are these tiny menacing things, but they're easy to kill. They are one of the few hostile creatures on Ornau and they live in the Bleeding Circle."

"Bleeding Circle?" I ask, avoiding branches and puddles of mud as we head back to base.

"Yeah, there's a huge tree with branches the span as far as twenty men lined up. The branches hang over a large pond, mixed with blood. The redcaps find their victims and the ones who are unlucky enough, get tied upside down and hung to bleed out from their scalps, until they dry out and die. Then the redcaps drink from the pond. It's how they live, they can't eat anything else." He speaks of the redcaps like it's normal.

"What happens to the bodies?" I ask, almost mortified at the misfortune.

"No one really knows. Everyone either dies before they find out, or they run before they're next."

We reach the base and the sound of the shop alley brings me comfort. I've never seen a healthy town life like this. In Halistyn, everyone is angry or hungry or jacked up on dragmist. There's no trading and peace like there is here, it brings me hope for a better time. A hope that I'm trying to bring to everyone.

"So, what do the redcaps have to do with anything?" I ask him, wondering what the reason for going after them would be.

"The Bleeding Circle's tree holds the bracelet. The book said that it's in the trunk. How we'll get it out, I'm not sure. But we'll cross that bridge when we get to it. And we have to wait for a full moon." In three days.

I take a breath as Zehlin heads back to the cafeteria and I go back to the shopping alley. I'm left feeling oddly warm, but cold being away from Zehlin. It's getting harder and harder to drown out this feeling of him, the feeling that there's a connection neither of us can ignore.

Chapter Twenty-Two

I lay in my bed with Torrid still sitting on the window sill. He tells me stories about his adventures centuries ago before he was captured and put into his little flask. He says he used to be able to turn into all kinds of forms and manipulate people into seeing things that weren't real. He said he used his power for bad but he never knew anything else. He didn't realize that he could use his power for good, and not just personal gain.

We talk for an hour about his adventures and about my life in Halistyn, as well as the few places around Ihrivan I have traveled to before.

Right in the middle of my sentence, we hear a blood curdling scream pierce its way through the camp. I hear some rustling and a few doors fly open in response.

Torrid's eyes go into a panic as he turns to me. "If you let me out now, I can be one of the jungle animals and watch over you while you go see what's happening," I give him a skeptical look as more muffled gasps are spoken. I did bring him here to let him go. I did promise him. "Please, I want to help. Let me help."

I nod, taking his flask in my hand and I pinch the brown cork holding the glass bottle shut.

"Do good for me, Torrid." I tilt the flask down into the window sill and he slides out, landing on his feet. He stretches for a moment and takes a deep breath. He looks at me and nods as he closes his eyes. The next thing I know, there's a small toucan flying around in my room.

"I've missed this, Artea. Thank you," he says with a scratchy, toucan voice. I open the window for him to let him fly out and slip my boots on. He flies with a gracefulness that makes it seem that he never stopped.

Before I went back to my apartment after experimenting with Zehlin, I grabbed a knife from one of the shops. I paid for it with a few Telikian coins, a very special currency that we decided to take with us. Also, the only currency we have. The new steel dagger with a black handle sits comfortably in the shaft of my right boot.

I have missed my dagger very much. This one is not the same as the one I lost, but it will do.

I run out of my bedroom and don't hear Aleck or Zehlin around so I'm assuming they're still outside. Zehlin has been doing a lot of resting, that's for sure. I make my way out and down the ladder and follow the noise. Some people are yelling and others are rushing away.

It takes a moment but I find where all of the commotion is coming from and find a circle of people gathered around a man lying on his back in the ground. He's in the middle of the shopping alley, laying still. I weave through the crowd and get a better look.

His head is bleeding onto the dirt and gravel floor, he has dirty brown hair paired with pale, almost white skin. He looks young, about my age, but I've learned that looks don't mean anything of age anymore. His clothes are blue and white, splattered with dirt and some blood from multiple injuries. No one stops me from walking closer to him.

The biggest and most distinguishing feature about him is his wings. He has large white feathered wings splayed out on the ground. They're also littered with patches of dirt and blood. The white of his wings matches the white of his outfit and skin, but his outfit isn't formal. He looks like he was traveling somewhere before this. He has hiking boots on with a bag strapped to him along with multiple coats and thick pants. His skin is as pale as snow.

I kneel down to his body and see his breath hitch, uncontrollable panic tries to rise in my throat.

He's alive.

"He just fell from the sky!" a lady behind me yells. She looks to be a baker and also looks as terrified as the others around me. "I heard a crack. Is he okay?"

I nod to everyone and make sure my gloves are on before I touch him. Zehlin and Aleck come running to the body with me.

"Where were you guys?" I ask them, still looking at the barely-alive man. I place my ear to his lips and feel, as well as hear, the breath slowly go in and out of his mouth. "It doesn't matter, we need to get him help right now."

"He's an Avian. From Avaris. He had to have flown for hundreds of miles to get here." Zehlin says as we all three go to lift the man's body. A woman directs us to the medical tent and we shuffle our way there. His wings make him that much heavier.

We place his body on a table in the tent. There are some lanterns that light the room along with trays of tools and medicines of all kinds and colors placed on shelves spread around the room. There are three nurses already in here when we set him down.

Some odd sense of panic is still pulsating in my throat. Is he going to be okay? How did he get here all the way from Avaris? Can Avians really fly for that long?

It was my job to learn about the people on the islands for the month that we waited and I know that Avians have wings and live on the upper island of Avaris. The lower level is full of dead plants and is a graveyard full of vile creatures, but the upper sky level is full of pegasi and faeries with wings. I know they can fly, but the distance between Boronia and Avaris is massive. How did he do it?

"What happened?" One of the nurses comes rushing over to the table, all of us out of breath.

"They say he fell from the sky. We don't know how high it could have been but he's barely breathing. Can you help?" Zehlin begs the nurse in a demanding way. Hearing his general voice never fails to surprise me.

The nurse nods and starts to put a thin pair of gloves on his hands. The other two do the same. "We will do what we can. There could be major spinal injury, but we might have the right thing to fix it."

"Do whatever you must." Aleck nods to the three of them and we all walk out. It takes me longer to leave than the rest of them as I look back to the man. Something is pulling at me, the man being here is pulling at me. Part of my heart aches with each step I take.

Who is he?

Chapter Twenty-Three

Over the next three days we've waited for the man to heal. He's made progress and there's good signs that he should be all right. He still lays asleep in the medicine tent but they're keeping him that way with treatment so he doesn't wake up too early and hurt himself.

Zehlin has had rest and is back to his regular self so we've been training with my power. I've gained most control of my power while my gloves are off, only one plant has died out of ten tries. I have learned to center my focus and take control of it.

Everyday Zehlin reminds me how the power is mine, and the day I can stop wearing the gloves for sure is that day that it's mine. And the day I become the most dangerous.

We have also tried to use the ring's power a few times and it's worked. However, one flashback was of Zehlin sleeping and the other was of him as a kid trying on his mother's crowns. A couple interesting, but insignificant things. Very different from the one of him and his now-dead father, or Mateo with the other dukes and duchesses fighting with the queen.

Torrid has stayed out all night using his abilities again, getting used to having to eat and relieve himself like he didn't have to do in his flask. So far, I haven't heard any children screaming or anything. He's yet to turn into his humanoid form yet, and I wonder if it's the same as the one in the flask or if it's a terrible looking old man.

He'd come back with stories of the animals he's met or the new places in Ornau he'd find by flying. He said he also had a fun time messing with Zazu as a woodpecker, flying around him like a fly in the summer heat. If that's the most mischievous he's going to get, my plan to keep him on the right track has worked.

On top of all of that, Zehlin and I still haven't talked about the time in the ring. But I've had dreams of it going differently. Dreams that make me embarrassed, and frankly a little pink. Has he thought of me that way? Does he wish he kissed me while we were sweaty and covered in chalk?

Why do I wish he would've kissed me?

I've been alone most of my life, tending to blankets and drunkards when I'm bored. And the more time I spend with him, the more I forget why I'm avoiding these childish feelings. Was it really his fault, the night of the ball? Was he ordered by his queen to not say a word? Why would the general of the archipelago disobey an order just for some girl.

And why in the hell am I thinking about this in the first place? Staring at my ceiling first thing in the morning pondering about a man who's five hundred years old and can breathe under water is not on my to-do list.

However, tonight is the full moon. Meaning we are going to make our way to the Bleeding Circle and try to get the bracelet. The second piece to the puzzle. The second piece needed for us to perform the ritual and relight the flame, bringing the bridges back and enabling preparations for war. It's odd that I might have to go to war with my parents without having to even meet them first.

I get up and get ready in my thick clothes and armor before strapping my bags and weapons to my body in secure places. I walk out the door and down the ladder to meet Zehlin at the bottom.

"Where's Aleck?" I ask him as he ties a rope to his side. Seeing him in jungle rags mixed with Telikian armor is an interesting sight, I'd think that the general would care about his looks, even on missions. But he does care about the right things, he doesn't just give orders. He gives orders and carries them out, he's loyal and will do whatever it takes to protect his country. His people.

"Oh, he thinks three fellows is too many for this. He's going to stick around here and probably frolic in bed with Mila." I tighten my straps and look at him in confusion.

"In bed? She's married, is she not?" I ask him as he starts to walk down a pathway, and I follow.

"Yes, to Mateo. But it was a marriage of convenience. Or still is, but they haven't seen each other in a hundred years. She benefited off of his title and he benefited off of her military knowledge. It's one of the reasons we're here on Ornau first instead of the other islands." He clears his throat as he leads us through more secluded paths to get ready for the journey to the Bleeding Circle. "Boronia is the safest base for us to be right now. Easiest place to start too."

We stay quiet for most of the walk.

An hour passes by.

Two.

And eventually it's starting to get darker outside. The light isn't as bright and each step is harder for me to take. My breath gets heavier and my limbs get more tired the more we weave through the endless trees and bushes. Zehlin looks unphased as he always does and I start to fall a few more steps behind him.

"Struggling, Angel?" he asks, tilting his chin to the side towards me.

"I'm doing just fine. And you?" I say through clearly broken breath.

"You can't hold us back too far, we need to get to the tree on the full moon. Tonight's your one chance unless you want to stay another month."

I decide to summon my magic and let it distract me while we walk. It's become so easy to summon it these past few days the more I practice. If I focus on making sure I don't turn any plants or animals to dust, it might distract me from the burning sensation in my feet.

I look at my magic as well as where I'm stepping, using the black mist as a pathway, slowly getting to the same pace as Zehlin.

"Why couldn't you just tesser us there?" I ask him with a dry throat. I will need water soon.

"The Bleeding Circle doesn't allow magic from outside to get in. We have to walk into the area and *then* use our magic. I might be able to get us as close as possible, if that's what you really need." I roll my eyes at him and scoff, but he opens his hand and I walk over.

"You really made me walk for hours, just to say you could have gotten us there in seconds?"

"I wanted to kill time because we have to wait until the moon is up anyway. Plus I didn't think you'd want me to hold you anymore than I needed to. Since you've been ignoring me."

"Ignoring you?" I ask, baffled by his statement. If anything, he's been ignoring me.

"When we practice, you barely speak to me. And when we're eating supper you only look at your plate, it seems like you can't wait to get up and leave. Like the thought of being around me after that morning in the ring is horrifying."

My mouth hangs a little open at the sudden confession of feelings. He's upset that I've been avoiding him. Which is true, but I thought he was avoiding me too.

He continues before I can say anything. "I get it, you're pissed at me and I'm a distraction. The last thing you need is a man to pick you up and tell you everything will work out while your life is constantly at stake. But we are in this together, Artea. I need your thoughts, I need your input. You've just been following Aleck and I around with barely any question."

I take a breath and look him in the eyes for the first time, we're both standing still. "I'm sorry, Zehlin. I didn't mean to ignore you, but you're right. That day in the ring was weird, and I am mad at you. But it's not my place to ask questions, I know what we're doing when we're doing it. You're more experienced. I'm trying here, but all of this is a lot for only over a month of being a completely new person. How do I give input on something that I know near nothing about?"

"Artea." He takes an irritated breath. My name on his tongue sounds like molten sugar as he speaks. "Your life doesn't just matter to me, or to the queen. *Everyone* is relying on you. You can't just follow around, I need you to be an equal player if you want to survive this. The seven pieces will be hard enough on you, now stack all the people who might want you dead and the war that we are trying to stop."

Before I respond, I realize he's right. I have been walking around and following whatever they do. Aside from Torrid or the visions, I haven't been on an equal level as them.

I breathe out a sigh, a heavy one. "You're right, I'll try to give more of my thought. It's just easier to assume you're right with so much already going on."

He smirks and shrugs slyly. "That is usually everyone's best bet." I ignore his ego and decide to be a little truthful considering he seems lonely.

"I brought Torrid with us." Zehlin is looking up but slowly turns to me after I mention that Torrid isn't in the basement.

"You did *what?*" he asks me, walking closer by small steps. By now my magic cloud has disappeared, my focus completely gone.

"He's not as bad as everyone thinks. He's just been hanging out with Zazu and flying around Ornau at night. I made him promise to keep to himself and only interject into anything if we need help. Just like now, he's probably flying over us with his little toucan wings scoping out the area." He looks weary but he's listening. "I'm being careful, okay?"

I open my hand to try and finish this conversation as quickly as possible. I gesture to him while he gets over his shock that I actually had an original idea. He opens his hand in response, deciding to drop it too. We lock palms and he closes his eyes.

I've been so worried about preparing to stay alive and hoping for the best. I've been looking for myself in every mirror, looking for who I am and why. I didn't even think about Zehlin or Aleck in all of this. The weight of the archipelago's military is on Zehlin's hands, the people are on his shoulders. If all of this goes badly, he'll blame himself. He's worried too and I've been so soaked up in my own sorrows that I've used him as a punching bag every morning and a tutor only because he has to. He has to make sure I'm ready, otherwise the people will suffer.

"Don't think of me as just an asset to your war," I nearly beg before he can tesser. He reopens his eyes and I see a hint of silver glimmer in the dusk.

"I never have, Angel," he whispers, quieter than normal.

And then we're gone.

Zehlin was right when he said walking was going to kill time. Now that he knows Torrid is here, I called Torrid down and we asked him to scout the area. Zehlin said he didn't know the exact area that the Bleeding Circle was at, and he wanted to be around it to wait for the moon to be high enough.

The moon, according to the spell, has to be in the middle of the sky when we get the bracelet. So, we are going to go in before then to get rid of the redcaps first. Then we will find a way to get to the tree and get the second piece. Torrid eventually came back and gave us a parameter for how close we should get.

We both sit together with our back against a large tree stump. The air smells like mud and death. It's almost like I can taste the bloody pond from here, the metallic sting in my nose is overwhelming. I start to hear the crickets rise while the birds' cries die down.

"Was walking better?" he asks me, I smile and look over at him.

"You trained me for skill, not for stamina."

"I guess I'm a flawed teacher, huh?" He smiles back and slips two knives from his side out of their sheaths and holds them by his sides, fidgeting out of boredom.

"How much longer will we have to wait?" I ask, looking out in front of me at the dark trees and endless green. I hear a waterfall very close to our left.

Water.

"About an hour, and then we'll go hunting." He uses each dagger to sharpen the other one, and I'm not sure how effective that is. I tilt my head towards the sound of water but don't say anything as the thirst tugs at my throat. "I might be able to hear it from a mile away, but you hear it too. Let's go."

How does he read my mind like that?

We both get up and start walking to the water. "Can you read minds too or something?"

"Angel, I've been in the military long enough to know when someone needs water. Even the most dangerous elves can't go on without some." He says in a dramatic tone.

Am I dangerous? Scary, even? I hate not knowing.

"Does anyone in Ornau know why we're actually here?" I ask.

"They know we're looking for an important object to help the islands, but that's all. Really only Fin and a few others know the extent. We can't share too much information. Plus, you're with me, so you get a free pass around here either way." I nod and grin in response. He's right but I still hate it, the authority he demands by just being in a room, not even trying to gain respect.

He just has it by default.

We reach the waterfall after only a moment and I bend down quickly, more thirsty than I thought, and drink. I cup my hands over and over, slurping the liquid and feeling the coldness drip down my forearms, similar to the cold I feel when I use my magic.

Zehlin does the same, but he's more graceful with it than I am.

After taking a sip out of my palms one more time, I hear Zehlin grunt. I look over to him but before I can see anything, something grips my head and pulls me on my back. It feels like every fiber in my neck is being pushed in on itself, collapsing like an unstable cave. I scream and scream, the pain not going away. I try to push away whatever is on my head and covering my eyes, but it won't budge. I try to use my power but I can't sense it anywhere. Everything is black until my body goes numb, not from cold, from something else. Something I've never felt before.

I hear Zehlin's muffled cries, just as mine sound as my whole face is covered. The pain on my head consumes me more until I stop moving all together.

Then it all goes black.

"Artea!" I hear someone yell. I look to my right and see Zehlin. He has rope tied around his legs and his abdomen, covering his limbs and holding them together. His hair stands up and is flowing free, yet caked in dripping blood. And then I realize he's tied upside down.

And I am too.

I can't move anything anywhere as I try to twist and turn to attempt and fit through the rope tightly constricting me. It's of no use so I decide to look around me for something to help Zehlin and I out.

It's near midnight now as the sound of water drops echoes through the area.

We're tied up to the tree of the Bleeding Circle. Torrid wasn't able to scout for all of the redcaps, he must have missed one. Unless he didn't say anything and was hoping that he could find an easy way to get rid of us, maybe he was using me to get out of his flask.

He's nearly the least of my worries right now. I push my worry aside, as well as the guilt of maybe disappointing Zehlin.

"Zehlin, does that hurt?" It looks like there's a lot of blood coming from his head. Each drop I see fall down creates a sound that instills more dread.

Drip. Drip. Drip.

And I hear that his drops aren't the only ones making any noise. The pain slowly seeps through after the shock of my wake. I look all the way down into the water and see my own blood getting fed into the crimson pool.

"Y—yes, but not too much." He grunts, also trying to wiggle out of his binds.

"Can you tesser out? Please, do *something*." I whisper as I continue to look around and see small figures start to walk out from the dark, night fog. They're almost shorter than dwarves but all of them are wearing one specific feature. They all have literal red hats on.

Pricks. Mocking death.

"We were running out, you know. The water was turning a little too clear, little ones." One of the little redcaps steps forward and speaks.

"Let us go," I bark, too frustrated with the worst headache of my life to deal with any banter.

"Your blood will not go to waste, don't you worry. We thank you, actually, for walking in here." His pale skin mixed with his white hair makes him look insane, and in a terrifying way. If I wasn't in these ropes, I would squash him like a bug.

"What will you do with us?" I ask him, silently angry with Zehlin for not being able to tesser, or just not doing it. "With our bodies?"

He smiles and tilts his head, making his teeth glisten in the moonlight. "We will leave you to Spinner. She takes care of all of the bodies for us. We get the blood, she gets the delicious meat." I scoff in response, already done with this and hoping for a way out.

This is not how we go.

"We all have to eat, you know?" He grins again.

Chapter Twenty-Four

What feels like a couple of hours go by. They walked away without another word, some of them taking a sip of the blood infected pond before doing so. I've fallen in and out of sleep, light headed and sickly. We aren't losing a lot of blood fast, but the loss is starting to pile up, making it harder to keep my eyes open.

If we miss the full moon, we might lose before we can even get started.

I hear a rustle in the foliage in between both Zehlin and me. I get confirmation that he's still awake because I see him look towards it too. It's the first sound other than our blood that we've heard all this time. The pain suddenly is drowned out with panic when I see three, four, eight. Eight legs attached to a black and yellow body crawl out into the clearing.

Spinner.

It says nothing as it crawls closer to us. The tree is like a web that the redcaps spin, and then Spinner comes in and takes care of the aftermath. She must be as tall as a human, not counting the massive span of her legs that reach out at a horrifying length.

I start begging for something, anything. Aunt Prim taught me a lot of things, but she never taught me how to not panic. My breathing quickens. This is how I die. After all this hope, all this effort, I'm going to be spun into a web and eaten.

She walks into the pond, her pointy black legs piercing the mud beneath it. I hear small chirps coming from her mouth, and I can start to smell the moldy scent she creates. The slime on her body starts to make itself visible the closer she gets. The next thing I know she's right in front of me.

Her breath whispers on my skin, making chirping noises similar to a bird. The sweat from my terror is almost enough to slip me out of my rope as I shut my eyes tight, avoiding the mutilation.

"Zehlin!" I scream, and before I can feel the sharp pain of a leg being stabbed into my side, or a mouth tearing open my stomach, I have orange Spinner intestines strung all over my body.

I fall to the ground and into the pond with a splash and Zehlin falls right after. The water is shallow enough that I don't hit the bottom. I wonder how many people have fed this river, how many victims of this parasitic relationship between Spinner and the redcaps have suffered.

The red is all over me, that's all I can think about before I feel Zehlin's arms wrapped around me. I gasp for air, coughing the water and blood out of my mouth. I rub my eyes and open them. There's no more rope, and Spinner's head is left to slowly roll into the red puddle. Her body topples over, and crumples as she shrivels into a ball half her original size.

"Artea, I'm here. I'm here." He cradles me like a child. I can't help but shed tears. So many tears mixed with the blood, the water, the guts. It takes too much sobbing before I realize that there's a man standing in the dirt a few feet away from the pond.

It's the same man that we saved from the camp with the large white wings and broken back. My heart skips a beat, in a good way and a bad way. He is holding a sword covered in the same orange gunk that's all over my body.

"You're here. You're okay? Why are you here?" I ask him, crawling and swimming through the blood. My blood.

"Artea, I'm okay. Please you guys need help, I need to heal you." I can't think of any reason to reject him as my hands meet the cold mud. I pull myself out of the water and turn around to make sure Zehlin is out too.

We lay on our backs, my feet barely touching the water still. I cough the rest of the blood out of my mouth and turn my head to Zehlin. He looks at me too and all I can think is how grateful I am to still be looking at his eyes, the silver voids.

The man with wings, the Avian, walks over to us, dropping his sword. We helped him after he fell from the sky, so I don't even care to flinch when he kneels down to me and twists my neck to the opposite side, exposing the cut on my head through my hair.

The pain seeps back in the more I think about it and my vision threatens to fade out, but he holds one of his hands there for a moment and the pain is gone. The tiny cut meant to drain all of my blood assumingly disappears. He turns to do the same thing for Zehlin and he allows him to.

We walk over after some struggling to the same waterfall we drank from earlier and rinse off some of the blood in the water, letting the crystal clear liquid carry all of it away. We don't say a word, none of us. I decide to cut the silence.

"You killed the Spinner?" I ask, already knowing the answer.

The man turns to me and nods as we walk back over to the tree. We still have one more thing to do before the sun comes up or the redcaps come back. We can't let them catch us off guard like that again. "Yes, I followed you guys here from the military base down south. Your nurses did a wonderful job but I can heal myself, plus I wasn't here to slay a spider. In fact I had no idea why you guys left the base. I just needed to talk to you guys."

"Thank you for your help, but it can wait." Zehlin walks to the edge of the water and pauses, not wanting to get back into the red water. We need to get the bracelet now, before it's too late.

"I can take you guys over to the middle, to the tree," he suggests, aware that we are in a hurry to get something done. We both nod as I look at his feathery wings. He looks like he feels the need to help us, like he's useless without it. I don't know if his begging is pitiful or out of necessity. The tenseness I felt when I left the tent once we found him calms now that he's here. Why?

"Okay, yeah. Also, you can heal yourself too?" I say.

"It's complicated. I can heal everything, and sometimes bring them back to life." I've heard of healers being able to cure others, but never themselves. He takes us each one by one, flying us over a few meters to the middle, to the trunk of the tree.

"How do we get it out?" Zehlin and I stand next to each other, I run my hand along the brown bark that's hard as rock, wondering how this tree could contain a bracelet for so long.

"What have you been practicing for the last few days?" The general smirks at me, I smile back but realize that I don't have my gloves on. Zehlin and this man have been touching me this whole time. What if I were to hurt them, send them to the same fate that the plants have faced? Does my power even work on people?

I'm just lucky that it didn't go that way.

My black fingertips almost blend in with the dark brown of the tree as I place my hands on it. Quickly, with my focus, my power slowly eats through the tree. The tree's bark turns into ash as I work through it more and more, pushing my hands deeper in the tree trunk. Zehlin summons his light, turning the moonlight into visibility for me to see.

I take one of my hands and summon my own magic, making another, bigger cloud of smoke and death.

It travels along the branches, turning each inch of the giant tree into nothing. The dust flies down into the water, making it made up of more ash and blood than any kind of water.

Eventually, my other hand makes it all the way through the tree, almost to my shoulder. It's almost as if I'm sawing it down, searching every inch of it for this bracelet.

I'm starting to doubt that it's even here. Almost all of the branches have turned to dust by now. "Maybe it's not here, maybe the book lied or someone took it."

"It's here," Zehlin says, convinced. So, I keep going. "There."

He points to a shiny speck of gold poking out of the tree trunk, right below my arm. I disintegrate the rest of the wood around it and grab the bracelet. It really is here. This makes my confidence in the books and spells much higher than before. I was questioning the authenticity of the information that the queen and the general were given.

I stand corrected.

I decide to get rid of all of the rest of the tree, letting it float away into the wind and blood. The tree dies with the spider, the bleeding circle will not be used as a death web anymore.

I'm sure the redcaps will find another tree and another pond to ruin, but at least they'll have to hide their own bodies.

The man flies us back over to the solid ground and I slip the bracelet on, letting it fall into my left wrist. It's almost like the metal has a mind of its own as it tightens, constricts against my wrist. Not uncomfortably tight, but just enough that I can't slip it off.

Just like the ring.

Nothing happens, I don't feel anything immediately, just like at the bar all that time ago. Yet it was such a short amount of time.

I turn to Zehlin and he nods. Blood water is dried, dripped down his face.

"Thank you." Zehlin turns to the man. We seriously need to figure out his name. "What should I call you?" Always reading my mind.

"Klord works just fine. And you're welcome, but I wasn't tracking you down to save your life. I needed to find you guys alone."

We both share a confused expression, but we want to hear more so we keep our distance and listen. Zehlin seems tense like he's prepared for attack, which seems justified weighing the circumstances.

"This might sound like a lot, but Artea, you're my sister. Twin sister, actually," he pauses, I don't find it in myself to interrupt. *Twin?* "We were separated, when we were placed on the islands for protection. It would have been too risky to keep us together. Twins are only an elvish trait. But I'm back, and you need to know a few things."

Hold on. What?

Klord is my brother. What if he's lying? The more I look at him, however, the more it makes sense. He has the same caramel hair, the same deep brown eyes. He even has the ears, the pale skin, and the freckles. He *does* look a little like me, only taller and with wings.

"How are you my twin if you have wings? Both of my parents are elves, elves don't have wings."

"When I was brought to Avaris, someone put wings on me and they used magic to grow over time. They're a part of me now, to blend in with the other Avians," He looks eager, like he's waited a long time for this. I feel funny doing it, but I sit down on the grassy, muddy ground. The other two surprisingly follow suit. "I was forced to take the fesch root too. Just like you."

He was altered as a baby, just like me. He knows about the root, but how does he know? Zehlin looks just as lost as me.

"What did you mean we were put on the islands for protection? I thought I was left there because they couldn't face what they made. A weapon." I glare down at my hands, now decorated with two pieces of jewelry.

"No, Artea. That's what I'm here for. I've seen things on the bottom level of Avaris. The Deadland is full of nasty creatures and forbidden grounds, but underneath is even worse. There are caves full of crystals, purple crystals. They mine them, and use them to make dragmist. They send it all over the country and infect our people–"

I interrupt him and hold my hand up. "Who's they?"

Zehlin looks as if he wants to punch him. "Are you assuming I don't know what's going on in my own country?"

"*They* are hired by the queen. She tried to distribute it one hundred years ago until King Ector, our father, didn't like the idea of everyone getting their hands on it. The queen knew that the drug makes you easily susceptible to orders if you don't know you're taking it, and makes you insanely strong if you do. She wants the military to benefit off of it"

"Stop," Zehlin cuts him off. "You're saying that the queen wanted to mind control the entire archipelago?" Zehlin doesn't believe him and has a glint of murder in his eye.

Klord shows up and accuses Zehlin's cousin of over five hundred years of being a dictator. I don't blame him at all for wanting to cave his face in.

"And she still does." He has a begging look in his eye. "I've known the truth for about a year, I just have never made it this far to tell you. I only knew where you were because of a few Avians who are placed in Telik to monitor the sky."

"You have *spies* in my castle?" Zehlin nearly grunts his words through gritted teeth. He's standing up now, pacing to distract himself.

"Please, the queen is lying to you. And they're not *my* spies, I only hear things. Our father tore the bridges down because he wanted everyone to be safe so no one had to take the dragmist without knowing. She wanted to distribute it through food." The very thing that we are all short of right now. Zehlin tries to listen, but is more upset as time goes on. "She wants the bridges back so she can take control of everyone and boost her armies. That's why she trapped the dukes and duchesses, why they're in the deepest prisons, dying. I know she's your family, I know you won't believe me without proof. But Artea, please give me a chance. Etiza is bad news, and we were left here because Josephine and Ector thought it was the last place she would look. But she found you, and for some reason she hasn't found me."

Zehlin and I switch from glancing at each other to glancing at Klord. If any of this is true, that means that we're trying to get the bridges back for nothing. It means that the queen has been working against Zehlin and the rest of the people for over one hundred years. How did she manage to keep this quiet? Why didn't my parents say something?

It makes me wonder if Klord knows that Ector is still alive, that he's not dead like everyone believed when the war ended. Do I tell him? Would Zehlin be upset if he found out that I've known all this time?

"When we heard about the birth of Artea, we didn't hear of a twin. Where is your proof?" Zehlin glares, not pacing anymore, only staring.

Klord bows his head, still cross-cross on the ground like me. I can only look at him, analyze how any of this could be true, but it's all starting to make many of my confusions make more sense.

"I–I don't have any." He shifts his gaze to Zehlin. Just from that sentence Zehlin looks even more furious. "I know how powerful you are. One moment and I could be sent to Telik and executed for treason. Why would I risk my life just to lie to you?" He looks at me now. "I've known about you for a year now, I've been waiting for this. I know you felt something when you saw me, I felt it too, even in my unconsciousness. You're the death and I'm the life, we make up Josephine's power."

I nod because he's right, I do feel something when he's around me. The first time I saw him he felt like my responsibility, like it was on me to save him.

Torrid. Again, Torrid could be our proof. I impulsively yell for him as we need a medium in between Zehlin's anger and Klord's eagerness.

"Torrid! Torrid, I know you're there!" I yell up to the night sky, avoiding the death stare coming from the general. I hear a squawk, and a funny thing to hear in the middle of the night, so I know it's him.

He lands on the ground right in front of us, looking up with curious eyes. Klord looks confused, understandably, as I start talking to the bright colored bird. "Klord here says that Etiza is trying to use dragmist to control people, and to make her military strong. Is that true?"

I don't even know if just because he's out of the flask if his curse still stands, but this is the only way I can think right now that I can get Zehlin to avoid killing Klord.

"Yep. Wait, I can still do that. I can still hear the wind!" I don't even know what to say to anyone right now. Especially Zehlin. "She even wants to use the soldiers against Queen Josephine and King Ector. She wants to get rid of elves for good."

Klord gives me a look that doesn't say I told you so, but a begging one. He doesn't know Torrid can't lie, but Zehlin does.

"I don't know what to say." The general looks at the ground, hands dangling down his sides.

"How did you even find this out?" I question him, more curious about this winged healer.

Chapter Twenty-Five

(Zehlin)

Klord stands up with me while Torrid flies away again, Numen knows where he could be going.

That report is all we needed to know, Klord is telling the truth. Torrid also said Etiza wants to go to war with Queen Josephine *and* King Ector. Is he alive? It wouldn't surprise me. After all, his wife can raise the dead.

"Your aunt, Prim, and my Uncle Leve are married. Prim is Ector's sister, and my uncle couldn't hold it in any longer. He said I was old enough to know the truth, that he felt terrible for keeping the secret for so long. But now that you're working with her I can finally tell you. And, General, I'm sorry I have to come here like this, but it's important."

I try to control my breathing. Artea just found out she has even more elvish family planted in Avaris, a twin brother, and the queen she was willing to die for is trying to control her people. As much as she seems at ease, I can't seem to be.

"If she is able to get the dragmist out to everyone, she could control an entire population, an entire army," Klord emphasizes. "The army that's one tenth the size of Perdita's could wipe the elves out if they're hooked up on that dragmist. She's mad that Ector told her no, she's mad that he put out the flame to get in the way of her plan."

Torrid can't lie, meaning Etiza really has been working against the good of everyone for this long.

"Then what do we do?" I ask. "The people are dying, we can't just stop. Plus the book says that we must finish getting all seven pieces once we start, otherwise if we wait too long, the power could start eating at the wearer. We can't just stop."

Cutting off the plan from Etiza would be the easiest option, if we want Artea to die doing it and let the jewelry die with her.

"I have an idea," Klord starts walking away. I'm not sure why Artea and I follow him through the dark jungle, but we do. The sun is starting to come up now, and I can't stop looking at the anxious way Artea walks. I hope the bracelet doesn't make her sick like the shift and the ring did. "Etiza is too strong for us to make her upset. The worst thing that happens is we all get killed out of spite. Best case scenario, we are kept prisoners. We need to find a way to get rid of the dragmist operation while also bringing back the water ways, and doing it without suspicion."

We keep walking behind him, heading in the direction of Boronia. I'm not sure who made him in charge, but he knows the most about whatever is going on. Artea keeps close to his left while I linger a little bit behind.

"How do you suggest we do that?" I ask him from a distance, looking at the dark blue sky, slowly being lit by the sun, my power begging to be used.

"Well, I am from Avaris, and I can find out who is working for Etiza and flying the dragmist from there to Mava. I can find out ways to stop the mining. You guys just need to keep getting the jewelry like you've been doing. That way, the operation stays quiet."

I understand what he's saying perfectly, I've been in the military for far too long. "So we don't create panic in Mava. If they knew what's happening, we wouldn't have their support."

"Right," he makes an assuring gesture from ahead. "And we have no way to tell Josephine and Ector that we know why they started that war." *Josephine* and *Ector?* So, he *is* alive?

Artea speaks now. "But haven't elves been known for their violent nature for centuries now? Including Ector?"

He shakes his head and lowers it, lunging past a tiny creek. We all do the same thing. "Yes, but only in the archipelago. A long time ago, one of Etiza's ancestors fell in love with someone from Perdita, a woman. He wanted kids and she didn't. He tried to kill her once he found out she didn't want to carry out his bloodline. She fought back and killed him out of necessity, defense. Everyone blamed her and eventually hunted her down. Ever since then, elves have been depicted as terrible creatures by artists, writers, everyone. No elf ever stepped foot on an island since. Until Ector came and decided to try and work things out about four hundred years ago. They were allies for three hundred of those, and you know what the rest looks like. Even when they were allied, the islanders hated it."

How did I not know any of this? How has it been kept a secret from me this entire time, for years. I fought a war for her, I killed and shed blood for her. I tore families apart, all because they were trying to save us.

From her.

They never ate children or lured people with lust to kill them, they never hated fae. They always only ever wanted an alliance against greater evil. All because of Etiza, my family.

If she's having Avian spies transporting dragmist to the islands, it has to be in small amounts, but it's still enough to get people hooked. I've been aware that dragmist has been an issue, but we haven't been able to find where it comes from. Until today.

Even more lies.

Artea doesn't speak, she just walks. I guess we're both trying to consume the truth. It just seems easier for her. "Where do we start then?"

Klord shrugs and looks up at the sun-kissed dawn. "We go to Avaris so you guys can see what I'm talking about. I've seen it. We can also get the third piece, I'm not sure what it is. You guys know all about that. Etiza will still think that you guys are on your little mission while we stake out the Deadlands."

"What happens if she finds out?" Artea asks him, and I was thinking the same thing.

"We hope she doesn't find you. She wants you alive to spread the dragmist, you're the only chance to bring the flame back, and she can control people with her ability. I would just make sure that you can protect yourself."

"Well the chances she finds out are slim," I mention, my legs starting to burn from all of the walking, but my curiosity drowns it out to a subtle buzz. "She is smart, but she trusts me so she won't check in unless she doesn't hear anything. I'm sending frequent letters of progress already. She also doesn't know Artea has a twin, so she has no reason to think her truth might come out."

"Who else knows?" Artea asks, her breath sounds sparse as we keep going, almost quickening our pace out of frustration.

"The entire country of Perdita and us three, along with Uncle Leve and Aunt Prim. How has she been since you left?" Klord asks her, familiarity blooms in his voice.

I already know this answer, I cringe at it before she speaks. "She's back in Perdita. I don't know who she is there. And now I know she was sent back there because she was protecting me. I was hidden, as a human, out of protection. And Etiza still found me."

"Yeah, she's powerful," I mumble, trying to avoid the anxiety of knowing what might happen if she knows that we found out about her plan.

"But she can't travel without me," I realize. She can't come and check in on us anywhere unless she wants to risk her life on a ship. Even the strongest queen can't cross these oceans.

"You're right, I didn't think about that. Until I can get all seven pieces and get the bridges up, she can't go anywhere." Artea glances at me behind her for a moment until she turns back around.

"So, we just keep doing what we're doing and hope we can finish this before Queen Josephine and King Ector find their way here. We don't need more bloodshed."

Klord points out, I almost forgot that we had intel that they were planning on infiltrating us again. I wonder why they would even bother. Maybe they want to help get rid of the dragmist, maybe they want to get rid of Etiza. Or maybe Artea's aunt went and told them we have Artea.

"Your aunt could have warned them that you were gone. Maybe they're coming for you. We didn't get word that they are sizing up for war until we found you. Maybe they want to avoid Klord getting captured too." I offer, sighing at the complications.

"No, they're smarter than that. They knew the fire had to be put out to stop distribution, they also had to realize that Etiza wants the bridges back. They know I'm powerful enough to execute it," her voice almost shakes, and I want to tell her I'm sorry. How sorry I am that I helped Etiza turn her into a tool, just to break down other people. All for a crystal. "They know Etiza is using me as a means to an end."

"Do we want to tesser back? It's getting light and I'm hungry." I suggest lightly, I need to get off of my feet and sleep. I could also use a moment to make this all make sense.

For five hundred years she's been my best friend, she helped me through murdering my father, I helped her through her parents' deaths. I have carried out every single order she's given me. We have been through every single stage of life together, in that very castle.

And now I have to throw it all away because she's sucked up in the power. She's too far gone. I don't know how I didn't notice it sooner.

The constant reading, the obsession with Artea's life, the curiosity of the cattle and the crops. She made it seem like she was concerned about the archipelago's food supply dropping. She covered everything up perfectly.

They both turn around, but Artea hesitates. She doesn't have her gloves and she's only learned to control her manifestations, not her hands.

"I can grab your arm." I smile and Klord looks confused as ever.

"You'll see, just take his hand." Artea says and giggles. I bet she's excited to see someone else's reaction to tessering.

Klord's hand takes mine, it's surprisingly soft, like a baby. I grip Artea's forearm and will us to the base. Artea is still standing, which is a first, but Klord tumbles to the ground on his knees and balances himself with his palms on the muddy ground.

Some of the base is waking up, some are running, others are opening shops, some have been out for what seems like all night training. Since there might be a war on the horizon, I made sure to let the other leaders know to have a prepared army.

"That... was." He coughs, and I tap his back hard enough to knock the wind out of him. He stops coughing and puts a hand to his chest, breathing heavily. "Better, thank you."

He attempts to stand and Artea only looks a little sick, an improvement from previous times. She lets out a small giggle and I smile in response. The reality of what just happened hits us like a brick. We're safe now, but we weren't.

The redcaps, Spinner, the blood, the new twin.

The truth.

Before he decided to head back to Avaris and get a place ready for us, Klord, Artea and I made a plan. After a day of rest, we will head to Avaris with Aleck and look for our next piece. I will keep sending Etiza letters as normal and let her know our progress, but I won't tell her I know what she's doing. We will do this fast, take breaks when needed, and try to stay alive. Avaris has spies for Etiza as well so we are going to make sure to stay extra vigilant. We are going to stay in Klord's neighborhood as he says he has an extra bedroom for us to use if we need to. Then after we get the next piece, which is another ring, we will move on to Seglona, the frozen island, which houses the necklace.

I don't know how long I can keep Artea alive, and I don't know how long it'll be before the reality of Etiza's betrayal will hit me. I know it's true, I know it makes sense, but I never thought she would do such a thing.

I swore to never end up like my father, and she swore to never end up like the rulers before. She wanted her people to be happy, and her dukes and duchesses to be equal. She didn't want to undermine their word on their islands. She wanted everyone to feel like they were meant to be here, and protected.

Now the dukes and duchesses are stuck in the basement prison, ordered by me because she told me that they were all secretly helping the King and Queen of Perdita. Even more manipulation so no one can be warned when the dragmist makes its way to the food supply.

Artea has been planted as the head of the people and the face of an operation that's a death wish. Even if she survives getting all the pieces, she might not even survive the vigorous ritual. That is only possible if we can keep this quiet and avoid the spies or anyone willing to sell our information for money.

This is why Klord had to leave as soon as possible. We didn't want anyone from here recognizing us with him, just to be safe.

The Bleeding Circle is temporarily taken care of, we've found the second piece, and we're on to our third piece one day ahead of what we originally planned before we started.

And I'm fucking livid.

PART IV

(The Intersection)

Chapter Twenty-Six

Avaris is a deadly kind of beautiful. All three of us get tessered on to a landing deck made for winged fae to enter on and off of. It's an easy way for transports to be carried on their backs and flown to other parts of the island. Or in our case, other islands.

Klord flew Aleck across at a quick pace, only taking about an hour so the tessering could be easier on Zehlin as he would only have had to carry me. He's not as tired looking as last time, but his pace is slow and weakened. How Klord is strong enough to hold Aleck, I don't know. We had to leave the wagons in Boronia unfortunately, but we all have our rucksacks and weapons.

We walk through the transport area and get many looks, but we don't care because there's no reason to. We are only going to stay here for the day, stay the night, and then leave in the morning. We make sure to walk and look as regular as possible because we don't know who could be a spy for the queen.

I want to scream.

I want to tell them to show themselves, that the dragmist is hurting people, that they're criminals.

Everyone is carrying crates or barrels and loading them into airships made of wood and steel or onto other's backs. Avians don't only fly, but they also can have their own unique powers. Most are able to control wind and sometimes weather. I learned this from one of the many books in the basement of the Telik castle. Because of this, they are able to make the airships soar in the sky, treating the air like water.

I walk over to what seems to be the entrance into the town, through a large white and silver archway that reflects the sunlight in a similar way that Zehlin does. It's magnificent.

Aleck and Zehlin stay close behind me, keeping a bored but hard look on their faces. In their eyes, my cargo is more important than any amount of dragmist that could ever be made. They're there for strategic placement, not because they're gentlemen. Or at least I don't think so.

I also realized that the dragmist has to be made, meaning it's mined in the Deadlands but is also tampered with here before it's transported out. Klord decided he will search for any suspicious areas or scientists to find the heart of the operation.

We pass people of all kinds of different looks. Some have all white hair and white skin, almost like walking snowflakes, similar to Klord. Others are all red, or all black, all with feathery wings like Klord's. They all have siren eyes and thick facial hair on the men, or accentuated figures on the women. Some of them shamefully are eating each other's lips as we walk by, not even bothering to glance in our direction. Most of them have very revealing clothing on, some wear nothing. The ones who *do* glance are calculating, and I'm sure it's because we look much different than them.

And we aren't as indecent or confident as them either.

The walkways are made up of white rock that shine in the skylight. We are very high up, so high that I could look at the clouds leveled with my feet when we were at the transport edge.

Tall structures stand even higher than the ground made up of blue, gold, and white rocks, carved hundreds and hundreds of years ago. Water falls down the edges of Avaris like tears, like the upper island mourns for the Deadlands, trying to feed it.

It's hard to ignore the dark void below us. I'm not totally sure what's down there, but I'm told that I don't want to know. Aleck said one time that the Deadland is the hell on earth. The creatures, the death, the smell.

It makes me wonder who the miners for the dragmist crystals are, and how dangerous they must be to run an operation so fragile, yet demanding in an area like that.

The looks don't stop as we continue our walk to the capital of Avaris. Zehlin said we needed to check in with the wife of the previous duke, Rognvaldr. He disappeared, now in a prison being held by Etiza just like the others. His wife is supposed to give us an idea of where the Dragonborn Witch is, then we will be able to take the next ring I need from her.

It's rumored that the ring is still in her possession, and that she practically lives forever. She is the offspring of a dragon and a fae, making her one of the most powerful and durable creatures in the world. I have no clue how those two creatures can breed and frankly I don't need to find out.

She's the stuff of fairy tales, like the Loch Ness Monster. Except she actually exists, and no one has bothered to confront her. Because people avoid her and her terrifying hut of magic and spells, King Ector decided that a safe place to put the ring would be with her.

The only problem is that she's notorious for her selfishness and inability to cooperate when it comes to magical items. So, it's not like we need to fight a monster or shatter a tree or bathe in blood, we just need to get her to hand over the ring. Apparently she's also notorious for making deals, expensive ones too.

But we don't know where in Avaris she resides, so we need Rognvaldr's wife's help to locate her. I don't know how she can help, but we will take anything.

"This is supposed to only take one day, correct? Does the duchess even know we're coming?" I ask the general behind me while I keep my pace even and stern, cloaking the scared girl with the elvish soldier.

"Yes, she knows we're coming. I actually had Torrid send her a message. He flew with Aleck and Klord." I smile at the trust that Zehlin has in Torrid. Maybe he's grateful that he was able to find out the truth about Etiza, about his closest friend. I'm also glad that Torrid must be safe,

I was worried about him. But he's free now, so he will come and go as he chooses, he deserves it.

I see a large white and blue tower with several points spread across the roof. There are large windows made of clear crystal panes lined with silver metal that shine in the light. The castle is smaller than Telik's but large, nonetheless.

"That's the place, huh?" I marvel at the architecture, barely able to pay attention to the flying horses and the winged fellow around me.

"This is her, one of the most intricate buildings ever made. I've been to many places with Zehlin, he's given me the privilege to see so many places, so much beauty." Aleck's mouth almost hangs open as we finally set foot on the main walkway that leads to a staircase, and at the top is the door. Everything is so white, yet my eyes don't burn. I take in the sights as all of these things are things I've never seen before.

They don't know how lucky they are.

We walk through the door, let in by two soldier-looking Avians with large navy blue wings and dark black hair. Their armor is black and silver, matching the silver lining in the windows and the pathways.

"Welcome. I'm so glad you made it," a woman's voice grabs my attention. I turn my head to the left, the men standing on both of my sides. She is young, too young to be a duchess even by marriage, at least I'd hope so. Her hair is dark brunette and her skin is a tan color, close to burning sand. She wears a purple dress that drags on the crystal floor as she walks towards us. She's also quite short, a couple inches shorter than me. I start to feel informal in my thin armor cloth and my straps.

"Tonya, it's great to see you again. Our travels were safe, and we have a place to stay after we find the witch tonight. We–" Zehlin gets ready to explain our mission before Tonya interrupts him.

"I know, you need to talk to my mother." So, she's Rognvaldr's daughter, that makes sense. "She's actually in her study now, if you'd like to get it over with. I know she's not excited, but it needs to be done."

I suddenly feel a short ache, right in my chest. The gold band of the bracelet from Ornau feels like it's tightening, but I look at it and don't see any changes. It's getting warmer, like a small fire is being lit on my wrist. It doesn't burn, it only simmers. I start to feel soft memories, like a distant one from years and years ago. One that isn't mine. It's similar to the distance I felt when I was searching Mateo's head with the ring from Ihrvian, or when I got the vision from Zehlin. This time, Zehlin is calling to me with this bracelet. The warm feeling I'm getting is his. He feels nostalgic about Tonya, he feels a sort of familiarity with her.

I can feel Aleck's emotions too, it seems, and he's annoyed. I'm not sure what he's annoyed with, but that's what the bracelet is telling me. Being able to sense what their emotions are feels like an intrusion so I push the feeling away before following behind the three of them deeper into the castle.

Out of curiosity I try to analyze what Tonya is feeling, if she's reciprocating Zehlin's, but I can't find anything. Every time I try to manifest the power, like I did with Mateo, it's like I hit a brick wall. I can't search for her emotions like I can with the other two.

"It's been a long time, Zehlin," she coos, I can hear the smile on her face. An embarrassing amount of jealousy rises in my throat before I shove it down. Who is she to him? "And you too Aleck."

"It has, how have you been?" Our footsteps echo across the wide ceilings. Her heels make an extra loud clink compared to the rest of us. "We left off on odd terms."

I sense a massive amount of discomfort in Zehlin after his statement, and regret. "You're right, we did, didn't we? I guess arranged marriages don't usually work out when the bride can't feel anything."

Tonya mentions this so nonchalantly I almost stop in my path but force myself to follow, and Zehlin is not only filled with regret but with sadness. I wonder if he missed her.

"I guess so." He subtly tilts his head toward me and looks ahead again, he's embarrassed for me. The memory of us almost kissing in the ring is as distant as any dream.

This also explains why I can't dig for Tonya's emotions, she can't feel them. I wonder who arranged this marriage, and why would they arrange it with such a young woman and an older general. He doesn't look like it, but he's five centuries old.

"Arranged?" I decide to ask. I hope Zehlin doesn't notice my jealousy and mistakes it for curiosity.

"My father and Etiza arranged it," Tonya answers. "The queen of the archipelago technically has the right to marry away anyone she pleases. But Zehlin and I were going to do it willingly once we heard. It was a good military based idea and benefited Avaris greatly. This was twenty years before the war, of course."

"Before?" I ask, confused by the youth reflected from this young woman.

"Yes, before. I look like this because Avians age slowly, just like elves. You should know this, no?" she asks, turning around and looking at me as we stop at a large wooden door. It strikes in comparison to the rest of the white, blue, and silver castle.

So, she knows I'm an elf. I didn't know how much she already knew about this whole endeavor. I guess I do look different from any regular fae. "I'm still getting used to the islands."

"I see." She speaks with suspicion.

Zehlin is tense as the wooden door swings open revealing another large library with a single desk at the very end of the room in front of us.

A woman stands at the end of it far away from us, her palms leaning on the wood. I assume it's Rognvaldr's wife as we all walk in the room and she looks up from the desk and smiles.

"Dear Tonya, Zehlin, Aleck. It's so good to see you two again. It's been a long time." She takes a couple steps to the side and gives Zehlin and

Aleck each a hug. They smile back and nod. "Well, you have a busy schedule, so we should get right into it."

She gestures her hand to me, guiding me to walk forward to the desk. I find out it's not just a desk, but a map table. It looks like a map of Avaris, though I'm not totally familiar with the island masses. There is the capital of Avaris, Hellon, and a few other towns labeled, however.

"I'm sorry, what's your name?" She asks me, I don't know hers either so I don't blame her. I walk into her castle as an elf and don't even bother introducing myself.

"I'm Artea, the exiled soldier of Perdita. I'm sure you know why I'm here." At the mention of Perdita, I feel a hint of fear linger from the wife. I try not to shrink from the shame.

It's all a lie. But we have to keep the truth quiet to avoid riots, or full on rebellion. The woman has sun blonde hair and cream colored wings to pair it with. Her icy blue eyes are hard to ignore in contrast to her long white dress, similar to Tonya's.

"Pleasure to meet you. I'm Duchess Sephyr, the late duke's wife. I'm in charge of most things around here, but mostly I'm here to help you locate my sister." Sister? How can a dragonborn woman be sisters with an Avian? "Half-sisters. Her father was a dragon but we have the same mother. She's older than me, quite older. But since I'm her only blood left, I'm able to track her. I haven't done this in decades."

I look at the table below us and see that not only is there a map, but there's also a bowl full of green and purple herbs mixed together with some sort of liquid. The bowl illuminates a small area with green light. It's faint, but it's magic.

Sephyr wastes no time. She dips her hand in the bowl and covers it with the liquid, leaving only the herbs inside. She drags her fingers and palm across the map and drenches the whole paper.

She starts a light chant, it sounds ancient, almost like the chanting I heard when Etiza cast the spell on me, unlocking my powers with her magic. It makes me sick that I was grateful for her at one point.

The map's edges start to disintegrate as she speaks, tiny flames burn the paper away. Tonya moves to her mother, gripping her arm. The look in her face is concerned, but she stays looming at her side. It looks like Sephyr is hurting as she chants, as she makes the map smaller and smaller.

Everyone is quiet and lets her make the map smaller. I think she's making it smaller by finding the witch. It starts to shrink in odd ways, taking paths in all directions. Then she stops chanting and slams her hand on the map aggressively. The rest of it disappears except for one small piece.

Sephyr points to it, smiling. "I still got it," Zehlin and Aleck smile too, both glad that we got her location quickly. "She's only a few miles north of the edge of Hellon. It shouldn't hurt you at all to tesser there. She's much closer than I thought she'd be"

It shouldn't surprise me just how much she knows about Zehlin, a general should meet with his fellow leaders often.

"I want to thank you, Your Grace, for helping us. I know we didn't leave on the best terms, but this means so much." Zehlin shakes the woman's hand and Tonya keeps her head down. But before I can look away from her, we make brief eye contact. She looks back to her mother immediately.

The marriage or proposal must not have gone well. Maybe Tonya rejected him last minute. Maybe Zehlin refused to marry a woman who couldn't feel anything. Maybe one of them wanted kids, and the other didn't. I'm dreading my constant interest in this woman who looks as young as me yet has to be at least ten times older.

"Mother, are you all right? That looked painful?" Tonya asks, holding her mother's hand that was previously covered in a concoction of unnamable ingredients.

"I'm quite good, I'm less in pain and more happy that I can still use my magic." Aleck secures a few of his straps and clears his throat before he speaks.

"We should go so we can finish by nightfall," he says sternly. I'm sure Klord debriefed him on the new information before we got here. He has been a little bit upset since we got here and hasn't spoken much. For someone who likes to run their mouth, he hasn't taken many opportunities to.

"Thank you, for the short hosting. It was wonderful to meet you both, your castle is beautiful. It has considerable competition compared to Telik's." I smile.

Tonya and Sephyr both smile back, almost chuckling. They look like sisters standing next to each other, deadly sisters. Something about Tonya's demeanor worries me. Maybe it's the inability to feel anything, or maybe she knows I don't belong here, that I'm a liar.

"We are more than happy to help Zehlin, he protects his people well. We trust him." Tonya tilts her chin down, walking toward him. "It's a big job."

They hug each other. Zehlin keeps his arms loose, but Tonya's are tight. He seems uncomfortable, he doesn't want to hug her. She glances at me while they hug, her ear against his lower chest. She grins, but in an unfriendly way. Something tells me she is trying to scare me off, or mark what used to be hers.

The real question that's bothering me is who called off the marriage?

Him or her?

They each pull out of the hug and Zehlin gives a pity smile. I feel more impatience roam from Aleck's body the longer it takes for them to say their goodbyes.

"Well, we'll be here if you need anything. Just avoid the Deadlands while you can, you know the things that roam that place," Sephyr warns us, looking at me and my ears subtly, or at least she tries to be subtle. Her wings flap like a horse's tail chasing a fly before she starts walking away from the table towards the door.

She escorts us out of the room and closes the door behind us. Tonya thankfully stays in there with her.

"She's bad news," I whisper to no one in particular while we walk out to the main door of the castle. I try to hold in my own frustration but the cold shivers of my power call to me. Great, my body wants to kill things when I'm upset.

Not very good for anger management.

"Bad news?" Zehlin breathes a chuckle as we walk out, the cool air hitting my face quickly. It makes sense that the higher elevation gives the entire upper island a constant cool breeze.

"When she hugged you, she looked at me like I was food. Yes, she's bad news. And there's obviously a reason the wedding was called off."

"Wait, why are you so invested in a wedding that almost happened over a century ago?" Aleck asks, seemingly speaking Zehlin's mind too. I can feel Zehlin's amusement and I want to kick him for it. This makes me sound like I'm obsessed with him. Aleck's right, why should I care?

"I'm not invested, I'm just curious." I shrug.

"Don't worry, Angel. She's no competition. She relies on her wings too often in battle." He shakes his head, joking. I stay behind the two of them to hide my irritation. Is she a soldier as well? Did she fight in the war with him?

"Competition? You're not territory, nor do I want to fight over you. You're the last person I would want to fight over. Especially since you sit around with your military crown on and expect everyone to give you what you want. The pet names, pinning me to the ground and almost kissing me, treating me like I can't handle this."

Even my own words surprise me. But it's all true. Zehlin's ego is the size of all of the islands combined and then some, he's been treating me like glass this whole time even when I've asked him to stop. I can sense Aleck's wave of shock like a brick.

"Angel, I think protecting you and treating you like a child are two very different things. Plus, I know you like being called these names, you turn red when I do. And this isn't me being cocky, it's me telling the truth."

I stop walking and cross my arms, feeling a little ridiculous. "I know you loved it in the ring, so don't even start with that."

I hate that he's right and I'm feeling more and more irrational the more I open my mouth. "Fine, if I need to be protected then don't bring me to the witch at all. Let me stay here in Avaris, explore. You said it yourself that I need to learn more, so I'll be hands on with it. You don't *need* me to get the ring, you just need to get it *to* me. Right?" I ask him. They're both turned around facing me, visibility irritated with my antics. I don't blame them, I only want to prove Mr. Right-All-the-Time wrong.

"I guess we can do that. You'd be safer here too, yes. You sure you don't want to go?" Zehlin grins and shrugs challengingly, his brown hair and sculpted face look like art in this light. It makes me wonder if he's doing it on purpose, shifting the light to benefit himself. His face is equally as testing as mine.

"Yes, I would like to stay. That is, if you think you'll be okay without me?" I claim, looking around at the streets of the capitol. The people are much different from me, I stand out. Plus the queen definitely has spies here somewhere, or at least folks that transport her dragmist.

"All right, stay here in Hellon. We'll convince the dragonborn to give us the ring and we'll get it back to you. Just please make sure you're taking care of yourself." He only mentions it for the hundredth time.

"Yes, see–?" I begin before he interrupts me. While taking a step forward, leaving only a foot of space between us, he speaks softly.

"You're important to me, Artea. And you're important to a lot of other people. All I ask is that you honor that. You're not a child, or a weak human, you're important. Do you understand that?" He speaks to me like a general. Not like a flirting friend, or a mission accomplice.

I can only nod in response because he's right as usual.

"Good. Just handle your own until we get back. I'm trusting you, that means I don't think you're weak, okay?"

Why do I care what he thinks? This is frustrating.

But he trusts me.

"Okay, yeah I'll be around. How will I know when you're back?" I ask him, happy that he's actually letting me stay here. I don't know if he'd actually stop me though.

"Wait, you're actually letting her stay?" Aleck asks, looking back and forth between us. I roll my eyes and consider knocking the guy over, not that I'd make much progress.

"I'll just go to Klord's at dusk and hope you're there or get there after," I say. Klord showed us his house before we got to the transportation dock. I think I'll remember it by the time dusk falls. Zehlin nods and Aleck gives a half-hearted one as well. "Just don't lose the ring on your way back."

I chuckle as I joke, but I'm also serious. That would severely mess things up.

Nobody says anything else which leaves it settled before Zehlin and Aleck disappear, tessering into the witch's territory. I wonder if it's a creepy hut filled with wood carvings and potions. Or maybe she holds gold like dragons do. Or maybe she's just a possessive woman who's very easy to persuade.

I doubt that last option, but I like to stay hopeful.

I also don't like that Zehlin was right at all, and when I was trying to prove that I wasn't a child I sounded extra childish. To be fair, he has a few centuries on me so I don't know if I can do anything without sounding like a child.

I decide to look around me as I'm in the heart of Hellon, the capital of Avaris. It's been described as one of the most beautiful cities in the archipelago and it is. It has more diversity than Telik, that's for sure. I look above me and see faeries flying solo, some on pegasi. The pegasi look like regular horses except they're about double the size and have wings that span teen feet wide. My mouth hangs open as I wonder what I'm going to do until Zehlin and Aleck get back.

I look at the people passing by me as I walk aimlessly through the side streets, they all seem upset once they see me. None of them are near as friendly as the fellow in Ornau, and I got a death threat there so the line is pretty low.

A light blue sign catches my eye while I walk. It's old and faded away, so it's hard to tell what it says, but it looks interesting. The building is made of molding wood but there's people walking in and out of it frequently. I walk towards the door and walk in.

It seems to be a tavern of sorts as drunken men and women lean over the counter for more drinks or stumble to the washroom. The air is muggy from the ale, but it's oddly easy to breathe because being so high up is a natural air filter.

I walk over to the main bar and look at the array of alcohols. I decide to settle on a simple faerie wine, so I ask the bartender.

I get a nasty look from him, but he doesn't refuse. I have a few coins in my pocket, and I assume it should cover it.

He doesn't take long before I have my drink and I take a sip. The goblet is large, bigger than what we serve in Halistyn. The taste is so sweet it seems to melt my taste buds and slither down my throat, it's better than anything I've served or tried before. The color is a deep red and almost feels like blood as I continue to take the beverage down.

It's empty before I can think about it and I ask for another. While I wait, I feel someone tap my shoulder. It's a young woman with pink skin, dark purple hair, and pink fiery wings that are smaller than others I've seen.

She takes the seat next to me and taps the table. The bartender hands me my drink and starts making hers. She didn't have to say anything, so I notice she's a regular.

"One of your friends will be dead by the time they come to find you at dusk," she says.

I whip my head to her and immediately feel sick and I'm not sure if it's the wine or the quick movement. "Excuse me?" I ask her, the disgust on my face is prevalent as I examine her face.

"I could feel Sephyr looking for me. It hurts you know, when she tracks me like that. Feels like a blade to the back while she burns that map." The witch receives her drink and swallows it in two gulps, then taps the counter again, visibility enraged.

"You're the witch." I laugh in hilarity. How did she find me? And if she's here, what is going on with the guys?

She smiles wide and deep, her pride in the title is clear "I am. But I'd like to say I'm more of a contractor."

"What do you mean one of them will die?" I clench my teeth but keep a stone stature. *You're an elvish soldier.*

"In my home, there's no powers allowed to be used except mine. And by contractor, I mean I make bonded deals." I already don't like this. Deals with a witch. "I promised them I'd make sure that when I met with you, you'd stay safe. In return, I wanted them to fight to the death using pure strength and skill. They reluctantly agreed. I thought it was extremely pathetic the way they wanted to protect a silly elvish girl. Wasting a life for you."

I start to break a sweat, hoping that they'll find a way out. Magic is a tricky thing, but even right now magic was used to take the flame down and I'm using magic to reverse it.

"How did you find me? What do you want?" I glare my eyes, trying to ignore the glossiness of them caused by the wine. The air in the tavern starts to feel heavy, and I know it's just the alcohol but it starts to get overwhelming quickly.

"It doesn't matter how I found you, what matters is I have what you're looking for in my pocket, and I want to make a deal for it."

She wants to run a deal for the ring, but what could she want from me.

Chapter Twenty-Seven

I shake my head, resisting drinking the next glass the bartender gave me. "I don't have anything to give you," I attempt to shut her down. "Where's the general?"

"Oh, darling, but here's where you're wrong. An elf is hard to find around here, damn near impossible. All I need is a vial of your blood, and the ring is yours. Of course I will tell you where your friends are, but you aren't allowed to kill me. Ever." She swallows her next drink and her purple eyes almost pierce through me. All she wants is my blood and I can get Zehlin and Aleck back, plus the ring. "That's my contract offer to you." She speaks so indifferently like she does this every day, and she most likely does.

It seems obvious what my choice should be. I'd probably have to magically bond the contract, she wouldn't let up such a valuable item without insurance. I sense a heavy feeling of confidence coming from her. She knows that the trajectory of my life is in her hands now. She feels powerful, and the bracelet giving me this feeling makes me receive a wave of intoxication because of it.

No wonder she comes in here and threatens my entire plan like this, she's strong and knows it.

"What do you need to use my blood for?" I know it's a stupid question, she's a witch, she needs all kinds of things to mix with others. I honestly don't care what she uses it for, I already know my answer.

She chuckles and shakes her head, taking a small brown bag out of her pocket just like the one Gunter took out in Halistyn. "That's none of your concern, young one. Are you taking the deal or not?"

I can save Zehlin and Aleck, neither of them have to die. I can get the next piece of the seven that I need. I can move on like none of this happened.

The wine starts to hit me like a gust of wind and I grab the small bag from her hand quickly. Well, as quickly as I can. "Fine, yes."

She nods and leans into my ear. "That's all I needed." She leans away, her back straight again. "They're exactly where Sephyr said they were. Walk only a few miles north, you'll get there before the sun goes down. And you'll find out what can break the contract soon enough. You'll be desperate, you'll break. Just pray to Numen that you can save both of them."

She holds a hand out, I assume she wants my blood now that the pleasantries are over. I give her my hand, but it feels like my arm moves on its own, the contract already in motion.

She doesn't use a blade, or anything other than her sharp, dragonborn fingernail. She cuts a large slit on my right wrist, not the left where the bracelet sits tightly. Blood starts trickling down quickly but I don't feel any pain. It's an odd sensation, not feeling anything at all. If anything, I feel like I'm on a cloud, literally and metaphorically. My eyes start to drift when I blink and the blood dripping into the vial the witch holds doesn't faze me at all.

It feels amazing, and I don't want it to stop anytime soon.

The vial gets full and she closes it up. She stands up, but before leaving she places a kiss on my cheek. "Pleasure doing business with you, Artea."

I don't ask how she knows my name, it would be pointless. Instead, I turn to the front of the counter and drop a few coins on it. I stand up, acclimating myself to the feeling. I've drank before, but this feels different. I feel out of my control in a wonderful way. I want to dance, I want to sing, I want to tell all of these Avians who I am. I want to shout that I'm going to save them all, help them be better again. I want to admit that their queen is a lying nightmare and wants to control them. Maybe one of her spies is in this very room.

I ignore all of that and walk out of the building, knowing my intent. The sun hits me hard and I squint my eyes, letting them adjust before heading north. I remember where Sephyr said we should go, so I continue walking until the city buildings die out and I find myself walking on dirt paths through cherry blossom forests. I'm a woman with a purpose, I will prove that I can do this by myself.

It took about two hours for me to walk, then take a detour, and walk again for me to find the area that Sephyr located. The map, luckily, was colored. She pointed to a spot with green trees, and there have only been pink or orange ones until now, so I know this is the place. I walk deeper into this chunk of the woods until I find a small wooden cottage. It looks very friendly, not very dragon-y or witch-y to me. Either way, I walk over to it and immediately hear muffled banging coming from the inside.

This walk has been very sobering, and the banging is too. I try to open the brown, rustic door, but it won't budge. I toss my shoulder and body weight into it over and over again, hearing wood splintering with each thrust.

The door breaks on its hinges and I almost stumble to the floor. I take a second to examine the cottage. It's warm with furniture, a stove, a few seats and sofas. There are book shelves that are now toppled onto the floor and there are two shirtless men slamming each other into walls right next to me.

Aleck pushes Zehlin into the wall where the bookshelf used to be and they both grunt, not in a light way either, they're both seemingly in a lot of pain. I see black eyes, so much blood dripping from cuts on their bodies, bruises already showing. I'm only hoping there are no broken bones.

Have they been at this for the past two hours? More? Are they really trying to kill each other like the witch said?

"Stop! Zehlin! Aleck, let go of him!" Neither of them respond to my cries, not even a turn of a head. They are by contract obligated to carry the deal out, unless I can find a way to stop it.

I summon my power, my natural one. The dark cloud rises from the wooden planks this time, slowly making its way into the air in front of me. Maybe if I threaten both of them, it will stop them from brawling.

I make the black mist hover over both of their heads, trying to avoid getting bumped into or hit by any flying debris. They have no reaction, so I make it hover closer and closer until I'm not comfortable with accidentally letting it touch one of them. Who knows what it would do?

I decide to take it away and hear a blood curdling groan from Zehlin. Aleck had taken a shard of glass and stabbed it into his back. Without his powers, and without the natural healing ability of the fae, he is just a body. He's as sensitive to any punishment as any human.

How are my powers working here? She said no powers can work here. Why am I so often an exception? It's getting tiring trying to know what rules apply and don't apply to me.

With no attention from either of them, and more cuts and blood appearing by the moment I dash into both of them. I use all of my strength and try to pry them apart, yet they still reach each other like cats in a rucksack. I can already feel the blood getting on my arms and hands making my grips on them slip. I turn to Zehlin, the fear of my hands killing him is far too gone in my mind. He has tears in his eyes, and they are almost falling. His under eyes are both black and his nose looks broken. I struggle to not tear up from seeing him like this, like a feral, lonely animal.

"Zehlin, look at me. I don't know how to stop this but you have to remember who Aleck is. This contract, it can be broken. But you have to hear me, please!" His eyes are glossed over and he still doesn't look at me. They both try to push me away but I hold on. I honestly have no idea how I'm still standing.

They stop trying to pry at each other, but they don't back down either. I push Zehlin by his chest as hard as I can to create some distance.

"Zehlin, it's me." He still doesn't seem like himself. He looks like a bear, only instinct, no thought. I know he's still in there, watching himself beat his best friend to death. "I'm right here, just remember where you are and who we are. You don't have to do this. Look, I have the ring. This is all pointless, you don't have to hurt him anymore."

I don't know how to stop this other than begging. He walks slowly to me, it's hard for me not to back away into Aleck as he makes his way over. He stops only a few inches from me, his chin only a breath's distance away from mine. I look up to his eyes, they're still grey. They still have the blue swirls, the sunlight seems to want to answer them, but it doesn't. He only stares at me. First my eyes, then the rest of my face.

He takes me in, but there's still no thought. He's so dazed into whatever trance the witch put him into. Why would they agree to this? Did they really want to sacrifice themselves for me? This makes me feel useless.

He brings a hand up to my face and I stop myself from flinching. "It's me, that's your best mate, your best soldier." I point to Aleck. "We have a war to prepare for, Zehlin. Just remember who you are." I whisper while his hand reaches my cheek, his calloused hands are rough on my skin but he's never been gentler. I've only been touched by him when we've fought, I never realized how much I needed his comfort.

I lean into his hand and just as I do, I'm across the room. The room starts to dim and my vision goes in and out. I rub my cheek and feel the warm tenderness of the hardest hit I've ever endured. I turn my body, groaning and twisting through the pain. He hit me so hard I broke a side table as I landed, I gain a few splinters while trying to get up.

They're back to fighting.

What did I think was going to happen? I was going to magically make him go back to normal? That I could snap him out of this daze he can't get out of? I want to kill that witch for not telling me how to break this spell.

She needed my blood for something, something important. So, she doomed my only protection I had and got what she wanted. Then walked away for the mess to be left to me.

My head is throbbing but I manage to keep my eyes open. Zehlin has Aleck in a headlock on the floor. The floor is starting to become more blood than carpet as they roll around only a few feet away from me.

I can't give up on them now, not when they have stood by me this whole time.

I lunge forward, my body practically moving on its own as I scratch and pry at Zehlin's arms to get him to let go of Aleck. I use the bracelet to feel for something, maybe I could get a sense of how they're feeling, maybe I can find out if they're still in there. I sense Zehlin's enragement but Aleck is *amused*?

Why would Aleck be excited to be fighting his best friend? Trying to kill him?

I continue trying to pull them apart, focusing on the task at hand. Zehlin is on the floor, his back to the ground while holding Aleck by the neck. Aleck is clearly struggling to breathe, his face slowly turning a sharp shade of purple.

"Zehlin! Let go, for Numen's sake!" I jam my arms in between the two men and use every bit of my strength to get them apart. Zehlin throws Aleck to the side and he hits a wooden piece of furniture, cracking to pieces like I did.

I expect Zehlin to run to Aleck and finish the job, but instead he turns to me. He sits up and jerks his body on top of mine. I get knocked on to my back and his hands go around my neck, his grip is deadly.

I immediately feel life being squeezed out of me from my lungs. I can't breathe, I can't move my body in any way. He's on top of me, completely covering every joint and every limb. The blood in my neck goes straight to my brain and I try with everything I have to take in any air.

I take a second to look at him, trying to avoid his true emotion but with no use. His eyes have tears in them, he's crying, the tears drip onto my own cheeks. My head is pinned hard against the wooden floor but my skull feels so numb I can't feel it. He's trying to get me out of the way and stop me from attempting to stop them.

"Z–Zehlin, stop." I manage to choke out. He shakes his head to the side as if he's fighting himself before focusing on me again. He doesn't let go, if anything he squeezes harder.

I'm going to die. Zehlin is going to kill me and all of this work will come to an end. They're going to keep trying to hurt each other, and my corpse is going to be forced to spectate the brutality. He's getting me out of the way so he can finish the contract.

I'm just a step in the staircase right now.

I can't let him kill me. All of those people who need my help, who need me to bring the bridges back. I can't die here, not by the man I intended to go through all of this with. I can't die from the man who's been by my side every day since I've been thrown into my real world. Into the truth.

I pray to Numen this doesn't kill him.

I summon the last bit of energy I have left to the surface. My hands manage to make it to his bloody, bruised chest and I push. I only push.

He gets thrown back to the side, his body rolls over onto his side. I can't look at him as I open my eyes, and adapt to the clearness of my vision and my throat.

I choke for air for what seems like an eternity. I don't hear anything. I don't see Aleck anywhere. I finally gather the strength to sit up and see Zehlin a short distance away from me laying down, unmoving. Still choking, I crawl over to him.

Nothing comes to me that I can sense from him, no pain, no anger, only nothing. The bracelet feels cold when I try to pull something from his body. I'm terrified to touch him, but I still do. I shake his shoulders, I run one hand through his messy, untied hair. I roll him to his back and beg in my head over and over for his eyes to open. I need them to open.

My head shakes involuntarily, I pound on his chest and bring my lips to his own. I push air into his mouth while pushing down on his chest. "Please, no, this isn't how you leave. Zehlin, I need you. I don't know who I am without you."

The tears just fall down, a warm stream falling onto his bare chest.

Where is Aleck?

My heart starts to feel heavy, draining of any hope I had when I came here. My throat fills with a rock the size of a boulder. Why wouldn't the witch tell me how to stop this? Why did Zehlin agree to being forced to kill Aleck, me?

In the moment, I thought I didn't have a choice but to get him off of me. I only wanted to hurt him, but I've never regretted anything more. I am supposed to be a powerful elf that's going to save my country. I'm supposed to be terrifying, yet I can't even save one person.

I keep pushing on him, I keep giving him air but nothing happens. The choking, the ale, the multitude of times my head has hit things, they all start to catch up to me. Zehlin's pale face starts to spin, alongside the rest of the room. Every inch of me fights it, but I fall over onto my back, the crook of my neck lays on Zehlin's limp arm.

He doesn't move, and neither do I.

He lays there dying, and I lay here with guilt.

I hope the witch comes back and takes me too.

This is easily the most pain I've ever been in. I've had many near death experiences, but this is the worst one. And it was at the hands of Artea.

She's still sleeping, laying on the only couch Aleck and I managed to not destroy.

Klord found us here after he went to scout out the Deadlands. He said he had some twin-sense thing happening, I didn't ask questions, I'm just happy he helped. Just like Josephine, Artea has the death gathering and Klord has the life gathering. He sensed the danger and claims he brought me back to life. I didn't know something like that was possible outside of Josephine's powers or other spells. I suppose it makes sense.

Klord wants to let her wake up on her own, he says it's better for her head to take its time instead of using his powers to fix it. He thinks there might still be some damage that won't get fixed if he goes the easy route.

I sit here next to her, refusing to move my hands from hers. I know what she did to me, for everyone else. She was willing to risk my life for the rest of the archipelago. She was forced into this position, and she still takes it as seriously as I hoped. Possibly a little too seriously. Klord saved me and I woke up next to her hobble, tired body. She tried to save me, she tried so hard there are bruises on her knuckles from prying Aleck and me apart and attempting to punch the air back into my chest.

She's definitely part of the reason I'm in so much pain. She has multiple bandages wrapped around all of her wounds, as do I. My own dried blood is crusted on her hands, arms, and even some on her face. Her tear streaks create deadly sorrowful marks along her cheeks. I wish I could have wiped them away as they fell.

But I was dead.

If Aleck hadn't agreed to the death duel, maybe none of this would have happened. That damn traitor. The witch proposed that she knew exactly where Artea was once we came here to find her. She said that the only way she wouldn't send multiple Avians and herself to kill her would be for us two to fight to the death. I wanted to say no, that it was a terrible idea and a wasteful way to die for both of us. I would never kill my right-hand man. I tried to convince him that we would find another way.

Subsequently, he agreed to it instead. Apparently the contract didn't need both of us to agree for it to go into effect. He seemed happy to want to kill me, to get me out of the way. My guess is he's working with Etiza, and has been this whole time. He's been gone off and on, insisting that Artea and I go on missions alone. Who is he spying with?

I don't know who to trust at this point. I watched Artea for weeks before she even knew what was going to come for her, she's the only one I know that can be trusted.

For now.

I debated running after him after Klord brought me back, but it's better if I stay here. The chances of the witch coming back are slim because she has to relocate every time someone finds her. She's very wanted around here for the messes she causes, so she only pops up every once in a while. I can only imagine the reason she needed us to be distracted while she found Artea. What did she need from her?

I found the ring the witch traded in Artea's back pocket. King Ector really wanted it to be hard to get our hands on all seven pieces. I don't blame him. He took the flame down to stop Etiza from spreading the dragmist any further than she's capable of. We killed him to stop him from doing so, but it was too late.

But maybe we didn't kill him. In the jungle in Ornau Torrid included both the elvish king and queen once he mentioned Etiza wanting to wipe them out. He could still be alive, maybe he didn't die for nothing.

I don't know what to feel now. My best friend, my cousin, even my right hand man have betrayed me. And for what? I still haven't figured that out yet. I understand how Etiza and her twisted mind wants to take control of the people, but why Aleck? Why is he working for her? And if I ended up dead in that fight with him, how would Artea have retrieved the other pieces? Even Klord can't fly that far over and over again trying to hold her as well.

I'm by myself now with only one job. Keep Artea alive, bring the bridges back, get rid of the dragmist operation, and make sure Etiza doesn't succeed.

I wish I could have had a reason to beat Klord's skull in before I knew that he was telling the truth, this is something I so desperately want to erase from my mind. Did Aleck already find a way back to Mava? Is he stuck in Avaris hiding from me? I pray I never find out, but I know that won't happen.

Taking me out of my deep tunnel I've dug in my own head, Artea shifts in her sleep. I hold her hand sitting at the end of the couch, hoping she knows how to control her powers better. The poor fruit.

It's an odd feeling, getting the life drained out of me like that. It felt like she had a grip on my soul and ripped it from its root in slow motion. It was the worst torture I've endured. Yet, I'm sitting here holding the hands that caused it. It's crazy what this world is capable of.

She starts to open her eyes, and as she does I can see the pain start to seep in. She groans an ugly groan as she attempts to sit up. I nudge her chest to lay back down.

"Hey, just lay on your back. You hit your head." I speak quietly so as to not startle her. It doesn't work very well, but she doesn't seem scared. She looks relieved to see me and I would be too.

My ushers to keep her on her back don't last long as she pushes herself forward into my arms. Her hug is warm, it's light, even though she pushed all of her weight, and then some, onto me. She squeezes me like I might disappear if she breathes too hard.

"Y—you're here. Oh my Numen." She holds my cheeks in her delicate hands now. Her pointy ears are tipped red, her glossy deep brown eyes are glittered with tears. It doesn't take long before they start falling. "I'm so sorry, you were right. I can't do this on my own. I never should have left you two alone. I should have gone with Zehlin. I'm so sorry. I didn't mean to hurt you. I didn't mean to please forgive me."

"I'm okay, I'm okay. Please don't cry." I wipe her face with my thumbs as best as I can. "I know what you had to do. And I'm so sorry you had to see me like that. I tried so hard to fight it."

An immeasurable wave of guilt weighs on me once I notice the bruises on her neck. I threw her across the room, I choked her until she almost died in my hands. She looks so exhausted, she looks like breathing hurts every time she lets air in. I start to tear up as well looking at her pleading, pained face.

"I know you didn't have a choice. I never realized how much I needed you until it was too late," she whispers, I can't help but smirk. I've been right this whole time and it took dying for her to admit it. Literally over my dead body. "Wait, how are you even here? Did I die too?"

She looks me up and down, assessing my injuries. I'm wrapped up in all kinds of places with white patches and cloth to stop different areas of bleeding or soreness. Klord helped clean me up a couple of hours ago until I was strong enough to do it myself. I was a little shifty about him, I didn't know how to feel until now. He saved my life and did everything he could to find out more about the dragmist. I owe him more than I've ever owed anyone else.

"Your brother helped me, saved me, actually."

"Oh, I don't even need to ask how he found us. I felt it, even in my sleep. It's odd, the way I can feel his presence."

"He says he felt something was wrong and followed his instincts. He found me dead and you dying." At this point, I have my back against the couch and she's sitting on my lap. Her chin rests on my shoulder as she hugs me, her breathing matches mine while we sit there together. Something about this moment makes me feel like our souls are intertwining.

"We pretty much just died together. It's odd how magic works." She giggles, but I don't find it funny at all. I *did* die and all I could think in that moment was how brave Artea was. How she risked everything to tear the contract apart. She fought for me with every inch of her life, it was excruciatingly beautiful to see.

I don't leave any more room for conversation. My lips meet hers in an instant, and my Numen I have waited too long for this. This majestic elvish girl who was nothing but a townsperson will now save the country. She's already saved me, given me a real purpose.

She turns warmer than a fire on a summer night while she kisses me back. Our lips and tongues wrap around each other slowly, but eagerly. Nothing about this kiss speaks of intimacy but more of longing. I want to eat her soul, I want to devour her every thought and share mine with her as well. I've needed her light, kind energy for so long and I didn't even know it.

My hands wrap around her waist and lay lightly on her hips as we consume what just happened, the near death. She is the reason I'm still here, and she's the reason I want to stay. We share the guilt and mix it together until all of the apologies are silently spoken and all of the tears are dried.

Chapter Twenty-Eight

He's alive. He's okay.

But I still killed him.

I can't imagine what it would have been like if Klord hadn't made it in time, if Klord hadn't been here at all. I would have eventually woken up and found him cold and pale, with the print of my palm on his chest. It's covered right now as I kiss him, but I saw the black stain I left on his bloody skin when I pushed him off of me. I marked him, forever reminding him that I was willing to kill him for the world.

I never meant to kill him, though. All I knew was that I couldn't die, not after coming this far.

Still, even after what I did he sits here with me. We share breath in a beautiful entanglement of words that don't need to be spoken. We tell each other we've needed this, we've waited for this. He no doubt feels guilty about letting Etiza dig into my brain, but that's the least of my worries. I worry for him.

He fought an entire war for her cause that ended up being a plan to take control, become a dictator instead of a queen. She betrayed him, the morals of royalty, and most of all she betrayed everyone in the archipelago. I can only imagine how Zehlin feels after being right by her side and command for so many years.

I've waited for him, even when I was human in Halistyn. I've waited for someone to show me what it's like to be strong, yet protected. I've never felt more safe than I have in this moment with him. Does he feel the same way? Is he upset at all that I subconsciously chose the people's lives over his?

And now that I think about it, I don't think I would have pushed him off of me if I were to live through it again. I'd let myself die, I'd choose to give up the islands just so I don't have to live with the fact that I ended his life. Temporary or not.

"Hey so I wanted to tell you what I—" Klord's voice appears in a corridor to my right that leads to some other section of the house. Zehlin and I turn towards him and I practically jump off of him, faster than a fly. "Oh, I'm sorry," he stutters and points behind him. "I can leave."

I shake my head and laugh nervously, the adrenaline from the kiss fading quickly. "No, no. Klord it's wonderful to see you."

I don't think much of it before I stand up and walk over to my winged brother. My arms wrap around him in an embrace warmer than my cuts and bruises. I lay my ear to his heart and close my eyes as I feel him return the hug. He doesn't only hug with his arms, but with his wings too. It's warm, and full of love. Something inside me feels complete hugging Klord. I truly have been waiting my whole life to see him again, I just didn't know it.

"Thank you. Not for helping me, but for helping Zehlin." A couple more embarrassing tears threaten to leave my eyelids as I hug him tightly and then let go.

"I know you need him, and so does everyone else. I wouldn't let a good man die like that. Well, *stay* dead I mean." He shrugs as I take a few steps back, he's feeling hopeful and full of pride in himself. Or maybe in me, it's hard to tell.

"Thanks for rubbing it in," I smile and the headache hits harder than expected. I wince but hide the reaction, we have things to do. "Where'd Aleck go?"

"He ran off, knowing I'd kill him when I had the chance." Zehlin grumbles like a pissed off puppy, I almost smile. However, I'm more concerned with why he wants to kill his best friend even without the contract.

"What did Aleck do?" I ask, now sitting back down on the couch avoiding making my heart pump too hard. Everything feels like it's pulsating in my body and it's quite unpleasant.

Zehlin shakes his head and grits his teeth. "The witch made the contract so that only one of us needed to agree to a duel. To death. Of course I said no because Aleck is my right hand and we could find a way to keep you safe. But before I could even say anything, he agreed, and I was caught in my own body. We fought for hours, our bodies have the same skill level without our powers so it took a long time. Then you showed up and tried to end it, ended up killing me, and that's what broke the contract."

I sigh at the realization. My hands go straight to my forehead, my headache seemingly worse than what it was before. "So, he ran because he didn't get away with killing you out of the picture."

"I don't know for how long, but he's been on Etiza's side. I'm not sure what she promised him but it must have been enough to make him try and get rid of me. My guess is that when he found out that we discovered Etiza's plan and were plotting against it, he needed a way out to tell her. He will lose whatever he's promised if he doesn't stop us from stopping her, therefore he needs to get rid of the one person who knows the most."

"You." I nod at her comment and Klord stands there with his arms crossed. "Well, do we know where he went?"

"That's the really bad part," Klord speaks. "If word gets to Telik that we know what she's doing, she will do everything in her power to end Zehlin and make sure that flame gets back up. Her entire plan would be ruined if we warned the people, but she doesn't know that we already agreed not to. It would definitely cause a rebellion and that's the last thing we need while the threat of war is on the line." It makes me proud that he's not afraid to say what he thinks in front of the general. I know I was at first.

"Why are Josephine and Ector trying to go to war again?" I ask both of them, hoping someone would have a guess.

"Josephine and Ector? Meaning he's alive?" Zehlin asks, turning to me while still sitting on the couch. The bruises and beatings are hard to ignore and it makes me feel terrible. If I just went with them, the witch wouldn't have put him through that.

"Torrid told me, weeks ago. When I first got to Telik." I wince at the admission, but it's time he knows. We shared death for Numen's sake, I can share a couple secrets. In addition to that, Ector would be a huge threat in war so Zehlin and everyone needs to know what we'd be up against. He knows Ector better than others, especially when it comes to war.

"I would ask you why you didn't tell me, but it doesn't matter. What matters right now is we find out where Aleck went, get the next pieces as fast as possible, and try to solve Perdita's issue before they strike war. We clearly already have domestic national problems, we don't need to fight. Plus, we can't even form an army right now, not with these waters." Zehlin stands up to stretch his legs and offers me a hand. I take it and stand with him. I'm assuming we're going to head over to Klord's place like he promised we could before we got here.

"Do you think the king and queen would go to war to try and get rid of the dragmist crystal completely?" I can't think of another reason they would do such a thing to an already broken country. It's broken because of them, no matter the reason they did it in the first place. The fire was taken down by them, and all of the deaths are on their hands.

"Seems likely, yes." Klord and Zehlin agree, and so do I.

"Are we heading back?" I ask heading to the door.

Klord nods and we start our walk back. We will rest for one night and continue our journey tomorrow. Zehlin will heal in that time, and I will take it slow for my head as I need to give it time.

On the walk, I slip my new ring on. I don't feel anything new, as usual. I'm sure it will take a while to kick in like all of the others did.

I feel warm seeing Klord walking with us, even though he could leave us and fly if he pleased. I hope he's in on this with his heart too.

I almost died today, I killed the man closest to me, I have the third piece. I feel unstoppable. Which, logically, I know isn't true. But I can't help but finally feel like I can do something for myself, even if I need help. I've always wanted to be something bigger than a drink pourer or a pot maker. This way, I can do something to help.

There is no room for failure, I will not stop until Etiza is dead. All of the blood is also because of her. This is all because of her.

While we walk in silence back to the city, I can feel the vibration of Zehlin's rage under my skin. It's the strongest emotion I've felt from anybody. He tries to hide it in his face, but I can sense the tension. He is out for revenge.

He will not be second in command any longer.

We are the command.

PART V

(The Puppet)

Chapter Twenty-Nine

B e careful, little bug." Momma giggles to me as she runs a little ways behind me, trailing my every step. I'm running and running on the side of the beach with her, my toes hitting the chilly water every stride I take. She's chasing me, but I know she's letting me win the race like she usually does. I hear the thud of her footsteps behind me and can't help but giggle too, I love when we play.

"You can't catch me! I'm too fast, Momma!" I taunt her and run even faster, starting to give her a little challenge. As I run further, I spot Klord and Pappa still working on the bird house in the sand. He brought nails and wood to teach Klord how to build things, just like Pappa does.

I get distracted by the pretty bird house and open paints in front of them, leaving an opening for Momma to scoop me up from behind me and tickle my belly until I can't stop laughing, until the joy hurts.

"You win, you win!" I choke through struggling breath. She lets me down and we both run over to Pappa and Klord.

Pappa smiles at Momma first, and then looks at my sandy hair and muddy feet. "Having fun out here, girls?" He shakes his head but he loves it when we have a fun time.

"So much fun! But the water is so cold!" I yell as I sit down next to Klord

"Why don't you go swimming, little bug? We are lucky we have the ocean, you know." Momma says.

Momma and Pappa exchange odd glances, but I don't bother to ask anything. Usually they respond with, 'Oh little elf, it's adult things.'

I've just stopped wondering.

I tilt my head to Klord and his project. "It's too cold Momma. How's your bird house building going, brother?"

"It's so good, I learned how to hit it together so it stays together, even in a raging winter." He smiles, he's so proud of his work.

Then, the oddest thing happens. A small orange cat saunters over to us and sniffs my Pappa's feet. He chirps a small meow, unusually unafraid of us. I wonder where he came from, and why he's not scared. "Kitty! Momma, look!" I've always loved cats and this one's colors are especially enchanting.

I walk over to it, closer to Pappa, and pick him up. He rubs his forehead on my chin, his little ears rubbing against my skin. I hug him tighter and hold him up to show Momma.

Right when I walk over to her, black smoke starts to take the cat's place. The weight in my hands is replaced with trickling dust, ash almost. I freeze, unable to find any words.

Momma looks terrified, she looks at me like she doesn't know me. Only for a second, but it's enough.

She hugs me, tightly she hugs me and doesn't let me go. We step in the ashes of the cat, unable to escape the spread. She holds me as I sob into her dress. Klord doesn't say anything and Pappa sighs.

"I didn't m—mean to, Momma." I cry.

She only holds me, she can only hold me.

Before she lets me down, a large man with a dark cloak stands far away behind us on a dune in the sand. I point to him, unable to speak. Momma and Pappa look behind them in his direction and each go pale, even paler than when they watched their daughter murder an innocent animal.

"How is he here?" Pappa asks in a near whisper, standing up and pushing Klord behind him in protection.

"We need to leave now." Momma says sternly. I only keep crying as she carries me, and we run. We ran away from the beach, away from the man, away from the half-built birdhouse.

I wake up with a jolt, already feeling sweat trickling down my forehead and soaking my back. I haven't had an important vision of the past since I used the power on Mateo, and now that I have, I feel torn.

I wasn't a baby when we were taken to the islands, neither was Klord. We were at least five years old in my vision, but I don't remember growing up with my parents, I don't remember them at all.

Josephine had dark chocolate hair with hints of auburn with deep brown eyes, and Ector had brown hair just like Klord with a scraggly beard and a lively looking face. They looked happy, we looked happy and full of love.

Is the threat of Etiza really worth giving your children up like that? Did they erase our memories? And why am I getting this vision now?

Who was the cloaked man that scared my parents so much?

I sit up in my bed and let the cool air of Seglona hit my face. I left the windows open tonight because I knew I'd need the air. After Aleck left the witch's cabin and we got the next ring, Klord stayed in Avaris to keep watching the mining operation before we try to stop it. He wants a clear picture of what we might get ourselves into if we infiltrate the site. Zehlin and I went to Seglona and found a small inn in a town called Rongh to stay at for a few nights. We still have plenty of the Telik currency coins to use and they're coming in handy in this way.

Liesl, the duchess of Seglona, was kidnapped by Queen Etiza as well as all of the others. However, she's one of the only ones who didn't have a partner or was married, so the island has been left alone for a hundred years.

As much as Ihrvian is struggling to grow crops or keep farm animals, and Avaris has a harder time finding people to harvest any vicious animals in the Deadlands, I didn't think another island could struggle more.

Seglona has always been an island full of ice and snow, covered by inches of the frosty white and frozen water. Lakes and rivers are all frozen, so water supply is nearly empty without faeries heating it up. They can't grow crops, animals are depressed and cold all the time, they almost have nothing. It suddenly makes me feel like a selfish islander for thinking I was living a bad life.

Most of the people here, if they don't have money, are struggling to live and keep their families alive. Before the bridges were torn down, the island relied on shipping and receiving, as well as trade to survive. The other islands helped Seglona and its people by giving them food and crops to sustain them.

I know people tried to flee the first few decades in the aftermath of the war, but most of them were unsuccessful. Now the rest of the people here are forced to scrounge for scraps and starve living in the cold, all because Etiza tried to ruin them and my parents took the flame down.

Was that their entire plan? Just take the flame down and then the people will be safe, without their rulers? Without food or other goods? The islands were made to survive in harmony with one another, they can't survive long without each other.

I see the vision, but long-term, their plan was terrible.

I wake up next to Zehlin laying on the floor with a couple blankets and a makeshift pillow under his head.

I turn to see him looking up at me, the dawn sunlight kisses his skin as he blinks tiredly at me. "Nightmares again?"

I nod and wipe the moisture from my forehead then scrunch my brows in question. I avoid describing him this one as it doesn't even make sense to me. "Again? How did you know I have nightmares?"

I see the face of the spiritless Mateo at night, the dying ghoul, the bleeding heads, the pond of blood and the reek of death. My own powers being able to drain the life of anything, anyone. It all becomes so hard to ignore.

"Even when you were still training at the castle, I could hear you at night sometimes. I wanted to come up and help you so badly, but that was a line neither of us should have crossed." I lay back down and remember his hearing ability. It makes me wonder if he's heard anything else I didn't think he'd listen in on.

"Yeah, they've happened since the night you came and killed the ghoul and dwarf. It feels like their eyes are always on me," I think back on my dream as I look up at the dusty, wooden ceiling, keeping my breath steady while I cool off being out of the covers. "But that's not what I dreamt about tonight. I think I had another vision."

I didn't *think* I did, I know I did. It worries me, though, using that power. It makes me feel like I'm going to find something I'm not supposed to know or something that will hurt me more than educate me. He stays silent, letting me talk my thoughts out.

"That night at the ball, you knew that Etiza had been keeping the dukes and duchesses, didn't you? And if you did, why didn't you say anything? Do you think they belong there, rotting?" I lean over the bed now, looking down at him. He looks surprised that I'd confront him about this, especially after everything. But I can't help but think about it. I can get over him letting her control me that night, but him not helping Mateo shook me and I didn't think about that until now.

"I— I don't know. I've always trusted her, she told me she was worried that they would take advantage of their ability to control the islands and their new solitude. I could agree with that worry, and I was always concerned that maybe she took too far measures. She kept coming to me with new stories about how there were attempts of murder on her by them and that they had plans to kill me and get her protection out of the way. I eventually grew to view them as prisoners." He looks into my eyes now, no longer talking to the ceiling. "How do you know she took them herself, and not a mystery magic?"

I pause and realize that he still thinks I can see the future, not the past.

"I know because I saw it, a vision. She took them the day after Ector got the flame down. It looked like they just wanted to go back to their people. They didn't seem threatening at all, just hopeless."

I glare at him, unable to immediately trust what he says. A few days ago, we had a moment, but we hardly spoke about it at all. I realize that even though I've needed someone like him, someone who encourages my growth and sees me as an equal, I still have a hard time putting all my trust into him. For all I know, he could up and leave just like Aleck did.

"Took? As in you saw the past? Not the future?" He sits up now, looking at me with curiosity. I prepare for the blow when he finds out I lied to him this whole time.

"It felt like something that I needed to keep to myself. When I had the first vision at the dining table that night. I panicked."

"Yes, you said Etiza was sick in the future, nothing more." He shakes his head, even more confused. I want to shrink into a ball as my lies catch up to me.

"When I threw up and passed out, it was because I had a vision of you," I say, now sitting crisscross on the bed facing Zehlin. "Of you killing your father in an office when you were much younger."

I talk quietly, unsure if I would be cutting open old wounds for him or not.

"Y–you saw that? And you didn't say anything?" He looks up at me, more defeated than I thought he would have. "That feels like an invasion, Artea."

"But it wasn't an invasion when I tore through Mateo's head in front of a bunch of civilians?" I scrunch my brow leaning further down towards him.

"Important civilians," he corrects me and I chuckle aloud. Is that seriously what he's worried about? "And I didn't know that the royals didn't do anything wrong. You have to understand that Etiza being the bad guy here is still fresh."

"I watched you murder a man and threw up right after. Do you really think that I wanted to see that? And I'm sorry that I lied, I didn't know what else to do." I shrug, empathizing with the recent loss of two close best friends.

"Maybe, I don't know, tell the truth?"

He's standing up now, pacing around the chilly room. "I was alone there, I didn't have anything to myself. My room wasn't even mine. Once I found an opportunity to keep something to myself, I did. I wasn't obligated to tell you guys the truth at the time, I didn't know it was important."

He gapes his mouth open and I can feel how upset he is, it feels like the bracelet around my wrist is tightening. "You watched me kill my father. That doesn't feel important to you?"

"It didn't at the time," I say softly, not meaning to make him feel exposed. There's a long pause, he hopefully recognizes that it wasn't on purpose. However, I'm sure his trust issues are just as fragile as mine. "Why did you do it?"

He sighs and slowly walks over to the bed. He plops down on the soft, small mattress right next to me. I sink a little bit with him and get a better look at his night clothes.

He wears a loose white top with a v-cut that has sleeves going to his elbows. He wears simple black cloth for trousers that run down the length of his legs. His long brown hair is disheveled from last night's slumber and he attempts to brush it out of his face and behind his ears as he thinks.

He looks at me, pity in his eyes, I'm not sure if it's for me or for himself. "I don't know how much you saw, but he was a terrible father and an even worse general. He didn't care for family or proper duty. He didn't care about his wife or his only son. He only wanted to carry on the family name of being the general," I go to hold his hand and he takes it. Even though it must have been at least three hundred years ago, these wounds don't heal. "He deserved it."

I nod in understanding. I saw the way his father treated him, like he was nothing. Even though mistakes happen, he was hurting him more than he already had.

"I'm sorry all of that happened. Was it Etiza's father, King Xeon that died?" I ask him, still holding his cold hand in mine.

"There was some insane fae mad at King Zeon, my uncle, for a call he made on the military. It's a little hard to remember now what it was exactly. Anyway, they claimed themselves as demon hunters and decided he was a demon. Xeon was sick at the time but I called a couple soldiers off duty to check out a potential murder in Telik. That's when they took their move and Xeon was too sick to protect himself," his face says it all, all the sadness. He feels guilty, so guilty that it starts to weigh on my shoulders too. The air in the room feels oddly crisp as we breathe in unison. "It was my fault, but I didn't do it on purpose."

"You're right, it wasn't your fault. And it's not your fault Etiza was put in as queen too early." It breaks my heart to see his memories flow through his mind, the tears threatening to slip through the crack of his hard gray eyes.

"I spent so long blaming myself for it, torturing myself for killing my own father. But ever since I became general, the islands have been at peace. We made peace with the elves, we brought back the alliances that spent so long in the dust."

I nod and scoot closer to him, speaking softly. "This whole time, the elves have been fucked over by the fae, by the humans, by the creatures that live here. We can bring that back, your efforts didn't have to be for nothing. All we need is to finish today, get the necklace, and we can move forward. Then we will only need three more pieces."

"Do you think there's any way Klord would be able to fly to Perdita and delay the war threat? You parents would have to remember him, right?" He asks me, the sorrow in his eyes becomes distant, now filled with determination.

"I'm not sure, he's still in Avaris observing the dragmist. Plus Perdita is very far south, I don't think he'd make it." I stand up, stretching my legs and splay my arms out, pacing.

He nods in agreement. "Well, he said he'd be here tomorrow with new information. We can wait until then to ask him," there's a short pause until he speaks again. "How long did you know Ector was alive?"

I wait and consider lying, that I was just guessing. "I found out when I first got here, from Torrid. I was visiting him a lot and had many questions. Again, I'm sorry I didn't tell you. I just needed something for myself, and I didn't know who to trust."

"Can't say I blame you, I shouldn't have trusted practically my own sister." He chuckles but I know he's hurting. Because of the bracelet, his heartbreak reverberates off the walls and onto me.

"The bracelet, it lets me feel you. I can feel anyone's emotions practically. Except the Tonya girl. I couldn't read her at the Hellon castle, nothing at all." I pry a little at the situation only because it was so confusing. She looked like she loathed me and was clinging on to Zehlin hard, I'm still ashamed at my jealousy.

He nods and rolls his eyes. "Her parents and Etiza wanted us to marry, badly. It would have been good for the military and trade between the islands. Plus they're an extremely powerful family that would make powerful offspring. But I found out soon enough that she doesn't have the ability to feel anything. Not love, anger, happiness, not even sadness. She never mourned her dad when he was taken either."

"Why did she react so negatively when I was at the castle? Is she always like that?" I ask him, the look on her face still sends shivers down my spine. "It all seemed so off."

Powerful.

"When I called off the marriage, her family was disappointed. Rightfully so. She can't feel emotions but she still knew what was best for her family. I think she still thinks there's a chance with me, and that would explain why she tried to chase you off like that. I didn't even notice."

It made sense, her trying to get rid of a threat if she still had a plan to get her hands back on Zehlin. "I just don't understand why she thought I was a threat."

He gives me a look while still sitting on the bed, he cocks his eyebrow and lets his smile take over his lips.

Numen, those lips.

"You don't understand?" He asks me, and I can't help but smile too. The memory of him kissing me brings up a flush to my face and immediate sweat on my back. The way his warm, calloused hands were so gentle on my cool skin as he ravaged my mouth like he'd waited years to do so.

"No, I really don't. I'm not a threat." I grin as he uses one finger to gesture me over to him. I walk over and stand right in between his feet, looking down on his morning appearance. He rests his arms gently around my waist and gives me no time to think before he pulls me into his chest and raises his chin to mine.

We interlock our lips once more and the feeling of home rushes quickly into my soul. The warmth, the tenderness, the way our breath merges back and forth shakes my reality. I might collapse if his hands weren't wrapped around me, keeping me stable. It's not fast, it's not desperate, it's longing. We kiss like we are still looking for our lips, like we want to find more, yet have everything we need.

It's merciful, it's forgiving, it's eternity.

Something about sharing myself with him in these moments, even when we're close in the ring, I feel grounded. I feel like I'm meant to be here, like I was made for him.

"Do you think Tonya would feel threatened if she saw this? Would you be a threat then?" He smirks through our kissing, chuckling at the thought. He clearly doesn't like her that much.

I can only nod, finally agreeing with him. His hands lower from my waist to my hips, slowly trailing even lower. Even sitting down, our heads are almost level with each other as we share each other, explore each other.

"Zehlin," I interrupt his exploring, the kiss, and look into his eyes. "Is this right?"

"Is, what right, Angel?" I heat up even more from the name, curling my toes in excitement.

"An elf, and a fae? Together like this?" I question. What if something goes wrong? What if we regret it and go right back to what we were before?

"Don't think, don't worry." He almost whispers as he grips my hair softly and brings my neck towards him, asking me to kiss him more.

Just for one moment, I don't think. For one moment, I don't worry about the lives I need to save, about the queen attempting to hurt thousands. I don't even think about what I have become and how different I am, how different this Artea is from who I used to be. Or who I was sculpted to be.

I trust Zehlin, I trust him as much as I can. This feels right, this feels like warmth and the sun and darkness, all stirred up in a perfect mixture.

"Please, Angel, say my name again."

I'm itching to become more of him, and for him to become more of me. I need his sun, and he needs my shadow.

I love seeing you take him over like that. Go on, say his name.

I stumble backwards, my back hitting the ground with a hard *thud*. I scratch at my head, almost hitting the voice out of me.

You let me in, savior. This was all you.

Etiza, no.

Zehlin falls from the bed onto his knees, his eyes filled with focus on me.

I'm not going anywhere, so I want you to listen to me and listen to me very well.

I try to open my mouth but I can't move my lips. My mouth hangs open leaving my jaw tilted and tight. I try to back away from Zehlin but I can't do that either.

I finally found a way to talk to you, to make you listen, make your body listen. I hear a light chuckle through the voice in my head, her laugh sends aches through my limbs. I feel a tear run down my cheek, the warmth covering me in fear. *Aleck will be here in a moment, and you will follow him.*

Please, don't do this. Let me go, I'll do anything.

You let Zehlin lie to me in those letters. Aleck told me everything, you know about the elves, you know about the dragmist. You will come back to Telik, to Mava. You will tell me everything you know. You will finish the ritual to get my bridges working again, and you will suffer the entire time.

I didn't do anything, please.

I'll see you soon, little bug.

Chapter Thirty

(Zehlin)

The door hinges get torn apart mercilessly by whoever has been banging on the other side since Artea fell back. She said Etiza's name and went pale, followed by complete silence and stillness. She never looked at me, only stared in front of her at the window in the tiny inn bedroom.

My body shoots up onto my feet and I conjure up my sword. My arms drink the sunlight and shape it into the white blade I'm so familiar with. Artea sits there, staring at me with nothing in her eyes.

Stay with me, Angel.

I'm pissed at myself for not remembering that anyone who takes a spell from Etiza also carves a pathway into their heads for her. I hope Artea can fight her as long as she can so I can take care of whoever just barged through the door.

I finally look at the person at the door and feel my hands almost give out. "We can talk about this, brother." Aleck walks in, his golden eyes almost pierce through me as I remember what he looked like the last time we came face to face. *Bloody, beaten, finally awake.*

"What is there to talk about?" He cocks his head and walks closer to Artea and me. I instinctively take one step closer to Artea, begging for her to move herself out of the way.

"Why did you accept the duel from the witch, Aleck? Why did you run?" I ask him, already knowing the answer but wanting to hear it from him. I couldn't stop fighting him, I couldn't stop bleeding, I didn't stop even when he would choke me, threatening my life. I only had the bruises and scars after he left to remind me of what he did. That he wasn't my brother anymore.

He chuckles and I almost toss my blade into his heart from where I stand. "You were in the way, General," he's never called me that before. My face hardens, gripping the handle of my sword. "The dragmist doesn't have an effect on you and your cousin is tired of it. She wants you at the castle for some... alterations."

"I'm not taking any dragmist." I scoff and hold my sword at the threat. I'm not going anywhere and neither is Artea. *Fight her off, I know you can.*

"Whose food have you eaten in the past one hundred years? Who have you leeched off of? Whose castle is *your* home?" He takes a step with every question he throws but I stand still.

So, not only is she trying to poison her people, but her family too. Etiza's true form becomes more and more disappointing the longer I'm away from her. How could her behavior be under my radar for so long? And why is Aleck siding with her?

"How do you know about her trying the dragmist on me?" I question him, wondering how long they've been working together behind my back, how long I've been too gullible to see it.

"The dragmist will help everyone, eliminating decisions, helping them take care of themselves. I don't know why you're trying to get rid of it, General." As he speaks I wonder if he's being manipulated too. I know he might've sided with her if he was threatened, but for him to fully agree with her is unfortunately a shock to me.

I shake my head and glance at Artea who looks purple and strained. She's trying so hard to get Etiza out of her head. I want to hold her, I want to help her. I need to help her. "No, it hurts them. You've seen it, it boils their insides, it burns them from the inside out the more they use it. They will all die at some point if you use it the way Etiza wants to. She only wants an army to fight Josephine and Ector. Aleck you're better than this."

"You don't know what I am, and you were never interested in figuring it out. Don't make this harder than it already is." He walks over to me completely, I let my sword face him point first sitting straight out in front of me.

"I'm not the one who's making it hard. Etiza has fallen out of line, you need to see that." He stands at the tip of my sword, breathing heavily in irritation. I never thought I'd be willing to stab my best friend, my brother.

"Maybe I've fallen a little out of line too."

He lunges forward after pushing my sword to the side. I manage to hold my grip on it as he uses his hands to shove my shoulders back. He's strong, but I keep my balance and avoid letting my weapon stray too loose. He's a better fighter than me, he's a better fighter than anyone I've ever known, my heart races at the thought of losing. Panic rises up in my throat as I dodge multiple punches and lunges towards me. My blade swipes left and right to him, always missing but never falling to the ground.

Please, Angel. Come back.

His eyes glare down, surprisingly full of life. Like he's waited to be able to take me in a real fight like this. We've sparred and tousled, been in a trance and tried to kill each other, but this is real. We use our powers, our strength, and our will.

He's able to land a right hook straight onto my jaw, dislocating it with a crack. I refrain from groaning so as to not let him know that it hurts. He still smiles, he still shows me that he knows I'm going to lose unless I use my power.

"You see," he pushes my back against one of the four wooden posts on the bed, pressing my neck back as well. "When you give a soldier who has unlimited fighting power some dragmist, it makes for a good battle, doesn't it?" He chuckles out of breath, his face only an inch away from mine.

"Seems like you need it to win against me." I taunt, knowing that he'd beat me in a fight any day.

But he doesn't have power aside from his fighting ability.

"You know that's not true." He smiles as his hand comes up to my neck, pinning me to the bedpost. I try my hardest to bring the sword up, but it still drags on the carpet. I open my other free hand after dropping the sword and gently create a smaller dagger. I bring my hand up and lift the sharp tip to his chin in one swift movement, threatening a lethal wound. The dagger has a shine to it as it's made out of sunlight. He eyes his side where I hold the weapon, seeing the glow below him.

"You—," I start to choke out, my face feeling hot and swollen as he chokes me. "You can still save yourself, Aleck."

My hand shakes as I push the knife closer and closer to his skin, pricking a layer of it drawing blood. "I'm already saved."

I use the last of my strength to push against him, throwing him off of his feet and pushing his back against the wall behind us. I take the dagger in hand and put the shaft of the blade against his bearded neck. "Don't make me do this."

He laughs and tilts his head back, allowing more room for my blade, wanting more. "Anything you do is because I let you. I could get out of this and stab you to death right here, right now. I have people outside this building waiting for me, waiting for us," he looks down at Artea, I refuse to take my eyes off of him and look behind me. "Waiting for her."

"You stay away from her, she has nothing to do with us." I can't help but snap back at him. He really has fallen off of his horse, I don't recognize him anymore.

"She has *everything* to do with this, General." A low growl escapes my throat as I push my knife into his neck, allowing for a few drops of blood to drip down his neck and slide on my hand.

I don't even think about anything past this moment, I only continue to dig deeper and deeper into his throat. Why does he let me go deeper? Why doesn't he stop me?

I stare into his eyes and the only thing I see is amusement. He's happy to watch me kill him, he's content with his brother ending his life with a blade. He smiles deeply now, almost laughing as I create a deeper line than I thought I'd be able to. I can't help but fight the water in my eyes as I gash him.

I remember the battles we fought together, always on each other's feet, waiting for the next move. I look back on the times when we were just children, running around in the woods with our poorly handmade bows and arrows, missing every shot. Dinners at each other's homes where our mothers would share recipes and gardening advice while we rough-housed in the backrooms.

Every single time he saved my life on the battlefield almost makes me forget who he seems to be now.

I get ready to give the blade one last push into his red stained neck before Artea slowly comes into view to my right. Before I can turn my head to her, before I can make sure that she's all right, her hand raises up to my dagger and grips the base of the blade, her skin reflecting the light from the blade in a dangerously beautiful manner.

The entire dagger disappears into thin air, her dark mist taking over the glowing blade. She tilts her head over to me while lowering her arm. I look to Aleck for a quick moment before Artea's hand shoots to my chest.

I feel the same dread immediately that I felt in the witch's cottage. Her power forces me on my knees and draws sweat and tears out of my body faster than I can think. I can't help but let the water from my eyes fall, I can't stop them. I feel the neglected carpet beneath my knees, I feel my fingertips become numb as my arms lay limp at my sides.

Out of breath, I slowly lift my head to see a lifeless angel in front of me. Aleck stands in the corner of the room holding a cloth to his neck. Artea stares down at me, almost a smile written on her face.

"She's mine now, she wasn't quite strong enough." It's at this moment that I regret ever letting Artea get her natural powers back. That's how Etiza is able to use her power from Mava inside of her even from this far, an island away. Taunting her, using her. "She's listening well, she did have some fight in her though."

I look into Artea's complexion, and even though it's her face, I can see Etiza's glare from her eyes. I can see the evil start to seethe inside her grin as she wears Artea's face.

"Let her go, Iza. You don't have to do this," I speak in almost a whisper. My voice is raspy from the silent screams as Artea's power still seems to drain me. "She's not your puppet. I know what you are now, let this be between you and me."

She laughs like I just slapped her, like she knows so much more than me. The shrinking feeling in my chest starts to tighten up more and more. My tears and my sweat start to soak through my sleepwear. I look down to my hands for a moment and see tiny dots of blood start to seep through my skin, like someone poked me with a needle one hundred times and left it to bleed. The holes start to appear everywhere, crawling up my forearms and my shins.

"Don't you see?" She starts to speak, leaning down toward my face now with a calculating, cruel look on the face she's wearing. "It can never be between you and I now. Artea is everything, she will determine the survival of every single person on these islands. She will finish the ritual, and she will bring back my bridges and restore the plan that was so devastatingly torn apart by the disgusting creatures down south."

"There will be a war!" I yell through the pain of the layers of my skin being ripped little by little. The blood starts to drip onto the carpet and seep into the crack of my fingernails and my toes. "It's not the time to control your people! It's time to protect them, it's time to fix what you destroyed!" I glare at her, painfully trying to remember that it's Etiza talking, not Artea.

"We will win the war once my army is built. And once I build this new army, I won't need you to lead it." She sneers, looking almost disgusted with me. I know I've lied in my recent letters to her, I know I've kept the fact that I know what she is from her.

I know that I've secretly been preparing for a war I know she can't win. Even with her drugged minions.

"If you tell the people that there will be an active threat, they will listen to you. They will volunteer, you don't need to take control of them, you don't need to hurt the people you love just because you are feeling *vengeful*." I spit out.

She barks a laugh and twists her hand gently in the air. The life-draining grip that Artea is being forced to use starts to tighten even more, curling my nerves and sending aches into places I didn't realize could hurt. I can almost feel my organs and my heart moving as she forces Artea's power on me, they beg for a release, for a breath. But I can never get a full one in.

"One hundred years ago, I proposed the dragmist plan to the elvish king. Ector and I were in love, I thought he wanted to be the ruler of both Perdita and the archipelago with me," she glares down at me and shakes her head. "I never wanted simple control, I wanted my people to be happy. I wanted them to realize that life is so much easier when you don't have to make the decisions."

It makes sense that she might think that. She was forced into a position of decision making and power since she was way underage for a queen. She had to fill a seat that had been filled for almost one thousand years by her father before her. I'm sure that after five hundred years in the seat herself, she's tired of the decisions. She's assuming everyone is tired as well.

"Why do you think controlling them like this would make them happy?" I'm almost sobbing now, not because of the pain or the fact that Artea is tearing me apart, but because I'm forced to. They feel heavy, like the life that's being pulled out of me are my tears.

"As long as we keep it a secret, they don't have to notice a thing. Everyone will start getting happier, healthier, quieter. My army will be aware of the dragmist so that they can be faster, stronger, sharper. They will get rid of the elves for good. Ector destroyed our happiness, I will bring it back and defeat the threat forever, and Ector doesn't have to bother us anymore. Especially that brute wife of his."

I cough, the breathing becoming harder and harder to sustain. I try to remember what Artea's face looks like when she is herself, when Etiza isn't wearing her skin and tormenting her mind. I remember how her brown eyes shine in the light, and how they create terrifyingly majestic caves in the night time. I remember the softness of her smile lines and the dullness of the bags under her eyes.

"There is no *we* in this, Iza." Iza is what I used to call her when we were small children. She would call me Lin. We thought if we both made up nicknames, we would have our own bond to ourselves, something only we had. She twists her hand in the air again, pulling more and more energy from me causing screams of pain to escape my throat. I feel my veins start to bulge from my skin, the blood inside starts to pulse louder but slower.

"Don't, call me that. Don't even consider me family if you don't want your people to be truly happy. If you don't want *me* to be truly happy." She lets go of me, her hand now laying at her side, almost limp like she disconnected her power from Artea's arm.

I manage to choke out a few words as I bend down gasping for air and wishing for water. "This isn't happiness."

She still looks down on me, her stare burning holes right through my body, all over me she stares as I try to recover from the torture. "Artea, your sweet angel, is mine. She will stay in the castle and watch you burn away as we finish delivering the last four pieces. It should be much faster than what you're used to, seeing as I have men with wings all over these islands."

I know Etiza won't let Artea go until she's in chains back in Mava, in the Telik castle. I know how she works, because even as powerful as Etiza is she is still careful.

And with war coming up within the next two months, she will waste no time finding the pieces and bringing the bridges back together to raise her army. To destroy the dignity and honor of the island's people for good.

We have to destroy that dragmist mining site, and we have to do it quickly.

I never thought I'd be praying to Numen for Klord to give us a miracle, but if he can realize that we are no longer here, that the room was left in a mess, when he comes here expecting to meet us and sees that he has to try something. If he's Artea's brother, the life to her death, I have a feeling he won't back down from this fight.

"Now," Etiza begins to speak. "If you try anything, I will not be scared to drain you within an inch of your life with this new power of mine." The way she speaks of Artea's power like it's hers makes me want to stand up from this place on the carpet and show her what it can feel like to be drained of life.

I know she would punish me that way too because if Artea could kill me with a punch of her fist, Etiza could make Artea use her power the same way, even if she fought. Etiza is using Artea as a puppet, a mule to carry out her deeds. She's using her to control me, control the rest of her people.

I can't conjure my weapons, I can't even bring any light into the room. My hearing radius has been dramatically decreased, only being able to hear a conversation from the other side of the wall.

Etiza forces Artea to use a drop of her power from a distance as she makes her walk out of the room. Aleck comes up behind me and picks me up from under my arms and we follow Artea out.

I can only imagine how she feels being trapped, being used and forced to hurt me. She fought better than I've ever seen anyone restrain from letting Etiza use her power, and it shocks me. It almost scares me.

Etiza has always been able to control people from the same room or same castle. In battle she could use her power from across the fields and the hills or in the middle of the ocean. Everyone succumbs to her immediately, she's too strong to fight or push away from your head.

Artea though, she fought for a good few minutes, longer than I could have.

When Etiza and I were young, she would make me slap myself or spill my water at the dining table while our parents talked. She would make me trip or make me pet our cat's belly so the cat would bite me, the cat hated being pet on his belly.

But we got older, we got more fair and she realized that it wasn't fair game anymore. I could fight her with my weapons, I could make her fall over with the force of my light, I could blind her with the sun. But none of that mattered when she could dig into my head and pick and choose what I could do.

We agreed that we wouldn't fight anymore and that we would be partners.

Then both of our parents died or went missing, and all of a sudden we were left alone and in charge of an entire section of the world.

How she is now, it makes me wonder if she's always been this way and I just didn't see it. Maybe the years of power finally took over and she no longer truly cares for the people. But it doesn't make sense that she would keep this as a secret from me if she thought it was a good thing, she knew I'd disagree with her. She knew that I'd know that it's a bad thing, that this will do more harm than good.

So, why does she lie about happiness?

What else is she keeping from us?

Epilogue

There are two constants in this world.

Death and hunger.

When people know that death can creep in at any moment, it becomes more and more likely for them to stay safe, stay certain, stay comfortable. When people see that food is plentiful and there is a royal gate surrounding them, they become more and more likely to commit acts of risk, of danger.

Why be scared when they know they have a net under them, a fire to keep them warm.

So, when the flame was taken down and the people were left with hunger or evil, all uncontained terrors, people hid away and became less prone to strength, to happiness.

The very opposite of what Etiza claims she could bring.

Because over hundreds of people have died in the ocean trying to escape the local cruelty. They have died trying to find food and shelter, trying to find food or selling their familial valuables just to get a couple coins and feed their children. I was considered lucky in Halistyn. I was fed, for the most part, and safe if I stayed out of the criminals' way.

The lords and ladies at this castle could be considered gods. They not only have the shield of Etiza and her power around them, but they have their own powers to share. All of the powerful faeries live in Telik, in Mava, and can give each other anything they could ever want with the flick of the wrist.

Lady Ideena, the old lady of one of Telik's territories can turn into animals. Lord Caston can wield the wind and the clouds, sometimes forcing rain and a storm down onto the earth.

Many of the other lords and ladies have powers that outshine Ideena or Caston, some have really boring powers like turning other items into glass or talking to birds.

I've learned all of this because I have sat at Etiza's side at every ball, at every event, at every personal luncheon.

I have been her lap dog for the past month, sitting by her in a throne-like chair, waiting and waiting for something to happen.

I haven't been allowed to see Zehlin, either. He's been stuck in the dungeon of the castle since we were brought here. Etiza told me that if I'm going to keep secrets from her and work against her, she might as well do the same thing. She's always saying how she wants me to be happy like the rest of her people, but I'm too valuable for her to risk trusting me.

She's right too. If I could escape, if I could get out of this castle and find the other pieces on my own, I would. I would bring the flame back and catch her off guard and kill her with my bare hands. But she creeps into my head every time I try to do something on my own, leaving me in constant mental chains.

I hope Zehlin is still alive, and if so I hope he's been doing okay down there. I wonder if he's been put with the other dukes and duchesses or if he's in his own cell, on his own floor, in only darkness.

The interesting thing about the dungeon is that the chains they use are the blackout carbide chains that Duke Mateo had on during the ball, when Etiza made me recite her speech. So, even if Zehlin was alone or with the other prisoners, it wouldn't matter because he can't use his powers with those chains on.

He's alone, probably cold, scarred, and defenseless. As powerful as one man or woman can be, there is always something that can stop them.

The queen has made bracelets and anklets out of the blackout carbide that I wear with me at all times. I still need to portray the image of the good elf that wants to bring the bridges back and save the rest of the people. I'm not allowed to expose her for her plans and I'm absolutely not allowed to go anywhere but by her side. The only place I'm alone is where I sleep, but even then I don't have a balcony like I did before, and I'm not allowed to bathe myself. Two to three guards are always outside my door equipped with even more blackout carbide restraints.

There are squads of guards out looking for the other pieces of jewelry right now. I have the ring from Ihrvian, the bracelet from Ornau, the ring from Avaris, and I also got the necklace from Seglona as the guards were able to get it before we left. It's gold with light blue gems that sparkle in the moonlight, like ice.

The queen still thinks that I don't know what powers the ring from Avaris or the necklace from Seglona gave me. I've done a very good job at lying to her. The necklace lets me understand different languages like ancient Elvish or Pixieish, written and spoken. The ring from Avaris lets me float in the air for short periods of time. Almost as if I'm defying gravity for only a moment.

However, I've had these blackout bracelets the entire time, since the journey from Seglona back to Mava. I'm not supposed to know what powers I have if they're being taken away from me.

I wonder how long it will be before she finds out they don't work on me.

Acknowledgements

I would first like to thank everyone who believed in me and my dream to explore my writing. I want to appreciate anyone who is even reading the acknowledgement page because its not often that it happens. My dad is my number one hero who helped me through losing family and raising me to be the resilient young woman I am. Josephine, my sister, is the best older sister a girl could ask for. My two younger sisters, Bridget and Liesl are two of the most caring and headstrong individuals I know. Alec, my first love and who should be my last, you saved me from some dark years and I'm lucky to have someone like you, and as cute . Emily L., my day one best friend from across the country, I miss you. Daniel, a built in friend with a cool little sister. Hannah, you are the coolest little cousin, you are missed dearly. Lydia, Hannah H., Maddy, Ashlynn, Mackenzie, Cecilia, Ciera, and so many other friends I met through high school, you have all been so amazing to me. Thank you Ray and Bandit for being amazing friends through the past few years. Thank you Anze Ban V. for the hard work you put into my beautiful cover. Thank you Belle Manuel for thoroughly going through my rough manuscript. Thank you to Mrs. Harms and Mrs. Atkinson for pushing me to be my best as well as more than just teachers.

To Ginger who has taken me in as her own, and Nana who does the same. Emily P. and Max, I hope I see you guys soon. Everyone's love and support has made this possible. I wish to keep growing and improving for those around me.

Author Biography

Tabitha Bull graduated Triton High School in 2025. She has a loving family, four cats, a much too long To-Be-Read list, and a hidden love for video games, sunflowers, and writing. She grew up in Vancouver, Washington and moved to the middle of nowhere in Indiana with her family when she was 15.

Contact Information :

Phone – 564-202-4100 (TEXT)

Email – tabithabull01@gmail.com